These are the sites where you can find R.L. Mankin

www.facebook.com/RLMankinFanPage

Twitter@RLMankin

www.myspace.com/rl.mankin

www.pinterest.com/rlmankin

I Can't Breathe

Blood Upon A Rose

R.L. Mankin

authorHOUSE®

AuthorHouse™ LLC
1663 Liberty Drive
Bloomington, IN 47403
www.authorhouse.com
Phone: 1-800-839-8640

Published by AuthorHouse 12/19/2013

ISBN: 978-1-4918-4649-0 (sc)
ISBN: 978-1-4918-4648-3 (hc)
ISBN: 978-1-4918-4647-6 (e)

Library of Congress Control Number: 2013923256

I dedicate my book
To
You!

I hope that you enjoy reading it.

Acknowledgments

I would like to say Thank You to my husband Jeff and my children for once again standing by my side. I love the encouragement that you have given and I love you with all my heart.

To my wonderful Fans,

The fantastic support that you have given means more to me then you can imagine. You are all wonderful and I hold you close to my heart.

To Christy Senalik,

We have known each other for so many years, thank you for being here for me the entire time as I was writing "Blood Upon A Rose." You have been so wonderful and patient with me as you listened to everything that I wanted to change and add to this book. You are truly awesome.

To Steven Shady,

We have known each other since we were very young and as time ages us we become better and wiser. Thank you so very much for creating the cover for this book. I cannot express enough as to how beautiful it is. You are a fantastic artist and a wonderful friend.

My wonderful Father in Law Charlie Mankin
owner of Charlie Mankin Films.com,

Thank you for working your magic once again for taking such a fantastic author picture of me to place on the back cover. I am very grateful to you and I love you very much.

Chapter One

As my body is starting to wake up from my rest, I can feel Marrick his arms are still holding me to his beautiful body. I am facing him as I have the side of my face pressing against his sculptured chest. I can feel that he is starting to wake up as well but we are not able to move our bodies just yet, the sun is starting to go down.

As I lay here thinking about Fred I know that it is going to take a lot of time to mourn the loss of him, but it will also take time to heal from what David had not only done to me but to Marrick as well because he knew everything that was happening to me from the powerful bond that we have with each other. But I do know that it has also affected Sarah as well.

I do understand that human and animal blood will keep us alive but it is the essence of the human blood that gives us all the powerful strength that we will need for our next encounter with David. We will need to consume as much human blood as we can to help increase our strength.

Now that I have made my complete transformation to vampire, my emotional feelings are much deeper and the physical part of me is now much stronger then when I was half human and vampire. Which was only a few evenings ago because it took two evenings for my body to completely die and also for Marrick's blood to transform me to a vampire. I finished my change to full vampire last evening.

I am now finally able to move, so I reach up to touch Marrick's face as I look at my pale white hand. He places his hand on mine and he holds onto it as he slowly opens his beautiful dark coal black eyes.

"Good evening Renee."

"Hello Marrick."

I reply to him as I look at his beautiful face.

As he continues to look at me I can see his yellow glow, it is completely yellow because his body is waking up and we have not yet consumed any human blood for this evening.

"Marrick there is such a great sadness within this house, because Fred is no longer with us."

He removes his hand from mine so that he can place his arm around me once more as he holds me close to him. Marrick's yellow glow has faded back into him.

"I will do what I can to help you, Sarah and Keith to make it through this horrible time Renee. You must also know that Damon will be here for you as well, we are all family now."

"Thank you Marrick. Will you please do me a favor?"

I ask him as I continue to look upon him.

"Renee I will do whatever I can for you!"

"Marrick if you are able to get a hold of David before I do, will you please kill him?"

"Renee, this is a favor that you do not have to ask for because we WILL destroy him!"

"Marrick, the sooner he is destroyed the better it will be for all of us. What is it that we need to do so that we are prepared for our next encounter with him?"

"Renee we need to make sure that we have plenty of blood supplied for us all, this is the most important thing that we will need to do. We are going to need to make sure that every human that is with us is half turned if not completely turned into a vampire. We are going to need everyone's powerful strength! But you must also understand that when David is destroyed, the evil he has created will also have to be dealt with. Renee, are you sure that you are up for this task because it will take a very long time until David's evil vampires that he created are destroyed."

He says to me as he is looking into my eyes.

"I will be by your side for whatever needs to be done. Marrick I feel such a heavy weight in my chest where my heart used to beat."

I say to him with great concern in my voice.

"Marrick can you feel anything at all from Maryann? I am worried about her."

"No Renee, she refuses to allow Damon or myself to feel anything from her, but we do know that David still has her with him."

He replies to me as I can now feel that Marrick is also worried about her.

"How do you know that he still has your Mother?"

I am now feeling very badly for asking that question to him.

"She is allowing us to hear her thoughts that she wants to see David destroyed. We cannot feel what she is feeling, Maryann will not allow us. But we can hear her thoughts but only when she allows us to hear them."

He replies to me as I can feel his arms tightening around me as we continue to lie in bed together as we are still facing each other.

"Marrick, I do not understand why she will not allow you to feel what she is feeling now that you and Damon have re-connected with her. Why can I not hear her thoughts from you?"

"Renee, Maryann has learned over the last two centuries how to block us! But trust me; she will be released from him. The reason why you do not hear her thoughts from me is because I am worried what she may send. I do not want you to be more frightened than what you are now."

"Marrick, I am glad that she is still, alive so to speak, even though David still has control over her. Thank you for protecting me but there is no protection for any of us for what we are heading into."

I reply to him as he loosens his grip so that I am able to lie on my back. Once I am comfortable Marrick tightens his grip around me once more as I am now holding on to his arm that is lying across the front of me with his hand tucked under my waist.

"Honestly Renee, we are happy about it as well, now that we know the truth that David commanded her to kill our families. But please remember you must not trust her, she is still as dangerous as a poisonous snake. Damon and I have not forgotten how she treated us when we were children but we still loved her, she is our mother. We must still watch every move that we make because David still commands Maryann to tell him where we are and also what he wants her to do. But we are must learn to block Maryann as well so that she can no longer allow David to know where we are at or what we are planning. And you are right Renee; soon there will be no protection for any of us."

He says to me as we continue to lie in bed together, I tighten my grip on his arm that is has lying across the front of my body.

"All I can say to that Marrick is that I understand what you are saying, but Maryann had said to me that she honestly regrets what had happened to both yours and Damon's family. Marrick they were her family as well."

I say to him as we continue to lie together as I turn my head toward him so that we are looking into each other's eyes once more.

"Renee there is no way that I can argue with what you have just said because you are correct!"

He says to me as he closes his eyes and I lower my head back down so that I am now resting the side of my head against his chest.

I am going to do what I always do best and that is change the subject.

I raise my head up so that I can look into his eyes once more.

"Marrick shall we get up so that we can go downstairs to warm up some blood?"

"Yes Renee, we should."

He replies to me as he removes his arm from lying across the front of my body, I move myself so he can remove his other arm from under my body.

Marrick sits up and he places his legs at the side of the bed and then he stands up. He turns so that he is now facing me and he holds out his hand out to me. I place my hand in his as he helps me to get up out of the bed.

I can feel from Marrick how he desires to be inside of me but I know that I am not ready yet; I do not know how long it will take for me to recover from what had happened.

Marrick does realize that I can feel what he is feeling but neither one of us is not speaking a word about it.

"Marrick this is going to be different for me not having to go to the bathroom after I wake up."

I say to him as I smile and trying to take our minds off of what I was just feeling from him a moment ago.

I look over at Luna, I watch her as she moves herself from her laying position on the floor she is now sitting up. She watches us as we make our way over to the cold storage unit in the secret room and Marrick grabs two bags of blood. He closes the door to the cold storage unit and we are now making our way to the door. Before we leave this room I bend myself down toward Luna so that I can pet her soft beautiful black fur. She looks at me as I pet her; Luna has decided that she no longer wants me to continue petting her because she moving herself to stand up in front of me. I move myself so that I am now standing straight up and I take a couple of steps and I place my foot down on the square outline piece of wood inside of our secrete room and I push down on it to open the door. As Marrick and I along with Luna walk out of our room we are now inside of the walk in closet. Marrick bends down so that he can pull up the carpet beside the secrete door and he pushes down on the marked wood to close the door that leads into the hidden room.

Marrick Stands back up and he places his hand on the side of my face as he looks down at me, I close my eyes as he is touching my face. When I open my eyes back up he removes his and walks out of the walk in closet and he goes over to the dresser he opens two drawers to pick out his clothes, I decide to remain in my pajamas. I am trying really hard not to look at him while he is changing his clothes.

When he has finished changing we make our way out of the bedroom as we walk down the stairs that lead in between the living room and the dining room, Luna is still with us. I can now hear the beat of her heart.

As we are walking through the dining room I can hear Sarah and Damon in the kitchen along with Keith. Marrick and I can now see them as we make our way into the kitchen. I see Beauty as Luna walks over to be by her sister's side they are now both laying on the floor together. As I stand here watching the wolves, I notice that they both have a dark red glow.

Why was I not able to see their glow when I was half turned?

Keith is sitting on the chair at the table and Sarah along with Damon are both standing by the kitchen sink.

Keith looks up as Marrick and I walk into the room to join them, I am gazing at his red glow with a hint of yellow because he is now half vampire and human.

"Good evening, how are the both of you doing?"

He asks to the both Marrick and I as his voice sounds so sad and tired.

I cannot help myself I go right over to Keith and I bend down to give him a hug and as I look at him I can see tears forming in his eyes. I move myself so that I am now standing beside of him so that I can hold him in my arms trying to comfort him as I start to remember the evening when David had murdered Fred. Keith has placed both of his arms around my waist as he rests his head upon my stomach. Sarah moves herself from standing beside of Damon; she has come over to us and she helps me to comfort Keith. Marrick is walking over to the blood warmer and he places the two bags of human blood inside of it.

"In time, we will get through what has happened to us all."

I say to Keith as we continue to comfort him, I can also hear the sound of his heart beating with in his chest and it is a very slow beat because his body is half dead because he is now part vampire.

"I do understand Renee that this is going to take time; it is just that right now it is very difficult, it is even worse when I am alone."

He whispers to us as he is trying to keep control of himself.

I do not reply to him but I do understand how he feels.

"Keith please always remember that we love you."

Sarah says to him.

"I do know that you both love me Sarah I feel the same way about you and Renee. I am having a very difficult time, I am not sure if I can make it through this."

Keith says to the both of us.

Sarah and I do not know what to say to him from what he has just said to us.

"I have a very bad feeling about Keith."

I say as I send my thoughts to Sarah as she looks at me.

"As do I Renee."

She replies to me with her thoughts.

Finally we release our hold on him as I kiss his hair then I turn from him as I make my way back over to Marrick. Sarah is now with Damon once again.

I feel so sad for what he is going through he was so in love with Fred. But we have also lost a wonderful friend.

I think to myself.

Marrick is now removing the bags out of the warmer and he opens up one of them with his long nails, he opens up a cabinet door to take hold of a glass and he pours the blood into it for me to drink. As I stand beside of him he hands the glass of blood to me, I can smell it by allowing the scent rise up into my nose as I hold my glass of blood close to my face and I can also feel my eyes turning completely black. Since I can't breathe, I cannot inhale but I can smell the sweet scent of human blood.

I look over to Marrick with my black eyes as I look upon the yellow glow that he has that is now mixed with the color red from the blood.

"Marrick am I developing a problem? I am the only one in this room whose eyes are completely black!"

I say to him as I look down at my glass that I am now holding.

"Renee you are not developing a problem, you are going to have to adjust to your eyes changing all over again."

I do not reply back to him, I just stand holding my warm glass as I gaze at the dark beautiful red color of blood.

"Renee I have allowed my eyes to turn so that you are not the only one with black eyes as we drink our blood."

Keith says to me as I look at him and smile.

I look over at Sarah and Damon as I look upon their beautiful yellow glow mixed with the color of red from the human blood that they are drinking.

"Good evening, how are the both of you doing?"

I ask them both because I did not say anything to them when Marrick and I first came into the kitchen.

"We are doing very well Renee, how are you?"

Damon replies to me as I watch their glow fade back into them.

"Right now my dear brother in law, I am doing the best that I can do for now."

I reply to him as I honestly try not to let what David had done while he had me captive slowly creep back into my mind.

"I do have a question to ask all of you, but I am not sure if anyone knows the answer, but if you do PLEASE tell me the truth."

I say to everyone as we remain in the kitchen.

"What is your question Renee?"

Damon asks me.

"We had found out that David had been watching me for some time, and he said that I was to belong to him. I need to know if Logan knew about this and if she had told anyone what he was planning?"

"Renee, Logan did not say anything to me about it."

Keith replies to me.

"We did not know either Renee."

Damon replies to me.

I can now feel my eyes changing back to normal; my eyes are hazel once more.

"Renee, do you remember that David is now able to block Logan as well, she only now knows what he wants her to know. I do not think that she knew anything about it, because if she did, I am sure that Logan would have said something to us right away."

Sarah replies to me.

"I hope that you are right about that Sarah. But there is something that I do not understand, please explain to me once more why is it that David cannot command Logan like he can command Maryann and the others that are with him?"

I ask to her as I try to keep what I am now feeling under control.

"How are we going to find him, if Logan can no longer feel anything from him?"

I am asking as I am also hoping to get an answer to this question as well.

"Renee when everyone rejoins us in two evenings, we will figure out a way to find him. I am sure that Maryann will not be able to tell us where David is but I am sure that she will be able to give us hints as to where he was at. Logan is special; he has no hold over her that is why David had killed her human lover Shawn. He was hoping to break Logan so that he could gain control over her. David has put Logan through hell since he turned her just because he cannot control her nor was he able to hear her thoughts until he had made himself stronger by consuming more human blood at all times while he is not resting."

Marrick replies to me.

"But what if he commands Maryann not to say anything at all to the both of you or what if he commands her to lie to you just to get us off his trail?"

I ask them.

"Renee, we will find him, and if he does command her not to say anything to us or has her lie to us as well, I am sure that we will still be able to find him. You must remember Renee, Logan tried to protect you from David. She defended you!"

Keith replies to me.

"I am so sorry; please forgive me for getting so upset. Keith you are right to what you have just said about Logan."

I say to him as I now remember that night when Logan was trying to help me, she was so frightened as well.

I remember David as he pushed his long nails into the skin of her arm then what he did next to her made me so terrified. As he still held onto her arm he licked the blood from Logan's skin. She was trying to demand David to let me go. He also picked her up and threw her against a tree.

"You have every right to be upset Renee, we all have that right as well!"

Sarah replies to me, the sound of her voice took me away from what I was just thinking of.

"I agree with you Sarah and you are correct."

I reply back to her.

I stand here in the kitchen with everyone and I continue to drink my blood. I honestly cannot help but enjoy how good it tastes and the way it makes my body feel. With each sip that I take, I can feel the human blood as it absorb into me. I feel such a powerful strength and the energy is coursing within my body.

I feel so strong!

Without looking up from my glass I cannot help but to say to everyone as we remain in the kitchen.

"If I am able to get to David before any one of you, I will cut his fucking head off for not only because of what he had done to me but also for what he had done to us all!"

No one replies to me, I do not even feel Marrick sending a thought to me.

But I can feel the blood tears forming in my eyes as I continue to drink from my glass.

Luna has gotten up from the floor and she makes her way over to me. I bend down to her and I pet her beautiful soft black fur as she stands here looking up to me. As I look into her beautiful blue eyes I place my arms around her neck to hold her as she lays her head upon my shoulder.

When Luna has had enough of me holding onto her, she gives me a soft moan and I release her as I stand back up, Luna remains standing in front of me. I find myself staring at the white fur on her chest it is bright and beautiful as the full moon in the night sky that is why I named her Luna.

Marrick comes over to me and he places his arms around me so that he can hold me tightly to him.

I have now realized that his touch is no longer cooling to me. I know it is because my body is no longer warm and alive, I am now dead and cold and the only thing that now keeps me alive is consuming blood. To be honest I will miss the feeling of his cooling touch, but I am now completely one with him and I am where I want to be. I am with Marrick, the vampire that I want to spend the rest of my eternity with.

Marrick knows exactly how I feel, as he holds me tighter to him.

How I love to feel him holding me close to his beautiful body.

As I think to myself once more.

Marrick lowers his head slightly so that he can look down to me.

"Renee, we must go out to hunt, we are going to look for humans that are causing harm and destruction to others so that we can destroy them before David gets ahold of them and we know that if they survive his sick torture he will turn some of them. We must do what we can to stop him in every way!"

Marrick explains to me.

"Marrick I understand but please forgive me, for this evening can I stay home? I do not want to go with you right now. I know that I said to you that I will do whatever it takes to help stop him, but I feel very uneasy."

"Renee, I understand that you do not want to go with us this evening. We have a very good supply of blood here; you can feed from that for now. But you must go with us the next time we go out to hunt."

"Thank you for understanding Marrick. I promise that I will go with all of you the next time."

I reply to him.

As we continue standing in the kitchen he gently takes hold of my hand.

"Renee, you must understand that when we start our search for him, you will not have a choice you will have to hunt with us and it does not matter how much blood bags that we will have with us!"

He says to me with a soft but demanding sound in his voice.

"I do realize this Marrick."

I reply to him with a soft low whisper as I can feel him letting go of my hand.

I can hear Sarah getting ready to say something.

"Renee, if you like I will stay here with you."

Sarah says to me as she walks over and takes my hands in hers.

"I will be ok. Please go out with Marrick and Damon. You can show me what to do when I go with you the next time."

I reply to Sarah as I try to force a smile for her.

"Ok Renee, we will be back soon."

She says to me, then right away she places her arms around me and I wrap my arms around her as well I am now holding onto her very tightly.

I am still trying really hard to control my feelings; they are so much more heightened then when I was half turned.

I feel more love for Sarah then I did when I was alive. She is truly my sister now because we each have a drop of each other's blood within us.

When we finally let go of each other, I turn myself to watch the three of them walk over to the sliding glass door and within a blink of an eye they are gone. I make my way over to the sliding glass door so that I can close it.

Keith looks over to me.

"Renee, please allow me to help you, would you like to talk about what had happened to you while you were David's captive?"

He asks to me.

Right away I realize that I am asking him questions.

"Do you want to talk about when David had murdered Fred, or do you want to talk about what he had done to me, or that I had killed 4 people? Or do you want to talk about Cindy; she was one of David's prisoners that he kept. She gave her life to help me so that I could get away, but that did not work because I was captured again. Cindy was killed right in front of me."

I say to him as I try very hard to remain calm and not to allow tears of blood forming within my eyes.

"Renee, we can talk about whatever you would like to discuss."

"Keith, I really do not know if I can talk about what had happened to me while David had me prisoner. I do not think that I am ready yet. But if you need to talk about Fred we can do that."

I say to him as I am trying to control the anger that I now have building up inside.

"Renee, talking is a good start no matter where we begin but you need to realize that you have just opened up to me. I now know more from you then what I did before."

Keith says to me as he walks closer to where I am standing.

I cannot help but lower my head as we remain in the kitchen.

"Ok Keith I am so sorry for what I had just said I am having trouble controlling my feelings. If I cannot keep myself under control I believe that I may go nuts. We can talk about Fred but should we wait for them to come back? I do know that Sarah would like to be a part of this as well. But Keith are you sure that you are ready to talk about him?"

I ask him as I am now looking upon his sad face once more.

"No Renee, but I have to talk about him, we will wait for Sarah to return. And I do understand how you must feel and it is ok. You will not go nuts I know that you will be able to control what you are feeling."

He says to me as we continue to stand in the kitchen.

"Renee, I know what will help you to feel better and hopefully it will help you to relax because your senses as well as what you are feeling is extremely heightened, now that you are a full vampire. I agree with what Marrick had said earlier, you must adjust to the changes that will occur within yourself and your body."

Keith says to me as he leaves me alone in the kitchen.

I walk over to the sliding glass doors to open it up so that the wolves can go outside, then after I watch them both walk outside I close the door to make my way into the living room with Keith. I can hear that he has turned on the sound system, right away I stop walking so that I can let the sound of the music completely surround me as I am now listening to the song "Whale and Wasp."

The sound of this music is so fantastic!

I close my eyes as I stand here in the living room just listing to the music. I can feel Keith walking closer to me, he is grabbing onto my hand so that he can lead me to the black leather sectional couch and with my eyes still closed I follow him as he leads me to sit down with him.

As I sit down I open my eyes and I am now looking at him I cannot help but smile.

"Thank you Keith for turning the music on."

"You are welcome Renee; I trust that the music will help you to feel better."

"Keith, music always has a way of helping me in so many ways. We have always believed that music has some kind of healing powers hidden with in it."

"Renee that is the first thing that Fred and I had learned about you and Sarah. When we met the two of you, we realized that music has a way of helping you both. When you both lost your parents you and Sarah had music playing at all times."

He replies to me with such a gentle sound in his voice.

I remain sitting on the couch, I look at Keith and I smile but I do not reply to him because I am allowing myself to become lost in the music as I am now thinking of my parents along with Fred. I close my eyes once more.

Finally I look back over to him as I give him one of my looks with a half-smile.

"Keith, I would really like to continue my training with the weapons, that is if you are still willing to show me how to use the cross bow."

"Whenever you are ready Renee, all you have to do is let me know when you want to start learning how to use it."

He replies to me.

"Keith, how about we start tomorrow evening, that way you will be able to get plenty of rest to continue my weapons training."

I say to him as I smile.

"Tomorrow night we will continue Renee. But you are the one who will need to rest."

He says jokingly to me.

He has made me laugh.

"Keith I am not human anymore, you are now half human and vampire so you will still tire before I will."

"Ok Renee, that is true but you have to go rest your body before the sun comes up."

He replies to me as we smile to each other.

We both stop our conversation because Keith's cell phone is ringing he stands up to pull it out of the pocket of his jeans and before he answers it he looks at me.

"Renee, it is Robert."

He says to me before he answers his call.

I watch Keith as he walks into the dining room and he makes his way into the kitchen as he continues to talk with Robert.

I can hear him open the sliding glass door so that Luna and Beauty can come back into the house. They both make their way into the living room with me; I can smell blood on them. The smell is different; it does not take me very long to figure out that they have been hunting for small animals. They both sit beside me as I continue to sit on the couch as I am now listening to the song "Out of My Head."

I am not going to listen to what he is saying to Robert; I know that Keith will let me know what their conversation is about. I wonder where my cell phone is, where did I place it?

I say to myself as I continue sitting on the black leather sectional couch as I glance around the living room looking for my phone.

I can feel Marrick and Sarah as they are out with Damon hunting looking for people who are dangerous so that they can consume their blood. Part of me does not want to feel them while they begin feeding on fresh human blood but the other part of me is now wishing that I had gone with them.

I continue to sit here with the wolves as I am trying to block what I can feel from Marrick and Sarah.

I am amazed that I am no longer interested in time. I was always looking at the clock needing to know what time it was. I no longer feel that way because time no longer concerns me.

I think to myself trying to take my mind off of Marrick and Sarah.

As I am petting both Luna and Beauty, Keith comes back into the living room and he sits down beside of Luna.

"Renee, when Robert and the others return, they would like for all of us to leave that evening to go after David. Robert and Michael have been tracking him. We need to make sure that we are all prepared and ready to leave because they had found out that David is regaining his strength. Does Marrick know what I have just said to you?"

"Yes Keith, Marrick does know."

I reply to him as I can feel Marrick in my mind.

"Renee, you must continue to drink as much blood as you can."

"I understand Marrick."

I reply back to him, I am trying to do what I can to be brave right now.

"Well my friend, it is time that we consume some more blood."

I say to Keith.

"I agree with you Renee."

We both get up from the couch and we make our way into the dining room, the wolves are following us.

As we are walking back into the kitchen, I cannot not help but look at him.

"Keith, what is that aroma coming from the stove?"

I ask him as we make our way down into the basement, Luna and Beauty remain in the kitchen.

"Renee, that is my homemade chicken and noodle casserole that I have just started baking in the stove. I am trying to make as much food to eat for us humans, because we cannot live off of blood alone for those of us that are half turned."

He says to me as we walk down the stairs to the basement.

"You must eat food as well; Marrick has said that to me several times! Keith I am going to miss eating the food that you cook."

I reply to him as he smiles at me.

"Well Renee at least you will still be able to smell it."

He says to me as I smile back to him.

We are now down in the basement. We are walking down the hall way into the big walk in looking safe; I make my way to the cold storage so that I can pull out a couple bags of human blood.

As I pass by the cots I begin to remember the night that Damon had turned Sarah into a vampire. He made it so romantic for her but I can feel the knot in my stomach once more from that evening.

I am now opening the door to the cold storage unit and I turn my head to look at him.

"Keith I am just going to grab as many bags of blood as I can hold in my arms to take up stairs for all of us."

I say to him as I am grabbing as many as I can carry.

With my arms full I move myself so that I can use my hip to close the door to the cold storage unit, together we start walking out of this room to make our way back upstairs.

"May I ask how does Robert know that David is becoming strong once again?"

I ask as I try to hide the fear from my voice.

"Renee, I am not really certain but I do know that he has people scattered everywhere looking for his brother."

I do not reply to Keith for what he has just said to me but I can hear anger along with fear coming from him as he answers me.

As we walk back into the kitchen I make my way over to the counter so that I can place all the bags down that I have grabbed, then I open the door to the blood warmer as I place two bags inside. I push the button and I watch the red heating lights come on to warm the blood for us. I can hear Keith's heart starting to beat a little faster as we wait for the blood to warm. I close my eyes as I listen to the sound of his heart beating from within his chest.

I turn to see Keith walking over to the refrigerator he now has the rest of the blood bags that I had carried upstairs, he is placing them inside of the refrigerator. I did not realize that he had picked up the bags because I was listening to his heart. Keith is also pulling out two raw steaks for both Luna and Beauty. They look very excited about their food, they both walk over to him and they take hold of the meat from his hands. We both watch as they walk over to the other side of the kitchen to lie down on the floor, they begin to eat the raw steaks that Keith has just given to them.

They are both very beautiful wolves.

I think to myself as I continue to watch them.

I turn myself so that I am now facing the cabinets I reach my hand up so that I can open up the door and I grab two glasses. When the blood is warm enough I open the door to the blood warmer and I take hold of them with my hands. I can feel the pain as the hot blood bags burn my skin but I know that my hands will heal within seconds. I cut open both bags of blood with the kitchen scissors so that I can pour the blood into the glasses.

I cannot help but look back over to Keith as he is walking toward me as I hold out his glass to him.

I wonder what station the music is set on.

I think to myself while I am listening to the song "About a Girl."

As I look at Keith, I can feel once more that my feelings are slowly starting to surface once again.

Without thinking I find myself saying.

"Keith, I do not want to talk about what I had gone through or what I had to do when I was a captive. Please do not make me share my pain with you; I do not want to make your heart heavier than what it is."

I say to him as he takes his glass of blood, I also notice that his eyes are also completely black once more.

"Renee, it is your decision but I am here for you if you change your mind."

"Thank you Keith."

I say to him as I can feel my eyes turn completely black as well.

He does not reply to me, we stand together in silence as we start to consume the blood from our glasses. I take a couple of sips from my glass and I move my eyes to look back over to Keith, I can see that he is enjoying the taste of human blood as well.

The burns on my hands are starting to heal.

I can feel them returning, so I walk over to the sliding glass door and I open it for Marrick, Sarah and Damon because I can feel Marrick and Sarah as they are coming closer to the house. I have finished drinking my blood as I stand here by the door waiting for them. I take a few steps to move out of the way as I watch them coming closer. I have placed my empty glass on the table in the kitchen. I can see their yellow glow and it has a very dark color of blood red mixed in to it.

I can feel my eyes turn back to normal as Marrick walks into the house to make his way over to me. He lowers himself down as he takes hold of my waist with both of his hands and as he stands back up he picks me up off the floor, because I do not want to let him go I wrap my legs around his waist and I place my arms around his neck as he places my body against his. He places both of his arms around my back as he also holds me very tightly to him. I can smell the scent of fresh human blood on his lips. I feel like a school girl in love.

If I were still human I know that I would say to him that I can't breathe.

Marrick is now walking into the living room while I am still wrapped around him.

He sits down on the couch and he looks at me for I am now sitting on his lap facing him, he places his fingers upon my face as he removes strands of hair away from my skin.

"Renee, you will be ok, please believe that."

"Marrick I do believe that but right now I feel very angry, please do not make me talk about what had happened because I do not want to."

"Renee, I understand how you feel about it, you know that I will not ask you to do anything that you do not want to do. Remember I can feel what you feel. "

"Thank you Marrick and I do know that."

I reply to him as I continue to sit on his lap.

"Marrick since we will be leaving in two evenings to find David, should we start collecting as much blood as we can?"

"Renee, we will get all of that taken care of, so you must not worry yourself about that."

"I understand Marrick."

I say to him as I remove myself from his lap I am now sitting close beside of him.

I can smell blood coming from the kitchen. I can feel that my eyes have turned completely black once more. I look at Marrick as he places his hand upon my face again. I close my eyes as he gently touches me but I can now taste my thick blood inside of my mouth my gums are now starting to hurt. This is the first time that this has happened since I have made my complete transformation to vampire. This pain is horrible; all I can do is place my hand over my mouth so that I can press it against my face. I am trying really hard to hold back my blood tears because of the pain that I now have. My mouth is throbbing with pain.

Marrick takes hold of my wrist to remove my hand from my face.

"Renee, open your mouth for me."

He gently demands to me.

I open my mouth so that he can see what is happening but as I do blood starts to come out of my mouth and it runs down my chin, I quickly remove my wrists from his grip to move both of my hands under my face, I am trying to catch my own blood before it drips off of me.

As he is looking inside of my mouth he begins to smile, his beautiful smile.

"My lovely Renee your fangs have finally developed, in time there will be no more pain as they grow long and sharp and you will no longer cut the inside of your mouth as you become use to them."

"Oh my stars, Marrick it feels like I have a very bad tooth ache on each side of my mouth!"

I say as I am trying to talk with my new fangs.

"Marrick this is going to take some time as I become use to these. Will I be able to control when I want my fangs to grow? You always know what I am feeling and also what is changing with me, so why do you still look?"

I ask him as I am still trying to stop my blood from running out of my mouth as I speak to him.

"Because Renee I do enjoy watching as your body changes. In time yes you will be able to control it, but until then your fangs will develop with your emotions, when you are angry, sad, and when we are making love, but most of all when you start to feel hungry for blood."

He replies to me as we continue to sit on the couch together.

Damon and Sarah along with Keith have come to join us in the living room, I am still wiping the blood from my chin because of the fangs that I now have.

Damon looks over at me and he smiles as well.

"Renee your fangs have finally developed! I must be honest, I knew about your fangs when we were in the kitchen because of the connection that I have with my brother."

"I also know that you have fangs."

Sarah also says to me as she makes herself comfortable next to Damon.

I look back at them because of what they both have just said to me and I cannot help but smile because I am a little excited that I now have them.

I am able to close my mouth but I can taste blood once again because I have just cut the inside skin of my bottom lip and so I am now swallowing my own blood once more. I am rubbing my tongue on the cut that I have just made hoping that this stinging feeling will soon go away.

As I continue to set beside of Marrick I can see his hand rising up from the corner of my eye and I can now feel his touch as he places his fingers under my chin to have me look at him. I am now watching as he is slowly bringing his face closer to mine, he is now pressing his lips to my lips, and as his tongue makes its way inside of my mouth I allow him to take my blood that is bleeding from the cut within my mouth.

I am trying to keep my emotions under control, because when I drank the blood of the thin red haired girl that David kept prisoner. David cleaned her blood from my face and neck with HIS tongue and mouth.

I continue to allow Marrick to take my blood as we sit on the couch together. He does not even say anything to me about what I was just thinking of as he continues doing this.

When he finally releases me we continue to sit together as we look into each other's eyes.

Sarah comes walking toward me and she hands me a tall glass of human blood and she also gives Marrick a bag of human blood as well. I did not realize that she had left the room. I take the glass and I continue to sit beside Marrick as I slowly begin to drink, Marrick is consuming his bag of blood. Sarah is now sitting next to Damon again; she has also given him a bag of blood also.

My fangs are still long and pointed, but I am able to slowly drink from my glass, but I am trying to be careful that I do not spill the blood as I sip from it. As the human blood from my glass washes over my new fangs it causes the pain to fade away.

I can hear Marrick in my thoughts as I continue to sit next to him as I drink from my glass.

"Renee, are you ok?"

"I will be ok Marrick."

"Are you angry with me for what I have just done to you a moment ago?"

"No Marrick I am not upset, but it did remind me of him. But I am here with you I am no longer his prisoner."

"No Renee, you are not, you are safe here with me!"

He replies to me with his thought as I am now resting the glass on my leg, he places his empty bag on the glass table in front of us.

I turn my head toward Marrick as he sits beside me; I place my other hand on his face. He slowly brings his face closer to mine once more so that I can kiss his lips with mine. I have cut the inside of my lip once more.

"This is going to get on my nerves."

I say to him as I tuck my bottom lip into my mouth.

I look into his beautiful dark coal black eyes as I swallow my own blood.

"Marrick I am not going to let this destroy us for what had happened."

"Renee neither will I, this I promise to you."

I move myself closer to him so that I can rest my head on his beautiful chest as he wraps his arms around me we are all now listening to the song "Be Yourself."

"I like this song."

Keith says to us all as he listens to the music.

I look over to him so that I can give him a smile then I look over to Sarah and Damon as they sit together on the couch across from us; she is snuggled tightly in his arms.

I know that I have said this so many times already, but I do love to see her so happy.

I think to myself as Sarah and Marrick both smile to my thought.

I raise my glass to my lips so that I can continue consuming the human blood.

As the music continues to play, "Over and Over" by Three Days Grace, I can see Sarah's look on her face begin to change as I finish drinking my human blood.

I can feel that she wants to talk about something; she is going to make me talk!

"Renee, I am so sorry about what had happened to Cindy."

She says to me with her soft gentle voice.

I am not going to look over at her, because I do not want to cry. I had myself opened as Keith and I were talking while the three of them were out.

"Sarah, Cindy was very brave for what she did, I will always remember her."

I reply to her with great sadness in my voice as I look at my glass resting on my leg.

I can hear Sarah as she is starting to speak again.

"Damon what arrangements do we need to make before we leave in the next two evenings?"

She asks to him.

I am grateful that she did not say anything else to me about it, but I know that she is slowly going to make me talk. In time she will have me talking about everything that had happened.

I think to myself as Marrick and Sarah can hear my thoughts once more.

One day I will have to stop thinking to myself.

I look over to Sarah and she is giving me her goofy half smile, I cannot not help but smile back to her I still have my head resting on Marrick's chest as he holds me to him.

I can now hear Damon beginning to speak and so I look over to listen to what he is going to say as I continue to rest my head upon Marrick.

"We must make arrangements to have as much blood delivered to us here before we leave. We will also need to have refrigerator trucks to keep all of the blood cold and fresh. This must be our number one priority."

As I sit here on the couch still snuggled in Marrick's arms, I am now watching Keith as he looks over to Damon.

"I will start making some calls tomorrow to get everything prepared for what is needed, let's prepare a list of what you want and I will get it taken care of and Logan will help us as well."

"Very well Keith I appreciate your help."

He replies to him as the three of them begin planning what we will need.

As Sarah is still sitting close to Damon she looks over to me.

"Renee, I think that we should gather up everything that we can find to be used for first aid. We can pack up the items and take them with us for the humans to use."

"That is a very good idea, Sarah, let's go ahead and get started?"

I reply to her as I remove myself from Marrick's hold.

Sarah and I get up from the couches while Keith, Marrick and Damon are continuing talking about the arrangements that are needed to be made. I take hold of Marrick's empty bag of blood off of the glass table in front of the couch; I have my empty glass still in my hand.

As we are now making our way into the dining room we stop next to the staircase that leads up to the second floor, Sarah places her hand upon my arm and I turn to look into her beautiful eyes.

"Renee if you like you can search in the kitchen for anything that can be used and I will go upstairs to see what I can find as well."

She says to me with her soft hand still resting on my arm.

As we continue to stand by the steps I give her a smile.

"Ok Sarah, I will do that."

I reply to her as we are now walking away from each other.

Sarah makes her way upstairs and I have made my way into the kitchen; I place my glass into the sink and I put the empty blood bag into the trash can.

I walk over to the closet in the kitchen and as I open the double doors to it I am somewhat happy that I have found a box on the floor of the closet. I bend down to take hold of it, as I stand back up I close the doors and I make my way over the counter by the sink and I set the box on top of it. I am now looking through all of the cabinets and I am placing everything that I can find that can be used as bandages into the box. I have also pulled out all of the alcohol so it can be used as antiseptic that is if no one drinks any of it.

I will miss drinking alcohol and chocolate milk.

I think to myself as I can feel Marrick, he is making his way toward the kitchen. I am standing by the sink waiting for him.

As soon as he enters into the kitchen he stops to look at me.

"Renee, there is something that you must know now that you are now a full vampire. If you do not consume blood, your body will be in great pain. This can also happen as your body wakes from resting during the day."

"Marrick, I do understand what you say to me, we need blood to keep us alive. I do listen to what you say to me! I also understand that I am to consume as much human blood as I can so that our strength will be increased for our next encounter against David."

I say to him as I can feel myself becoming very angry.

"Renee, you are correct I am sorry please forgive me for upsetting you."

"Marrick, you did not upset me, I am sorry if it seems that way."

I say to him as I look into his eyes once more.

"Please remember that you have nothing to be sorry for Renee."

Right away I start walking toward him so that I can place my arms around him, Marrick holds me tightly to him once more as I stand here with him as I now have my eyes closed while we are embracing together I do not want to let go of him. I can feel my skin start to tingle with excitement.

Am I ready to be with him once more?

I think to myself as I feel myself wanting his touch upon my body.

I can feel Marrick as he listens to my thought but he does not reply to me.

He places his beautiful hand under my chin and I look up into his dark coal black eyes.

"We will get our revenge Renee!"

"I know that we will Marrick, I am on count down for that to happen."

I reply to him.

"Renee, I will let you continue gathering up the first aid items. I am going to go back into the living room with Damon and Keith so that we can continue making our arrangements. Since Logan has turned him in to half vampire, she is communicating to him as we continue to discuss our plans."

He explains to me.

I move my head so that I can look up to him, I am watching as he bends down to kiss my nose. He moves himself to stand straight up and as he looks back down into my eyes he places his hand under my face so that he can rub my chin with his thumb. He gives me a gently smile and remove his hand from me as he turns to make his way back into the living room. I stand here watching him as he walks out of the kitchen.

I have just realized that my fangs are gone; my teeth are back to normal. I now find myself running my tongue over my top teeth.

I am starting to feel very badly about what I had said about Logan earlier this evening. Was Keith opened to her? If so she is probably very upset and hurt for what I had said. I know that I would be feeling that way if someone had said that about me. I really do like Logan. I really need to learn how to control my emotions.

I say to myself.

I do believe that I have gathered everything that I can find to be used for bandages, but I am checking one more time just to make sure that I did not miss anything.

I have now gathered up all the towels and every bottle of alcohol from the kitchen and my box is very full. I close the flaps and I pick it up as I carry it over to the table in the kitchen. I pick up my empty glass of blood from earlier and I take it over to the sink so that I can wash both of my glasses. I place them back into the cabinet.

I make my way to the other side of the kitchen to look in the half bathroom and I have found all the first aid items that I had gathered from my house. They are under the sink; Marrick must have placed them here when he unpacked my Dodge Journey when we first arrived here.

I cannot help but wonder if I will ever see my house again and also be able to listen to my favorite radio station 99.7. Someday I am sure that I will but not right now.

I think to myself as I carry these items to the kitchen table and place them with the rest.

The tips of my fingers are now starting to hurt; it feels as if my nails are being pulled out of my fingers tips. I cannot not help but put my hands into fists as this feeling continues.

I walk out of the kitchen and I make my way upstairs, this feeling that I have in my fingers is causing me to tighten my fists. I am now at the top of the stairs she is standing outside of the second floor bathroom waiting for me.

I am walking toward her and I look at her as I come closer to where she is.

"Sarah what is happening because my fingers feel so strange."

I am now standing in front of her and she takes hold of each of my wrists.

"Renee, hold your fingers straight out so that you can watch what is now starting to change."

I do what she has said to me, and we are now watching as all of my nails are growing long and sharp. This feeling of my nails being pulled on while we watch them grow is becoming stronger. The pain has gone away but I can feel a pressure as I continue to watch them grow. I cannot help but watch with amazement.

The color of my nails are still natural looking but long and sharp as if I have took a nail file and sharpened them myself. Now that they have stopped growing the feeling of them being pulled out of my fingers has gone away.

"Sarah, why do the nails grow out to be so sharp?"

I ask her as I continue looking down at my hands.

I am now moving my fingers so that I can get a better look at them. I am touching my nails and I can see and feel that they are very thick.

"Renee, I think it is because we can use them as weapons."

"You are probably right Sarah."

I reply to her.

I remember Marrick allowing his nails to grow just so that he could cut open a bag of blood for me to pour into a glass. I also remember David killing two people with just the movement of his hand. I also remember Damon and Marrick shredding those four men that were following us from the festival that David had sent after us.

"Sarah is there anything left that we can use for bandages?"

I ask her trying to stop myself from remembering David as I watched him murder Cindy and one of his half turned demons.

"Renee I think that I grabbed everything that will be needed. I am glad that the half turned humans will be able to heal their wounds as they consume human blood."

She says to me.

"Do not forget, they can heal but they can also die as well Sarah."

She now looks very sad to what I have just said to her.

"Renee, I am going to check around once more just to make sure that we have everything, but Renee we can also be destroyed."

She replies to me.

I now know that she is now remembering the night that Fred was murdered because I can feel her sadness for him.

I do not reply to her as I look down at my hands as I look at my long nails.

Sarah turns from me and she is looking through a closet she has found some sheets. Sarah takes hold of them and places them on the floor. She looks at me but she does not say anything to me I can see the blood tears starting to form in her beautiful blue eyes.

I am going to everything that I can to try and get her mind of what we were just talking about.

"Sarah one day we will have to paint our nails when they are long."

I say to her changing the subject and hoping that I am able to get her to smile.

I look down at the floor and since I do not have any shoes on, I think that I am now grossed out because my toe nails have grown as well. My toe nails are very pointed but they are not very long. The point of my toe nails are slightly past the tips of my toes. I move my foot to place the sharp point of my toe nail on the wooden floor I can feel the pull of my toe nail as I drag it on the floor. As I look down to watch what I am doing I can hear and see the deep scratch mark that I am placing upon the floor. I raise my foot just slightly to pull my nail out of the wood. As I place the bottom of my foot to rest on the floor I look to Sarah once again.

"Sarah, my toe nails look really nasty!"

"I know Renee; I thought the same thing when I looked at mine for the first time."

There is a thought that has just come into my mind that causes me to start laughing.

"Sarah, can you just imagine that having finger nails this long and sharp while still being human, we would cut the hell out of ourselves after we had to go to the bathroom."

"Oh I have to say Renee that is just so gross! Only you would say something like that."

She replies as she is now laughing as well.

"Sarah, why is it that Marrick and Damon's nails are so dark looking when they change?"

"Renee, maybe it has to do with their age. They are much older than the both of us."

"I will agree with you Sarah, they are much older than us."

I say to her as we both smile.

We both can feel someone making their way up the steps to the second floor. We know that it is Keith.

We are watching him as he is walking closer to us I am holding up my hands so that I can show off my long finger nails to him.

"Renee, I will say that your long finger nails are cool looking but your toe nails are really ugly."

He says to me as he walks closer to us while he is looking down at my feet.

"Keith, you do not like my toe nails?"

"I am trying really hard not to vomit Renee."

"Keith you are just jealous that you do not yet have long nails."

He smiles to us as he shakes his head.

"I have only come up to let you both know that Logan and Richard will be arriving tomorrow evening."

Keith says to the both of us.

"Thank you so much for letting us know that they will be arriving early."

Sarah says to him.

"You are welcome."

He replies to her.

"I thought that she was going to be here the same evening as Robert and the others."

I say to Keith.

"Logan has told me that it is very important for them to be here tomorrow evening. Renee, Logan also would like for you to know that she had no idea that David was targeting you."

"Keith I just needed to know if she knew about it. Please tell her that I am so sorry."

"I have myself opened up to her, and Logan's reply is that she understands exactly how you feel Renee."

Keith says to me.

As we continue standing outside the bathroom of the second floor we can smell blood, Marrick and Damon are warming bags of blood for us all once more. The three of us make our way downstairs and we are carrying all of the first aid items along with the sheets that Sarah has gathered. As we walk through the dining room we make our way into the kitchen to with them. I notice that the food that Keith was baking in the oven is now cooling on top of the stove. We walk over to the table in the kitchen and we place these items that Sarah has gathered with the rest of the boxes and the alcohol that we will never be able to drink again to use for first aid.

This time I hope that we will be better prepared.

I say to myself.

As the three of us walk away from the table we move over to join them, Marrick and Damon hands us each a bag of blood. I can feel my fangs starting to grow again but I notice that the pain is not as bad as it was earlier this evening as they were forming for the first time.

As Marrick hands me a bag of blood he looks at me.

"Renee, I do not want you to cut this bag open, I want you to sink your fangs into it."

I look up at him and for some reason I now feel very nervous.

"Renee, you need to learn how to do this."

Marrick says to me.

I remove my eyes from him and as I look down at my warm bag of blood and I can feel my eyes turn completely black and I look at my nails still remaining long and sharp. As I am holding the bag I am trying not to puncture a hole into it with my long nails. I slowly bring the bag up to my lips as I open my mouth and I can feel my fangs thumping in my mouth for they are now long and sharp and it feels as if they cannot wait for the blood to wash over them.

I now have both of my hands on the bag and I begin to place my open mouth upon it, Marrick continues standing in front of me as I do this. I place my lips on the bag of blood and I slowly force my fangs into the very thick soft plastic of the bag containing the blood. I close my eyes and I can also taste the plastic as I touch it with my tongue.

This really feels good as I am sinking my teeth into this bag of human blood.

When my fangs are finally inside the bag I can feel the blood flowing up into my mouth as I begin to squeeze it with my hands. I cannot help but to keep my eyes closed as I am sucking the blood from it, I am trying not to let any of the blood escape from me because I want every last drop.

I am so amazed as to how much I love the taste of human blood as it fills up into my mouth as I slowly let it run down my throat. I also love the feeling that it gives me as it absorbs into my body, I am developing such a powerful strength as if I am ready to take on anything or anyone!

My bag of blood is now empty there is no more left in it for me to consume. I look up to Marrick as I remove my fangs from inside of it. I was holding my bag so tightly to my mouth that my lips are sticking to the soft plastic; my lips slowly peel away from it as I continue to remove the empty blood bag from myself.

I can see that he looks very pleased with me.

"Renee, you did very well."

He says to me with a smile, I cannot help but to glance at his mouth as I am now looking at his sharp white fangs.

I stand here in front of Marrick and I watch him as he is raising his blood bag to his beautiful pale lips. He is now consuming his bag of blood. I cannot help but watch him as he drinks the blood because he is looking right into my eyes.

I must be ready to be with him because I can now feel my blood coursing through my body as I am now craving for his beautiful mouth to clamp down upon my skin so that he can drink from me once more.

I think to myself as I continue to watch him, he is still looking into my eyes as he is consuming the blood from his plastic bag.

I can feel my blood boiling inside of me.

Marrick is now finished he releases the empty plastic bag from his mouth and he moves his hand toward me so that he can take hold of my empty bag from my hand, as he removes the bag out of my hand his fingers are touching the back of my hand as he takes hold of it. If my heart was still alive it would be pounding like a loud drum within my chest. Marrick places empty blood bags into the trash can.

I can tell that Marrick is going to say something because I can feel him. I want to feel him!

"Now is the time that we must start consuming as much human blood as we can. We must be ready for what is coming!"

He says to us all as Damon is handing every one of us another bag of blood.

I can see Damon walking back over to Sarah and he picks her up into his arms and he makes their way into the dining room to go upstairs to their secret room inside of their bedroom. I can feel from Sarah that they are going to make love. I cannot help but close my eyes as I can feel what she is now feeling.

As I open my eyes Keith looks over to Marrick and I as he holds onto his delicious bag of warm human blood.

"Renee if you and Marrick do not mind I am going to go rest for a while, so I will see you soon."

He says to the both of us.

"Good evening Keith and I hope that you sleep well."

Marrick says to him as Keith walks over to the stove to take hold of his casserole, then he begins to move toward the refrigerator. He opens the door and places the food that he had baked on the shelf then he closes the door. Keith looks over to us and he gives us a smile but does not say anything to us. He turns away from us as he is now making his way into the dining room as well so that he can go upstairs to his room. Keith has taken the attic for his resting place.

While Marrick and I remain in the kitchen I look up to him as I am still holding my bag of blood that Damon gave to me a moment ago. I have now realized that I can hear the music coming from the living room "Remember Everything."

I look up to him as we are still standing together in the kitchen.

"Marrick, is it ok if we go outside?"

"We can do whatever you like Renee."

He says to me as he places his pale white hand upon my face he rubs my bottom lip with his thumb.

We turn and walk toward the sliding glass doors Marrick opens it for us and as we step out into the back yard we notice that both Luna and Beauty are lying in the grass together. Marrick closes the door and they both lift their heads up as they watch us walk past them. Someone else has let them outside.

We are now walking by the swimming pool that has two large concrete slabs resting over it.

Marrick and I walk over to the trees and he lowers himself to the ground as he is now sitting in front of one with his back resting against it. I stand here watching him as he raises up his hand to me I place my hand inside of his and he gently pulls me down to have me sit in between his legs. My back is now resting against the front of his body. He moves one of his hands to place it upon my leg; his fingers are resting inside of my thigh.

"Drink from your bag of blood Renee."

He whispers in my ear and then he gently kisses the skin of my neck.

I now have a gentle tingling sensation running through my body.

I am now doing what he has just told me to do. I hold the bag up to my lips as I did while we were in the kitchen just a few minutes ago. Again I feel my fangs forming.

I really do like this feeling as I push them into the thick plastic.

Again I am squeezing the bag as I continue to drink the human blood from it. I am being careful that I do not lose any of it.

I am now realizing how my body is starting to feel as I continue to drink the blood that I am holding as I am still siting between Marrick's legs with my body resting against his.

This feeling that is now developing within me is very powerful and so strong, I am not sure if I can keep control of myself because I now want to feel Marrick inside of me!

He can feel what I am feeling because of our powerful bond. We both finish consuming our blood and he moves his arms. He places one arm across my stomach and his other arm is now resting across my breast. He is holding me very tightly to his sculptured body.

"Renee, you do not have to give in to it, you can control what you are feeling."

"Marrick, I do want to be with you and I want so very much to lose control of myself with you."

I say to him as he loosens his grip on me so that I can turn myself to look into his beautiful eyes.

"Renee, are you sure that you really do want this?"

"Marrick you commanded me to sleep before David forced himself upon me. Yes I do want to be with you in every way. But are you ready to be with me because you know what he had done."

I reply to him as he places his fingers under my chin so that he can look directly into my eyes.

"Yes Renee, I want to be with you, I want to feel myself inside of you once more. I want to feel your gentle loving touch upon my body."

He replies to me as we move closer together and our lips are now touching, we both open our mouths so that our tongues can slowly rub together.

This feeling is making my body tingle once more as I am craving to feel the touch of his beautiful naked body next to mine.

Right away Marrick takes hold of me so that we are now pressing against each other as he stands up and very quickly picks me up in his arms; he is making his way to the house as he moves us to the speed of light. I can feel the warm breeze as we are passing through it. Both Luna and Beauty are running to the door and as Marrick opens it up he allows them to go in first then he carries me into the house and right away he closes the door. I tuck my head close to his shoulder and I have my legs around his waist as he moves very quickly through the house to make our way to our bedroom so that we can go into our secrete room. I can hear the music as he moves us through the house and the song that is now playing is "So Cold (acoustic version)" by Breaking Benjamin.

Marrick is now standing by our bed; he continues to hold me very tightly to him and I remove my legs from around his waist as he has my body press down against his body. His hands are on my bottom that way as he slides my body against his I am able to feel his extremely hard erection as he lowers me, my feet are now on the floor.

He places both of his hands upon each side of my face as his lips are now embracing mine once more I have my hands placed upon his chest.

I feel like I am going to melt as he continues to kiss me. He slides his hands down my face and down the skin of my neck. Now he is using the tips of his fingers to touch my shoulders as he slowly slides down my arms. As he slowly slides his fingers down my skin I can feel his gentle stokes from the tips of his finger nails. Once he touches my hands Marrick removes his nails from my flesh so that he can now take hold of my shirt. I raise my arms so that Marrick can remove it from me.

My vampire blood continues to boil inside of me, I feel as if I am on fire for Marrick.

He places one arm around me to hold me tightly to him as he caresses one of my breasts with his other hand.

I am getting so lost in this feeling that I have for him; I can truly feel the powerful love that he has for me and that I have for him as I also want to feel him deep inside of me. I am so lost in love with him!

He releases his hold on me as he moves himself to stand face to face with me. I look up into his eyes. Marrick bends slowly down in front of me as he is now removing my pajama pants along with my panties; he continues to look into my eyes as he is removing them from me. As he stands up Marrick gently picks me up in his beautiful pale white arms so that he can place me on the bed. I watch him as he removes his clothes we continue to gaze into each other's eyes. He is now lifting his leg to place his knee upon the bed and as he brings himself closer to me. I close my eyes as he moves to lay on top of me. I cannot wait to feel his beautiful touch to be placed upon my naked body once again.

As he slowly moves himself on top of me I can feel my fangs forming once more and my eyes are now completely black, I can also feel that my nails are long and sharp.

As he touches my naked body I can feel his touch going completely through me. I can feel every part of him as we touch each other, and it is such a wonderful beautiful feeling to be able to experience with Marrick.

I can feel Marrick raising his up hips as he is now placing his beautiful hard shaft inside of me as he lowers himself back down upon me.

I am trying so hard not to melt all over him as he is moving deeper inside of me. I honestly cannot control myself!

"Let yourself go Renee."

Marrick whispers into my ear with such a soft low voice as he continues to move himself inside of me.

I am now melting all over him, but I still want him inside of me and I begin to move with him as we are now making love together. This is my first time being with him as I am now a full vampire.

We are slowly thrusting against each other and as we are moving as one I can feel his grip on me become tighter, I move my head so that he can place his mouth upon my neck. I can feel his fangs pushing very slowly into my skin as he is now drinking my thick sweet vampire blood. This feeling has such a powerful over whelming feeling; this is such a different feeling then when I was half human and vampire because now it feels special so very important and personal.

Marrick continues to drink my blood as we are making love, he is slowly thrusting himself deeper into me and I continue to move to him making him feel every part inside of me.

He releases his mouth from my skin and he then starts to lower himself closer to me, I place my hands on the back of his arms and as I feel his skin now touching my lips I place my mouth upon his soft pale white flesh and I slowly force my fangs into him. I can taste his thick sweet blood as it fills my mouth I slowly swallow his blood into me. I close my eyes as I continue to drink from him as we move together making love. This is such a beautiful feeling to be making love with him and drinking each other's blood.

I can feel myself welling up deep within me and I release his skin from my mouth as we continue to move together for I am now melting all over him once more, he continues to move as I can feel him getting ready, he is now releasing his blood inside of me as he comes.

As he is still on top of me with his hard beautiful shaft still buried deep inside of me Marrick is looking right into my black eyes and I have my head tilted slightly back so that I am looking back into his. He lowers his head closer to me so that he can kiss me once more, then he slowly slides himself out of me and he is now lying on his side next to me. I move onto my side to have my back against the front of him. Marrick covers the both of us with the quilt that is upon our bed. He takes hold of me very tightly in his arms holding me once again to his tall beautiful naked perfectly sculptured body he also places his leg on top on mine to hold me even closer to him. I can feel my eyes turning back to normal as well as my fangs and nails.

I can feel our bodies slowly starting to shut down, the sun is starting to come up.

Our bodies are now resting but I can still feel him as he continues to hold me to him. I am so happy that I can feel his touch as our bodies continue to rest but we will not be able to move again until the sun starts to go down.

"Marrick can you hear me?"

"Yes Renee, I can hear you."

"Are you going to help them, to turn the humans?"

"No Renee I will not."

He replies to me with his thought.

"May I ask you as to why you will not help to turn them?"

"Renee the only one that I want to be connected to is you and to my brother. Damon will not be turning any one either."

"Marrick I do not know what to say to that but I do understand. I only want to be connected to you and Sarah."

"You do not have to say anything at all Renee. But I am glad that you do feel the same way."

He says to me as I lay here against him wishing that I could move my body to face Marrick so that I can wrap my arms around him.

"Have you every turned anyone else other than me?"

"No Renee I have not. You are the only one that I have and will ever turn."

I do not reply to what he has just said to me mostly because I do not know what to say or maybe I am scared of what he may say.

I cannot help but now worry as we continue to rest our bodies now that the sun has risen.

"Marrick, Keith will not be able to protect us if for some reason David sends his people after us during the day."

"Everything will be ok I promise you. Renee, Logan is going to send some of her half turned humans to us today while we rest. I assure you that you will not need to worry. They have been consuming human blood nonstop so their strength is now evenly matched with David's half turned creatures."

"Thank you for letting me know about that. Marrick I hope that I will be able to rest my mind."

"Renee, for now everything is safe but as you had said earlier, soon it will become dangerous for us all once more."

Marrick I do understand that and I will do everything that I can to be ready this time."

I reply to him as we send thoughts to each other.

"Renee, I want you to rest your mind so that when you wake this evening, you will feel completely rested."

"Marrick, will you please command me to sleep?"

"Renee you must go to sleep and I want you to awake when the sun starts to set!"

I hear him say to me in my thoughts as I am now starting to rest my mind.

Chapter Two

As I am starting to wake up I realize that I am not able to move my body yet. I find myself listening to beating sounds within my ears. I am still lying in bed unable to move but yet I can hear so many beats but they are not in rhythm.

I am now able to slowly move as I continue lying next to Marrick I can feel his arms around me and his leg is still draped across mine as I am still being tightly held against him.

I do love being held so close against him.

I say to myself as I am still listening to this sound that is still beating with in my ears.

I am craving blood, I want to feed! I can feel myself slowly starting to change, as I open my eyes I can feel them changing completely black, and I can feel my nails slowly growing long and sharp as well as my fangs are now forming.

I AM HUNGRY!

I want human blood and I can feel the pain as it starts to develop within me.

But I am now scared to leave our secrete bed room. Logan's people are here it is their hearts that are beating within my ears.

Marrick is waking up and he is able to move his body; I can feel his arms tightening around me to hold my body tighter to his.

"Renee, you will find that if you feed before you leave our room that you will be able to control yourself."

He softly whispers in my ear.

I can feel Marrick as he slowly releases me from his hold and he removes himself from our bed. I can hear him going to the door of our secrete room to open it up. The pain that I am feeling is because my body wants blood and this feeling is becoming stronger!

I now understand what he was trying to explain to me last night.

I move my head so that I can look at him as I gaze at his beautiful pale white naked body.

As I continue watching Marrick, he is returning to me with four bags of blood and he hands me two of them. As I hold them in my hands I can feel the warmth from them.

"Renee, Keith has prepared this for us."

Marrick says to me as he sits down upon the bed next to me.

I place the bags of blood upon my stomach as I sit up in bed. I cannot wait to feed.

Marrick gently runs his fingers through my hair as he sits next to me. I look down at my two warm bags I move my hand. I am slowly sliding my fingers across the top one of them I am now sliding my hand under the warm bag of human blood. I am holding it in the palm of my hand as I gently place my fingers around the bag to hold onto it, careful not to put a hole in it with my long nails. I can feel the warmth pulsating as I hold it.

"Renee after you consume your blood you will feel much better and you will not be so scared to leave this room. I know that you will not hurt anyone and you must also trust in yourself."

"I will try Marrick, to trust myself."

I reply to him before I place the thick soft plastic bag that contains delicious warm human blood to my lips. I slowly push my fangs into it and I close my eyes as the blood starts to flow smoothly into my mouth. As I feed from it I can feel the warm essence of the blood beginning to absorb within my body.

I have finished the first bag and I pick up my second bag of warm blood as I place it against my mouth. Once again as the blood slowly fills my mouth I allow it to flow gently down my throat. I am no longer worried about leaving our secret room behind our closet.

As I look back over to Marrick he is looking back at me with such a loving look in his beautiful dark coal black eyes. I remove the bag from my face and as I continue to look at him I cannot help but to smile. I notice that he has also consumed his human blood as well.

"Renee, we should go down stairs Logan and Richard will be arriving soon. We will always be able to hear the beat of a living heart; it is up to you if you choose to listen as the heart beats within their chest."

He says to me as we continue to sit together upon our bed.

"I understand Marrick I was able to hear the beat of Keith's heart last evening for the first time. I could also hear Luna's as well. Will you please allow me time to get ready? I would really like to take a shower."

I say to him as I look upon his beautiful pale white face.

"You can take as much time as you need Renee."

He replies to me as he gets up from the bed.

He walks over to the door of our secret room once more and I find myself watching him again.

He slowly turns his head to look over to me as I look upon his beautiful naked body.

"Renee, I will stay here with you while you get ready."

He says to me as I am now getting a very strange feeling from him.

He walks back over to the bed and he reaches out his hand I place my hand inside of his as he helps me to get up out of bed. Marrick gently wraps me up in the blanket from our bed then we both walk out of our secret room and into the bedroom. As I pass by the window in our bedroom I cannot help myself, I feel that I need to stop, that there is something I need to see.

As I stop right in front of the window I turn to face it Marrick is right behind me with his hands placed on my arms. As I am now looking out the window into the back yard, I have tears of blood forming in my eyes as I look upon what Keith has done. There is now a beautiful marble birdbath surrounded by beautiful bushes of red roses in the place where David had murdered Fred. Keith has made a memorial for his loving partner and our good friend.

I place my hands over my face I am now crying. Marrick gently places his hands on my shoulders to turn me around so that I am now facing him as he now holds me to him. He allows me to continue crying for Fred. As I am finally able to calm down I place my arms around his body and I hold on to Marrick as tightly as I can. He has placed one arm across the back of my shoulders as he places his other hand in my hair to rub the back of my head.

Finally I look up at him with my blood stained face from my tears.

"Marrick, if you do not mind I would like to take a shower."

I say to him as I try to stop my blood tears from forming with in my eyes.

"I do not mind at all Renee. Would you like me to wait here for you?"

He asks me as moves his hand from the back of my head so that he can place it on the side of my face, he moves his thumb to rub the skin of my cheek.

"No, I will be ok. Marrick you should go and wait for Logan and Richard."

I reply to him as we are still standing by the window, I still have my arms wrapped around him.

"Very well, I will see you down stairs when you are finished."

He says to me as he lowers his head down so that he can kiss the top of my head.

We release the hold that we have on each other, I watch Marrick walk away from me so that he can gather some clothes for himself. I go back into the closet to gather some clothes for myself as well and I also walk over so that I can close the door to our secrete room. After Marrick is dressed I can hear him walk out of the bedroom to go down stairs.

As I walk out of the walk in closet I am now back inside of the bedroom I stop once more by the window so that I can look upon

Fred's memorial once more. I can now feel a very powerful anger growing within me as I am now craving once again to be the one who kills that fucking monster.

As I stand here by the window I do not hear any thoughts coming from Marrick but I can feel him. I am concentrating on him as I am trying to control the way that I am now feeling. Because of Marrick, I am able to calm my feelings.

I walk into our bathroom and I place my clothes on the floor by the shower.

There is a mirror in the bathroom I am scared to look into it because I do not know if I will have a reflection. I do not remember if I have ever noticed that Marrick has a reflection or not.

I open up the door to the shower I turn on the water and I adjusted it to the warmth that I like. I release the blanket that he had wrapped around my body and it slowly slides down onto the floor as it falls into a circle around my feet. I step into the water and I close the door, I turn around and I move myself into my very hot shower as it runs down the back of me. I raise my hands up to my head so that I can run them through my hair. I take hold of my bottle of shower gel and I squeeze a small amount into my hand as I begin to wash my body. I place my shower gel back down on the rim of the tub and I take hold of my shampoo, I tip it upside down over the palm of my hand and I squeeze some out, I begin to wash my hair. After I rinse the soap from my hair I place my hands upon the skin of my legs and I move them around to feel if I have any hair stubbles that need to be shaved and there are none. So I turn the water off and I open the shower door once more so that I can grab my towel that is hanging on the bar of shower door and I begin to dry myself off. I look over to the mirror and it is covered with steam. After I have finished I step out of the shower and I bend down to grab my clothes and I begin to get dressed. I walk over to the steam covered mirror I place my hands upon the counter as I lower my head down I am now looking down at the floor. With my head still lowered as I continue to look at the floor of the bathroom, I raise my hand up and I wipe the steam covered mirror and I close my eyes as I slowly raise my head back up to look into the mirror.

If I could breathe I know that I would be taking a deep breath right now to help prepare myself but because I am no longer alive, I can't breathe.

As I am thinking of this I slowly begin to open my eyes.

I am now looking into the mirror and as I am doing this my reflection is looking back at me. I am a little excited that I still have a reflection as I stand here looking at myself.

I still look the same except that my skin is no longer flesh color I now have pale white skin.

I cannot help but say to myself as I continue to stand in front of the mirror looking at myself.

I grab my hair brush so that I can brush my reddish brown hair. I brush out of my hair tangles I place the brush back down onto the counter. I am now reaching for my tooth brush and my tooth paste.

I have always brushed my teeth while I was alive, so why should I stop now?

I say to myself as I begin brushing my teeth.

The tooth paste does not taste the same; it has a very strong disgusting taste to it. I am trying really hard not to gag from the taste of the tooth paste that it now has but I still want my teeth to be clean and my breath to be fresh. I am now forcing myself as I continue to brush my teeth, the taste is so horrible.

I have finished brushing my teeth I put my tooth brush and tooth paste away and I reach for my deodorant when I am done with it I place it back on the counter. As I look into the bathroom mirror one more time I find myself looking at my hair because it seems to have grown. I turn myself to walk out of the bathroom to go back into the bedroom and I put my shoes on. I am now looking forward to Keith showing me how to use the cross bow.

But when I go outside I will be in the back yard with Fred's memorial. I can do this, I can control my feelings!

I say to myself in a very demanding way as I am trying to maintain control.

I walk over to the bedroom door to open it up; as soon as I step out I can smell blood. I am now in a hurry to make my way into the kitchen and so I decide to see how fast I can now move. As I am making my way down the steps and into the kitchen I am running through the house so fast that as I pass by, everything looks like a blur. Within seconds I am now standing in the kitchen waiting for my blood.

I can see that Marrick is waiting for me he has a bag of human blood for me and as I walk up to him he holds it out for me to take. I am grabbing onto my bag of blood as I am now tilting my head back so that Marrick can lower his head down to kiss my lips with his beautiful soft pale lips.

After our kiss he slowly moves his head over to my ear.

"You will never lose your beautiful reflection Renee. But our hair will still continue to grow even though we are no longer alive."

He whispers to me as I now have a smile upon my face.

"Thank you Marrick for letting me know. But I am not happy that I will still have to shave."

I say to him as I look into his beautiful eyes as he smiles to what I have just said to him.

I have my bag of blood in both of my hands and I am now raising it up so that I can place my mouth upon it and I am forcing my fangs into the thick soft plastic and I am now consuming human blood.

When I am finished I can feel Sarah, I know that she is behind me. She is placing her arm around the front of me as she is now kissing my cheek.

Marrick reaches for my empty bag and he places it into the trash can along with his.

"Good evening moon beam how are you doing?"

She says to me as I cannot help but smile once more.

I place both of my hands upon her arm as she continues to have her arm draped around the front of my shoulders.

"Good evening my beautiful blood sister, I am doing well this evening and how are you doing?"

I ask Sarah.

She releases her hold on me and I remove my hands from her arm, she is now standing beside of me.

"I am doing good thank you. Renee, Keith has told me that you are going to learn how to use the cross bow this evening."

"Yes I am going to learn how to use it, Sarah I just hope that I do not shoot anyone."

I reply to her as she starts to giggle at what I have just said to her.

"Renee I do not think that you will shoot anyone."

She says to me with a smile on her face.

"If you like, you and Sarah can go meet Keith out back he is waiting for you. Logan and Richard will be here shortly."

Marrick says to the both of us.

"Ok we will go join Keith in the back yard while we wait for them to arrive."

I reply to him as Sarah is taking hold of my hand to lead me out into the back yard.

As I am walking out of the house I am looking for the wolves, and I do not see them. I do not even see the people that Logan has sent over but I can still hear their hearts beating.

I am looking up into the sky and it is a beautiful clear night the stars are shining brightly and I cannot wait to look upon the beauty of the full moon once again. Soon it will start to appear.

"Sarah I hope that Luna and Beauty have not wondered off to far."

I say to her as I lower my head from looking at the sky.

"Renee, if anything happens to them I know that you will feel that something is not right and we will go after them right away. We can listen for the sound of their heart beats; the wolves' heart beat will sound very fast because I am sure that they are hunting."

"Sarah I will let you know right away if I do feel something bad. I did not even think about listening for Luna and Beauty's heart beats."

I reply to her as we both turn our heads to look at Keith as he starts to make his way to us.

As Keith continues to walk toward us I set my gaze into the trees just to see if I can find where Logan's people are at. As I continue to look within the trees I have found them. I can see their dark red glows with the color of yellow mixed in. There are so many of them and every one of them are half turned. They are all waiting for something to happen as every one of them are watching from within the trees. As I continue looking at them I can also see they have their weapons clutched tightly in their hands. There are so many of them that I am not even going to try and guess as to how many there are; they are scattered throughout the woods. I have found Luna and Beauty they are in the woods as well; Sarah is right they are hunting for small animals.

The wolves are part of our family, I do not know what Sarah and I would do if anything were to happen to them.

I think to myself as I continue to watch them.

I look over to Sarah and Keith.

"Why is it that Logan's people are not here in the yard with us?"

I ask the both of them.

Keith looks over to me.

"Because Renee this time, we are prepared for a surprise attack from David!"

Keith replies to me.

Marrick is right, I am still frightened!

I think to myself as I stand here looking at him.

"But David's people will see them hiding within the trees, they will be able to see their glow!"

I reply to Keith as I am now feeling confused.

"Keith how is that going to work for us?"

"Renee, we want them to be noticed we want them to know that we are absolutely one hundred percent ready for them to attack us again. But do not worry because we will soon be attacking them."

Keith says to us as if he sounds like he is ready for his revenge.

This time it is Keith who is changing the subject to get our minds off of that monster.

"Well before you start your lesson, I have something for both of you ladies."

"A present oh Keith how exciting!"

Sarah says to him with excitement in her voice.

Just the way she said it I cannot help but laugh.

Keith walks over to the trees and we stand here watching him as he is now picking up three bags from the ground. He is now walking back over to the both of us, we continue to watch him, as he is now standing in front of us once again he hands us each a brown leather bag but he keeps hold of the third leather bag for himself.

I am not going to look into the trees any more this evening, well try not to anyway.

I say to myself as I take hold of the bag from him.

"Keith, should I be scared to open this?"

I ask him as I stand here holding the bag; I am giving him my half wondering smile as I try to take my mind off Logan's people as they are waiting in the woods.

I can hear Sarah laughing as she is looking into her bag that Keith just gave to her.

"No Renee, there is nothing that you should be scared of, just open up your bag."

He says to me as he starts to laugh as well.

Sarah and I both are pulling out of our bags a belt and some kind of wrist halter with a metal track attached to it.

"Ladies these belts are designed to hold wooden daggers and the small wooden arrow heads and also the wooden arrows that go along with your cross bows. The wrist halters are designed to hold your cross bows in place on the top of your wrist. As you can also see that these brown leather bags have shoulder straps so that you can carry all of your supplies inside of them with the bag resting on your backs."

He explains to us.

"Keith this is awesome, thank you so much."

I say to him.

"You are welcome Renee."

"Keith how are we to place a very large cross bow on these wrist halters?"

Sarah asks him with a concerned look upon her face.

"Allow for me to tell you how. Your wrist halters are designed for a very small cross bow that has been made just for the two of you by me."

Keith explains as he is now placing his bag onto the ground, he is reaching into it and Keith is now pulling out two small cross bows and hands them to each of us.

As we are both looking at the small cross bows we both notice that they are no bigger than our hands.

As Sarah takes hold of her cross bow she is also looking at the wrist halter.

"Keith I take it that we slide the cross bow on the metal track that is on the wrist halter and it will stay in place?"

Sarah asks him as she is still looking at both of her items.

"Yes, but when you slide the cross bow on the track you must push it all the way up and then slowly back down the track until the cross bow locks into place."

Keith explains to her.

So as I am listening to them I put my two pieces together then slowly slide my right hand into the wrist halter. It does not buckle or tie nor are there any snaps all I have to do is slide my hand into it, there is also a hole just big enough for my thumb to go into and the cross bow is now securely resting on top of my wrist.

I look over to Sarah and she is doing the same.

I am now looking at Keith.

"So tell me where is the trigger to this and how do we fire our wooden arrows from this?"

I ask him.

"Well for now Renee, I am sorry to say that you will have to use your left hand to push down on the button, it is on the back of the cross bow."

I am holding my wrist close to my chest I am looking for the button that he is talking about. I have found it; it is right behind the track that the wooden arrow locks into so I hold my right arm straight out in front of me as I place my left index finger on the button to see if it will seem difficult or awkward in some way but for now it seems ok to deal with.

I am not sure if I am going to like this.

I think to myself as Sarah is looking at me.

Now we are placing the belts around our waist so that we can feel how they fit and also how we will want to place the wooden daggers and arrow heads along with the cross bow arrows inside of the loops that Keith has made for them to be placed within the belts.

I feel that I have come up with a very good question that I need to ask.

"Keith by any chance would you have some sort of item to protect our chest and our necks?"

He looks over at me with such a wondering look upon his face.

"Renee, to be honest I have been working on that, as soon as I can figure out what will work for everyone I will let you know. I promise that I am working as fast as I can on this project but it will also take some time."

Keith replies to me.

"Please hurry up with that so that our bodies will be better protected."

I say to him in a begging kind of way.

As we are all standing here in the back yard we have stopped what we are doing and we look toward the house. We can hear the loud sounds of several large trucks shifting gears as they slowly drive on the dark road that ends in the front of the house.

"Logan and Richard are here, and they also have refrigerator trucks and an abundant supply of human blood that will last us for a good while. Robert and Michael are also supplying blood as well when they arrive tomorrow evening."

Keith explains to us as I now realize that the three of us are gazing upon Fred's memorial as we continue to stand in the back yard.

"Renee, Logan said that there is something that you must see."

He says to me right away with a worried look upon his face.

As I am standing here listening to what he is saying I begin to have one of my feelings.

"Something is not right, I do not have a bad feeling but again I am going to say that something is so not right."

I say to both of them.

"Keith do you know what it is that she wants me to see?"

I ask him as we continue to stand together in the back yard.

"No Renee I do not. Logan has not said what it is, except that you must go to her."

He replies to me.

"Do you want us to go with you to meet Logan?"

Sarah asks me.

"If you both do not mind, I would also like to know why I am having this strange feeling."

I reply back to her.

"Renee, I do not mind walking to the front of the house with you."

Keith says to me as we look at each other.

"Well then, shall we go to her?"

I ask to them both.

We start walking from the back of the house, we are now walking by the side of the house and we are getting closer to the trucks that have just pulled up to the front. As we are getting closer we notice that one of the trucks is a semi and there are two other trucks that have box trailers we can tell that those are the refrigerators trucks for us to store the bags of human blood. The three of us are moving as fast as we can.

This feeling that I have is now becoming stronger.

I say to myself as we continue making our way over to them.

We can see a man standing by the trucks, he looks so familiar. He must be Richard.

I really did not pay that much attention to what he looked like when Sarah took me to Logan's bar with the big colorful WELCOME sign on my birthday. He is the bartender that served us. But as we are walking closer I can see that he looks to be maybe 5'8 and he has short brown hair, he does not look very muscular but he does have a very nice body tone.

I remember Sarah saying to me that Richard is in love with Logan but she does not yet know about his feelings. I am sure that she does know in some way about how he feels about her.

I think to myself as we continue walking toward him.

As we are getting closer Richard turns his head to watch us as we coming closer to him. We are now standing with him and I can see his eyes. His eyes are amazing, they are grey.

As we continue to stand here with Richard I can smell a sweet scent in the air, it is human blood it is very strong. I look over to Sarah and she has her head tilted slightly back, she has her mouth slightly opened and I am watching her fangs as they begin to grow.

We do not talk to Richard because the smell of fresh human blood has our complete attention.

I can feel Marrick and I know that he is very close. We all can smell the scent in the air; we are starting to crave the taste. I can feel myself changing. I turn my head just slightly so that I can look at Keith, his eyes are now completely black.

"Renee, I need you to come to the back of this semi-truck."

I can hear Marrick's voice and I am amazed that he did not send his thoughts to me.

I take off my wrist halter that is now attached to my cross bow and I hand it to Keith. I start walking to the back of the semi-truck and I begin feel a great over whelming feeling of sadness. I stop walking; I can also feel fear as well as regret. I move myself closer to the side of the trailer I raise my hand up so that I can place it on the side. I am trying very hard not to cry because of what I am feeling and it has also taken my craving for the blood away. I close my eyes and I concentrate on the gentle breeze I can feel it as if it is playing with my hair. I am now ready to walk to the back of the trailer and I remove my hand from it as I start to walk once again. I am now at the back of the semi-truck and as I look inside of the trailer I can see a women lying down upon a cot. I can see that there are several cots that are bolted into the floor.

Is this where we will be resting during the day while we are searching for David?

I ask to myself as I am looking inside.

Yes Renee you are correct.

I hear Marrick reply to me with his thought.

I slightly move my head so that I can look over to him; he is standing at the opening of the trailer waiting for me. As we look at each other he holds out both of his hands for me to take hold of as he is now bending down from inside of the trailer. I take a few steps toward him so that he is now in front of me and I raise my arms up so that he can take hold of me. Marrick is now pulling me up to him as he lifts me up inside of the trailer. As he releases me I walk over to the woman that is lying on one of the cots and once again I can smell her blood as it drips onto the floor. Logan and Damon are also in here as well I can hear them as they move closer they are now standing beside Marrick. I can feel Sarah I know that she is with Keith and Richard.

I must control myself!

I say to myself as I close my eyes for a moment.

I am here for you Renee.

Thank you, Sarah.

I reply to her with my thought.

I have not changed back to normal; I know it is because of my emotions. As I open my eyes to look down to the woman lying on the cot I recognize who she is right away.

She is the healthy woman with the short dark hair. I remember seeing scars all over her I also remember her not being so sick looking as she is now but she was so very sad.

"Marrick, she is the one who gave me blood while I was a prisoner and she had also left the door unlocked to the room that I was in for me the evening that you and along with everyone came to rescue me."

I say to him as I am now lowering myself onto my knees so that I can be at her side.

"HE did this to you; David tortured you because you helped me."

I say to her as I try to keep myself calm.

She slowly moves her head to look at me as she opens her eyes. She is so very weak; I know that she will not live much longer.

"You need to know that he is becoming strong and powerful again."

She says to me in a very harsh whisper.

I can hear the rasping she is having trouble breathing and I can see that she is in so much pain.

"Please allow us to turn you!"

I ask to the dark hair woman.

"No, I do not want to go on as a vampire I need peace, please you must allow me to die."

She replies back to me as she tries to keep her eyes open.

I do not know what to do or say to her, I feel so lost right now. All I can do is look upon her, if she did not help me she would never have happened to her. She would not be dying.

Her left eye is so swollen she can hardly see out of it, her face is bruised and she has a very deep gash in her bottom lip. She has so many bite marks upon her body and very deep cuts within her skin. I can also see that her wounds have been cleaned; I can smell the antiseptic that was used. Both of her hands are wrapped in bandages that have blood slowly dripping from them.

The bite marks and the deep cuts in her skin I know that this has been done by David because these are the same marks that I had on my body.

As I continue to look upon her I can see that the way her hands are wrapped she is missing three fingers, two on her right and one on her left. Her clothes have also been torn.

SOMETHING NEEDS TO BE DONE!

I scream as loud as I can inside of my mind.

"Renee, please do not make me suffer any longer."

She begs to me.

"May I ask you for your name?"

I ask her as I move my hands toward her I gently take hold of her hand that is closest to me.

"My name is Becky."

She slowly replies to me as she starts to gasp for air.

Again I do not reply back to her. I continue sitting on my knees in a small pool of blood that is lying on the floor of this trailer that as escaped from her soaked bandages.

"Renee please forgive me."

She begs to me as she moves her had so that she can now look upon the celling of the trailer.

I am now watching as her tears are escaping from her eyes as they slowly run down her temples and into her hair as she lies upon the cot.

"Forgive you? Becky there is nothing to forgive because you were doing what you were ordered to do! So please do not feel this way."

I reply to her as I can feel my anger growing within me once more.

"Please Renee allow me to die. Take the blood that I have left inside of me and let me be at peace."

Becky begs to me once more with such a soft whisper in her voice.

Right away I look up to Marrick.

"I really do not want to be the one to do this, and this is bringing back my memory of the thin red hair women."

I say to him as I now have tears of blood streaming down my face.

I look at Becky once more as I can hear her heart barely beating and her eyes are now closed.

"I am so very sorry but I cannot do this for you."

I say to her as I have now lowered my head, as I continue to sit beside Becky holding her hand I place my head upon my arm crying quictly to myself.

Marrick gently grabs hold of my arm I let go of her hand so that I can stand up. We both walk to the opening of the trailer he places his arm around me and we jump out together; we are now on the ground. As Marrick still holds on to me we walk to the other side of the truck.

I need to know so I am sending him my thought as I see Damon walk over to Sarah.

"Please tell me, who is going to be the one to put Becky at peace so that she does not have to suffer any longer."

"Logan is going to be the one to help her to die."

He replies to me with his thought as we continue standing by the side of the truck.

I raise my hands so that they are level with my stomach and I turn them over I am now looking at my palms. I have Becky's blood on both of my hands and I am not the one who has beaten and tortured or cut off three of her fingers. I also have her blood all over my pant legs because I was sitting on my knees so that I could be at her side.

As I am looking down I slowly bring my fingers in so that I can make a fist with both hands. I close my eyes as I am now trying to calm myself once more.

"I am not sure if I am able to control what I am feeling."

I say to Marrick as I now have my fists against my chest.

He takes a couple of steps so that he is now standing in front of me I can feel his hands as he gently takes hold of my arms pulling me to him. Marrick is holding me close to him and I now have my fists between us still resting on my chest. As I open my eyes I can see that Keith and Sarah along with Damon are now walking toward us. I remove my arm from between our bodies so that I can hold out my right hand to Keith and he is now handing back to me the wrist halter with the cross bow still attached to it. Marrick slowly releases his hold on me as I am stepping away from him. I am now putting the halter back onto my wrist as I slide my hand inside of it once again. I still have Becky's blood on my hands and pants.

I look back over to Keith as he stands here; I know that he is worried about me I can see the look on his face.

"Keith I am ready to continue my training with the cross bow."

I say to him as I am now walking away from them, I am heading into the back yard.

I do not know what to do or say about what had happened to Becky. But I do feel very badly that I could not be the one to give her what she wanted.

It does not take Sarah very long for her to be by my side as we are now in the back yard waiting for Keith to join us.

I am unable to say anything at this moment, but I do reach for Sarah's hand as we are now holding onto each other as we stand side by side next to the covered pool. She does not mind that my hands are still covered in blood.

I set my gaze into the woods once more and like before I can see all of Logan's half turned humans hiding within the trees. There is movement on the ground from within the woods, I can see both of the wolves now, Luna and Beauty are now running toward us. Beauty makes her to next to Sarah's side as Luna is now next to me.

We can hear Keith coming closer to us and we can smell that he has blood with him. As he comes up to us he is now handing us each a bag of blood.

"Ladies this is now the time that we all must consume blood rather if we are hungry or not. So Renee and Sarah you need to feed on it the same way you both used to drink ice tea and your favorite alcohol drinks, pretend that you are drinking chocolate milk if you must. You must have human blood with you at all times for now on! You can place the blood inside of a plastic bottle when you are around humans. It does not matter what you carry it in, just as long as you are constantly consuming blood."

He explains to us as we each take a bag from his hands.

As we start to drink from it Sarah and I pull our bags away from our mouths right away.

"Keith this is not warm it is very cold."

Sarah says to him as I have realized very quickly that I do not like cold human blood.

"We cannot be picky; we must consume human blood at all times from this point on. Warm or cold we must do this if we are to match the strength of David and his evil creatures!"

"We understand Keith, and we will do what is needed."

I reply to him as we are now continuing to consume our very cold bag of human blood.

I can feel Marrick I know that he is coming closer to us. I turn to look at him and Damon along with Logan and Richard.

I am not even going to ask what they did with Becky's body; I am not going to bring her up at all.

I say to Marrick as I cannot help but to send my thought to him.

I look over to Sarah as she looks back to me there is a very strange feeling coming from her and she has such a concerned look upon her face.

"Very well Renee, then so be it. But I must warn you, Richard is going to test you, he does NOT want us to interfere in anyway."

He says to me as he sends his thoughts back to me.

"Marrick I do not understand what do you mean by he wants to test ME?"

I reply to him right away.

"Renee, why did you not give Becky what she wanted, she was begging you to be the one to end her suffering and you did not do it? WHY?"

Richard asks me with such anger in his voice.

I cannot help but to feel guilty for not doing it myself.

"Because I did not want be the one to do end her life!"

I reply to Richard as I am now looking at him.

"She wanted YOU to do it; you are nothing but a COWARD!"

He yells to me.

A COWARD!

I reply back to him.

I now have such a very strong powerful anger and sadness as well growing inside of me as my body begins to shake.

I want so much to kick his ass! I also want to cry. Why is he saying this to me?

I ask to myself because I feel that I do not understand what he is trying to do.

How come Marrick has not said anything on my behalf, why is he not defending me? No one is helping me. NOW I AM ENRAGED!

I say to myself as I feel so angry with everyone.

Luna is standing directly in front of me and she is growling as she is showing her teeth to Richard. Luna slowly takes a few steps toward him.

"What is wrong Renee, does the truth hurt you?"

He asks to me his voice still sounding very angry. Richard quickly lowers his eyes to looks down at Luna watching as she continues to move toward him. He raises his eyes and now he is looking at me once more.

He better watch what he does because she will attack him!

I release what is left in my plastic bag of cold human blood as it falls to the ground. I look over to Fred's beautiful memorial surrounded by the bushes of red roses. My anger is strong!

As I now look down at my hands I remove the wrist halter from my right hand and this time I hand it to Sarah. I look down once again as I turn my hands over to look at my palms still coved in Becky's blood and this anger inside of me is growing very powerful that I can no longer hear the words coming from Richard but I can see that Luna is now ready to attack him. All he has to do is take one move toward us. I look back at him, I can see his lips moving but I am so angry I still cannot hear his words.

I can no longer control myself and without even thinking of what I am going to do or say I find myself walking closer to him and my right hand is now in a form of a fist I pull my arm back and as fast and hard as I possibly can I push my fist toward him, I can feel his skin move as I punch Richard in his stomach. Luna is barking at him once again, I know that she is giving him his last warning because she continues to slowly move toward him.

"Richard I do not know what you are trying to do but I really want to hurt you right now!"

I say to him as my voice is low with a very nervous and angry sound.

I have also come to realize that my eyes are still completely black and my fangs along with my nails are still long and sharp. But as I remove my fist from his stomach I realize that my long nails are digging into the skin of my hand because I have blood now dripping from me.

I make myself walk away from Richard. Sarah is now with me she is trying to calm me down but I am too angry to listen to her.

"Renee, you must try to relax yourself."

She says to me.

"Now Renee, do you really think that your punch can hurt me? I still think that you are nothing but a COWARD you always rely on Marrick to be here so that he can save and protect you. I think that you are nothing but a SELFISH LITTLE BITCH!"

His voice is ringing in my ears and I am still shaking with anger and so right away I turn to face him as I start running toward Richard as fast as I can. I have my right hand opened with my fingers stretched out and my long sharp nails are pointed directly toward him. I am now standing in front of Richard and as I look up into his grey eyes I am forcing my hand inside of his stomach.

"HOW DARE you say these things to ME!"

I say to Richard as I push my hand farther inside of his stomach.

I can feel his thick vampire blood as it is pouring out of his body and off my wrist I can also hear his blood as it pours onto the ground. As I have my hand inside of him I can feel his intestines and I wrap my fingers around it and I start to squeeze as hard as I can. I know that I am causing him pain.

Right away he takes hold of my arm with both of his hands and he lowers his head just slightly so that he can look into my eyes.

I have lost control of myself!

"I needed to see what you are capable of doing Renee. You do not know me so there for I knew that you would not hold yourself back by making you angry with me."

Richard explains to me as he slowly bends his upper body toward me with my hand still inside of his body.

I notice that his eyes are no longer grey they are now completely black and his fangs have formed as well.

"The test, Marrick tried to warn me, he said that you were going to test me!"

I say to him as I now remember what Marrick had said to me with his thoughts.

"Renee, I must say that you have passed my test so please very slowly remove your hand from the inside of my stomach so that I can heal."

Richard says to me softly as he still has a hold of my arm.

I release the hold that I have of his insides and I slowly start to pull my hand out of his body.

I feel so badly that I can feel my eyes filling up with blood tears once more because I allowed myself to lose control.

I can feel that someone is walking toward us as Richard is now watching this person coming closer.

I know that this person is not alive.

"Renee I would like to thank you for doing what you have just done to him because from time to time I have thought about doing that myself. Richard can be such an ass at times."

Logan says to me.

I look to Richard again because I feel so horrible for what I did to him.

"I do not understand Richard why did you not stop me?"

I ask him as he is now slowly starting to heal. I can see that his eyes and teeth are now back to normal.

He looks back over to me as we continue to stand in the back yard.

"If you really must know Renee it is because I did not believe that you would do anything like what you have just done by forcing your hand inside of my stomach. But I will never take you for granted again."

He replies to me as Luna continues watching his every move.

"Richard, are you going to be ok?"

I ask him as I watch him slowing standing his body straight up.

"I will be fine Renee; it will not take very long for my body to heal."

He replies to me as I watch Logan hand him a bag of human blood.

As Richard takes hold of it he raises it up to his mouth and he begins to consume his bag of blood.

Logan gently takes hold of my wrist.

"Renee, please do not feel bad for what had just happened. He really wanted to find out what you are capable of doing. I must say that I am very proud of you. I also meant what I had said earlier, he really can be a total ass at times."

Richard cannot help but look at Logan while he is consuming his human blood because of what she has just said about him.

I force a smile for her but I still feel very badly.

I look over to Sarah as she is now standing beside me once more she is grabbing onto my hand again. But as she takes hold of my hand I am remembering that I still have Becky's blood still on my skin and now I have Richard's blood as well. I also have my own blood because I was so angry that I stabbed my own nails in the skin of my hand.

I can feel Logan letting go of my wrist as Marrick is now placing his hand upon my shoulder.

"Renee, you should go inside the house so that you can clean the blood off from yourself."

Marrick says to me as he speaks so softly with his words.

"Yes, you are right I should go clean my hands and change my clothes."

I say to him as I turn myself to look into his loving dark coal black eyes.

I start walking back to the house and I can still hear Luna growling so I turn my head to look at her and she is still watching Richard. She is still watching every move that he is making. I look to see what Beauty is doing as I continue walking toward the sliding glass doors and she is standing right in front of Sarah as if she is guarding her. Beauty is not growling but she looks as if she is ready to attack if she feels that she has to.

As I am now at the sliding glass doors I place my hand on the handle so that I can open the door.

"Luna would you like to join me?"

I say to her before I walk inside of the house.

Right away Luna is running toward me and I allow her to go in the house first then I step inside and I close the door behind me.

I walk over to the kitchen sink and I turn on the water and I grab the liquid soap and I am now scrubbing the skin of my hands and also my wrist as I am trying to remove the thick stained blood.

I look over to Luna and she is standing at the sliding glass doors as she is looking outside.

"Luna, are you still watching Richard?"

She does not look at me but she makes a high pitch sound as she is now sitting on the floor still looking into the back yard.

As I continue to wash the blood from my hands I look at her once more.

"Luna, it is ok I promise. Richard wanted to see what I would do if he made me angry. He was testing me Luna, I passed his test. So please do not worry about what he will do while he is with us. Please remember that he also helped to rescue me when I was captured."

I say to her as I look down into the sink, the water running down the drain is mixed with dark red blood.

I move my head so that I can look over to Luna while I am still removing the stained blood from my skin. She gets up from sitting in front of the sliding glass doors Luna is now walking over to stand by my side.

I have successfully removed the blood stains from the skin of my hands and wrist. I continue to run the water so that I can clean the blood from the sink. I turn the water off, since I have packed up all the towels to be used for first aid items I am rubbing my wet hands on my shirt so that I can dry them.

I bend down so that I can look into Luna's beautiful blue eyes.

"I am so amazed that you can understand what I say when I talk to you. You are truly special Luna."

I say to her as I pet her beautiful soft black fur as she gives me a gentle moan.

As I stand back up I hear the sliding glass door open I am watching Logan and Richard walk into the house.

"Richard did Sarah invite you into the house?"

I ask to him as I watch them both come toward me.

"No Renee, I do not need an invite to come into your house."

He replies to me as I now feel so confused.

"Renee, you must give your house over to a living human that you can trust if you do not want other vampires walking into your home."

I now feel very upset that we have forgotten about this.

We need to find someone that we can trust to give ownership of our house to.

I say to myself as I stand here in the kitchen looking at them.

"Sarah and I will work on doing this right away."

I reply to him.

As Richard and Logan are in the kitchen with me I have realized that Luna is no longer growling or watching his every move.

Richard looks over to Luna then he looks back over to me.

"I am amazed that you and Sarah are capable of having wolves as pets."

He says to me with a strange look upon his face.

I cannot help but give him such a very stern look.

"Richard, Luna and Beauty are NOT our pets, they are our friends. They come and go as they please and I will say again they are not our pets!"

"Then I stand corrected, I am still amazed that they stay with the four of you knowing that you are all dead. Animals do NOT take to the dead."

He says to me as he is trying to explain.

I can feel myself becoming angry once more for what he is saying to me.

"Richard is this another one of your tests?"

I ask to him as I am trying to stay calm.

"No Renee I promise you that I am not testing you. I am just amazed that the four of you have two wolves living with you. Wolves are so unpredictable and they will attack without any warning."

He replies to me.

I do not know what to say to him about all of this.

I say to myself as I stand here looking at him.

"Richard do you think that Luna and Beauty are some sort of supernatural creatures?"

Logan asks him as she is now looking at him.

"No Logan they are pure one hundred percent wolves."

He replies to her as he is now looking into her eyes.

"Then I think that you should not worry about their wolf friends. Richard, do you know the story as to why Luna and Beauty stay with them?"

"No Logan I do not know of it."

"Richard, they tried to save the wolves' mother but she was so badly hurt she passed away from her injuries. Luna and Beauty understand what they were trying to do and they have all been together ever since."

She explains to him, I can hear in her voice that she wants him to stop asking his questions.

As I look at Logan, she very quickly gives me a smile as she grabs hold of Richard's arm to walk him over to the sliding glass door to go back outside.

As Luna and I remain in the kitchen together I look down to her.

"Luna we do trust you and Beauty I hope that you do understand that Sarah and I also love you both. But now I must go upstairs so that I can change my clothes."

I say to Luna as she continues to stay with me.

I walk out of the kitchen and I am now making my way into the dining room so that I can walk up the stairs to the second floor. As I walk into our bedroom I am taking the belt off of my waist that

Keith gave to me earlier this evening as I am now standing in front of the bed and I find that I am saying to myself.

We will probably never use this bed again because we now sleep in a secret room hidden behind our walk in closet away from the sunlight.

I place the belt on to the bed then I make my way into the walk in closet so that I can change my clothes so I just decide to wear pajamas because the sun is going to be rising soon and our bodies will have to rest.

As I am removing the jeans from my body the material is very stiff from the dried blood.

"I am not going to keep these jeans."

I say to Luna as I can hear her jump up onto the bed that we will never use again.

After I have removed every piece of clothing that I was wearing I put my pajamas on and I grab my blood stained jeans and I carry them down stairs. Luna is still with me. I walk over to the trash can in the kitchen I bend down as I am pushing my clothes into it as far as they will go into the trash can. I stand back up and I begin to walk back over to the sliding glass doors but before I open it to go outside I stand here looking out into the back yard.

The words that Richard had said to me earlier this evening that I rely on Marrick to protect me, he is correct because I do rely on Marrick to do just that! I need to make myself become brave for now on. I should of never have gotten so upset with him.

I say to myself as I continue looking into the back yard.

Finally I raise my hand so that I can place it upon the handle of the sliding glass door to open it and then I walk out as Luna follows me I close the door and I walk toward Marrick as he is standing by Fred's memorial talking to everyone.

Marrick holds his arm out for me as I walk closer to him and I take my place next to him. He gently places his arm around my body he tightens his hold on me that the front of my body is now pressing against his side. He places his other arm around me. I cannot help but feel safe. As I am standing here with them for the moment everyone is quiet and once again I am being me because I need information.

I slightly move my head so that I can focus my gaze upon Richard.

"Please tell me how you found Becky!"

I ask to him as I try very hard to control my feelings.

"Renee if you really want to know then I will tell you."

Richard replies to me.

As I continue to stand here with everyone I am still looking at him.

"Yes please I really do want to know, will you tell me how you found her?"

I reply to him with the same question.

"Very well Renee. A few nights ago we went back to the airplane hangar where you were being held along with the others that he had captive. We searched the property to see what we could find because we were trying to figure out what direction he had went. Logan wanted to see if she could try to feel anything from David but she could not make a connection to him. We did not find anything or anyone. So we started searching further away from the hangar the following evening, again we found nothing. We had gone at least 150 miles away from the hangar when Logan found Becky. But while we were searching trying to figure out what direction he might have gone Becky was being tortured because her wounds were fresh."

Richard explains to me.

"Did you find out where she was being tortured, where were they at?"

"No Renee we did not but we did send another team out to search again during the day to where Logan had found her to see what they would be able to find and they did not find anything new. Becky had said to us that she was dropped off by his followers. So what was done to her took place somewhere else, but we do not yet know of the location. She also said that she needed to see you."

He replies to me.

"Is that why you and Logan are here now?"

"Yes Renee it is the reason why because if we would have waited until the following evening Becky would have died before she was able to see you."

I move my eyes from him and I lower my head so that I can look at the ground. Again I am trying to control myself.

As I raise my head back up I look at Richard and then I move my eyes to look at Logan.

"I am so sorry that you found Becky in that condition. But will we be able to find where he had Becky?"

I ask to the both of them as I tighten my hold around Marrick as I try to stay calm.

"It is ok Renee, but she DID ask to see you, we did everything that we could to keep her alive so that we could honor her wish. But as far as finding where he tortured I am not sure because he is always moving he never stays in the same place."

Logan replies to me.

"Thank you for what you both have done for her. Logan thank you for giving her peace Becky is now free from the suffering that was forced upon her."

"No need to thank us Renee. I only did what was needed to be done."

Logan replies to me as we continue standing together in the back yard.

I can see Keith as he looks over to Marrick.

"Is there any ideas as to how you are to consume human blood as your bodies are resting during the day for you to become stronger? You need be able to match David's strength."

As soon as Keith has asked his question a memory has surfaced from when I was his captive.

"Keith I have a suggestion as to what may be able to help us."

I reply to his question.

"Renee I know what you are going to say, it is a good idea and I am sure that it may work but are YOU sure that you want to do this?"

Marrick asks me as I am now looking up into his eyes.

"Yes I am sure, and I must do what needs to be done. I must be brave for now on!"

I reply to him as Marrick continues to hold me in his arms.

"Renee, what is it that you are thinking of?"

Keith asks as I also notice that Logan and Richard are also waiting for me to answer.

Before I answer him I look over to Sarah and she has a concerned look upon her beautiful pale white face.

I look back over to Keith.

"Is there any way that we can have I.V's placed into our arms so that our bodies can have human blood while we rest during the day?"

I ask him, I am trying not to sound nervous.

I remember having an I.V. needle inserted into my arm to have my blood drained from my body. I also remember David ripping out the needle because he was becoming impatient for my blood to drain out of me so he placed his hands upon both of my arms and pushed his nails into my skin.

"Renee that is an excellent idea and yes we can do this. We can start this evening. I am confident that your idea will work for us."

Logan replies to me as Marrick is rubbing my arm that had the needle ripped out from it.

"Logan, do you have everything that is needed to be able to do this?"

Damon asks her.

"Yes we do, we have everything that we need in the refrigerated truck that contains the human blood bags. We have everything just in case we need to do an emergency blood drive to fill bags of blood while we are searching for David. Feeding our bodies' human blood is something that we should do every time our body rests, that is until he is destroyed. This is an excellent suggestion Renee."

Logan replies to him.

"I will have Lizzie take care of the I.V's and changing of the blood bags for us as they become empty."

Richard says to us as he glances into the woods.

"It may be a good idea if she waits until our bodies are completely at rest."

Marrick says to Richard as he tightens his grip around me.

I know that he is making this request because of me.

I cannot help but think to myself.

As we continue standing outside in the back yard by Fred's memorial, Sarah looks over to Richard.

"Is Lizzie close by?"

"Yes she is Sarah; Lizzie is with the rest of our team within the woods. They are waiting and watching for movements from David and his group."

He replies to her as he looks in the direction of the trees as if he is now looking for her.

"I am sorry to interrupt but it is almost time for the sun to rise so there for we must make our way into the basement so that we can rest."

Marrick says to us all as I can see a blue tint in the sky.

"Marrick must we go into the basement?"

I ask him as I send my thought to him.

"Yes Renee I am sorry but we must. It will be much easier for Lizzie as she takes care of us while we are resting."

Marrick replies to me with his thought.

"I understand."

I reply to him as we begin to walk toward the house.

As we are walking toward the sliding glass doors, Keith is getting ready to say something. I can hear that he is taking in a slow deep breath.

"Marrick is there anything that you would like for me to do while you are all resting during the day?"

Keith asks to him as we are getting closer to the house.

We are now standing at the sliding glass door and as Marrick is placing his hand on the handle to open it as he looks to Keith.

"Yes, I want you to get as much rest as you possibly can before we leave."

Marrick replies to him.

I can see that Keith looks somewhat relieved that he was told to rest.

"Marrick, Logan also agrees with what you have just said that I should rest. I cannot promise that I will sleep but I will try to relax."

Keith says to him.

Marrick has opened up the sliding glass door and we allow Keith to walk in first so that he can make his way to his room in the attic. Marrick and I are now standing by the double closet doors that lead into the basement.

"Renee, it is time for us to go down stairs."

"Then let us make our way into the big safe."

I reply to him as Marrick is allowing me to go down the stairs first.

As we are both walking down the steps together I reach my hand behind me so that I can take hold of Marrick's hand. As we are in the basement standing by the steps we can see Damon and Sarah now coming down into the basement as well. Marrick and I are watching them as they are walking down the steps together.

"Logan and Richard will be joining us in a moment. They are both talking to Lizzie about how to insert the I.V's so that our bodies are able to consume human blood while we are resting during the day."

Damon says to the both of us as we are now making our way into the huge walk in looking safe.

As soon as we are inside the room Logan and Richard are making their way to join us.

I am standing inside of the safe room and I am following Marrick with my eyes as he is walking to one of the cots. He turns his back to it and he slowly sits down upon it. He is lifting his legs up on the cot and turns himself to lie down. He is resting on his back and he is moving his head so that he can now watch me. As I look back at him, I cannot help but smile to him.

I look over to Sarah just to see how she is holding up. She is sitting on the cot with her legs straight out in front of her.

She is slightly tilting her head back and I can feel that she is going to say something.

"Beauty and Luna please come!"

She has yelled out to them.

Right away we hear them barking as if they are replying to her request and we are listening to the sound of their paws hitting each step as they are running down into the basement to join us as well. As Sarah is now lying down upon a cot next to Damon I watch Beauty as she jumps onto of Sarah's legs to lie down upon her. I am now lying down on a cot right next to Marrick and as soon as I am comfortable Luna has jumped upon my body and she is now making herself comfortable upon me. I am listening to Logan and Richard as they are now resting their bodies upon the cots.

Before my body shuts down I look at Marrick once more so that I can see him before my eyes close and he is looking back at me with such a loving look upon his beautiful pale white face and now my eyes are slowly starting to close.

Our bodies have shut down to rest; we have no choice to do this because the sun has now risen.

"Renee, would you like for me to command you to rest your mind?"

Marrick has asked me with his thought.

"No, I need to be able to do things for myself but thank you for asking me."

I reply to him as I send my thought back to him.

"My beautiful Renee, are you positive that you do not want my help?"

"Marrick I am positive, please allow me to do this for myself."

"Very well Renee but if you change your mind all you have to do is to tell me. You must know that it is my will to protect you, you are my life and my love."

Marrick replies to me as our bodies continue to rest.

"I promise that I will tell you if I need your help Marrick my love. Thank you for what you have just said to me, I feel the same for you."

I do not hear anything else from Marrick because he is allowing me to figure out what it is that I need to do to so that I can rest my mind.

As I lay here upon this cot I cannot do what I use to do and that is concentrate on my breathing. I no longer can inhale or exhale because I no longer can breathe. But I can feel the energy coming from Luna as she lies upon my body I feel a warm tingling sensation as she continues to lay upon me. I am listening to the beat of her heart and not only can I hear her breathing but I can feel her inhale and exhale. I am listening to the sound of Luna's heart I am now able to quite my mind so that I can completely rest.

Chapter Three

I am starting to wake up but once again I cannot move my body because the sun has not yet gone down.

Being able to move after I wake up is one thing that I am starting to miss but I am sure that with time I will become use to this.

I say to myself as my body continues to rest.

As I continue to lay here upon this cot I have realized that Luna is no longer lying on my body but I know that she is still in this big safe of a room that we are resting in. I am once again listening to her heart beating. I can also hear Beauty's heart as well.

I can hear someone coming down the steps entering the basement; I am now listening to this person as they are now making their way into this room. I know that it is not Keith as I am still listening to this person now walking around within this room.

"Hello, just in case you are starting to wake up my name is Lizzie and I am here to check the bags to see if anyone is in need of more human blood while your bodies continue to rest."

She explains to us as to what she is doing.

I listen to her words as she continues.

I can now feel the needle with in the pale white skin of my arm, and I am NOT freaking out.

I am very proud of myself that I am now able to finally remain calm. If she had not said what she is doing I do not think that I would have noticed the needle.

I think to myself as I can now feel Lizzie beside of me; she is giving me a fresh new bag of human blood.

I can feel Marrick in my mind as he is starting to wake up as well.

"Renee I can feel that you are now able to control your feelings."

"It feels good to hear you say that to me Marrick, but I must admit that I was starting to feel as if I was going to go nuts because my emotions were so heightened. I am glad to have myself back!"

I reply to Marrick.

I am once again listening to Lizzie as she continues to check everyone that is resting within this room.

"I am finished and every one of you now has a fresh bag of human blood. But I must tell you that each of you has had seven bags of human blood this is your eighth one. Your bodies have consumed the blood very nicely there were no complications at all. "

She says to us all as she is now walking out of this room.

"We must make sure that we thank Lizzie for taking care of us while we were resting."

"That we will defiantly do as soon as we see her Renee."

He replies to me.

As I continue to lay here on this cot I can feel the blood as it enters into my body from my arm that has the I.V needle attached into it. I am concentrating as to how my body is reacting to it. The blood is so very warm and as it enters my arm I can feel it as it makes it way down into my fingers and now it is working its way up toward my shoulder. I can still feel the warm blood as it is now entering into my chest. Now it as it is working its way over to my other arm and through the rest of my body from my toes to my head. I can feel the energy coursing within me. I love how the essence gives us our powerful strength!

I wish that the sun would set soon I am ready to get up from this cot that I am still laying on.

I do not feel hungry since I have human blood coursing within my body and so there for I am NOT scared of being around the half turned humans and I CAN trust myself!

I think to myself as I no longer have fear of being around them.

I am now able to move a couple of my fingers but my eyes are not ready to open yet. I slowly move my fingers as I realize that my nails have grown long and sharp. I am now able to move my arm as well.

"Marrick the sun is finally going down."

I say to him as I am now able to move my mouth to talk.

"Yes Renee it is. Robert and Michael along with the others will be here soon."

He replies to me.

I have come to realize that my fangs have formed and as I am now able to open my eyes they are completely black. I feel so powerful and stronger then I have ever felt!

As I now look at Marrick he has changed as well and his glow has such a strong yellow color with a very dark color of blood red mixed into it.

"Marrick it has worked."

"Yes Renee it has. Your idea that you had, let me just say that it worked very well."

Marrick replies to me as I cannot help but smile to him.

"So Marrick if I were to challenge you to a race, who do you think would win?"

"My beautiful Renee, one day I will take your challenge. But I do believe that I would still be the one to win because as I told you before, I am much older then you and a lot more powerful then you will ever be."

He replies to me as he is now lying on his side resting his head upon his arm.

"My beautiful Marrick please let me know when you are ready to accept my challenge."

I say to him as I can hear Sarah laughing to what we are saying to each other.

I move myself on the cot so that I can sit upon it with my legs crossed in front of me.

As I look at my arm with the needle still inside of it I look over to Marrick once more.

"Is it ok if I remove the needle?"

"If you want to be the one to do it then yes Renee your bag is empty as well."

He replies to me.

As I look down at my arm I move my other hand over to take hold of the tape from the corner. I am now pulling the tape off of my pale white skin as fast as I can. My skin now feels a little irritated. As I continue to look down at the needle I place my palm under the thick plastic I.V. tube that has the needle inside of it and I wrap my fingers around it. I close my eyes and I very quickly pull it out of my skin.

"I am no longer alive and I still do not like needles. Pulling out the needle really did hurt."

I say to everyone so that I can complain about the discomfort.

As I sit here on the cot I am watching Logan and Richard they have both removed their needles as well and they are now getting ready to walk out of this room.

"We will meet you upstairs."

Logan says to us as they both walk past us.

"We will be upstairs soon."

Damon replies to her.

I look over to Sarah as she gets up from her cot. She is placing herself next to Damon as they are now sharing one cot.

I know what they are going to do.

I say to myself as smile I can feel Marrick listening to my thought.

As I look back over to Marrick he is still laying upon his cot and the soft gentle look that he is giving to me I can no longer resist. I am now getting up from my cot and I am now walking just a few steps so that I am now standing beside of his cot. Marrick moves himself so that I am able to lie down with him. I sit down upon his cot and I am placing my legs onto it and now I am lowering myself so that I can lay on my back and as we look into each other's eyes he places his hand on the side of my face as I continue to look into his beautiful eyes that are still completely black as the night sky.

We do not say anything to each other because we do not need to; we know exactly how we feel for one another. Marrick now has his body lying completely on top of mine.

I can hear Sarah and Damon for they are now making love to each other. I cannot help but look over to them as Marrick is now slowly forcing his fangs into the skin of my neck so that he can drink my blood.

I place my hands on the back of his head so that I can hold him tightly to my skin as he drinks from me.

I do love the feeling of his fangs slowly pushing into my skin and the way he moves his mouth on my neck as he drinks from my body it is such a powerful erotic feeling.

I am moving my body so that he is able to tighten his hold on my neck with his beautiful mouth.

As I am lying under him I am enjoying this feeling as I can feel my blood leaving my body and flowing into his.

As I am once again watching Sarah and Damon move perfectly together she looks over to me and our eyes are locked together as we now begin to watch each other.

I can feel Marrick as he slowly slides his hand down into my pajama pants he rubs the skin of my pelvic area. He is sliding his hand down lower so that he can place is fingers on my lips as he places two of his pale white fingers inside of me as he continues to drink my thick sweet vampire blood.

As he continues to do this I close my eyes and I move my lower body as he continues to move his fingers inside of me.

I am now moving my hands down his back and I take hold of his shirt and pull on it as to say.

"Please do not make me wait any longer!"

He gently and slowly pulls his fangs out of the skin of my neck as he is now looking into my black eyes. As I look back to him I see my blood slowly dripping from his beautiful mouth. He places his hand on my waist he is now sliding my pajama pants down my thighs. Marrick slowly moves his body away from me to move upward so that he can sit up to remove them from me this causes me to let go of his shirt. He allows my pajama pants to fall onto the floor next to the cot.

I glance over to Sarah and Damon once more they are still making love. They are thrusting very slowly against each other.

Marrick stands up in front of me he is now removing his clothes; I can hear them as they gently fall onto the floor as I lay on the cot watching him. He is now bending his body down to me as I spread my legs for him as he brings his body close to mine I can feel him placing himself gently inside of me. We are now making love as we move to each other.

I reach my hands up so that I can allow my fingers to become wrapped within his beautiful dark wavy hair. I look up so that I can gaze upon his face as we continue to make love together and his hair gently flows back and forth as he moves his body with mine. He lowers his head down to me so that our lips press against each other. He removes his lips from mine and he gently drags his tongue down to my neck as he kisses my skin.

I look back over to Sarah and Damon as they hold each other embracing one another in their arms. Sarah is now sitting upon Damon as they continue to move together as she now has her mouth upon the skin of his neck taking his blood into her. Damon has his eyes closed as she continues to drink from him; I can see that he is holding her tightly to him.

I move my head back and close my eyes as we as we continue to make love I raise my head slightly up and I am placing my mouth upon Marrick's flesh so that I can push my fangs into his skin. As I do this he is now thrusting himself deeper into me as he is grinding his beautiful hard shaft inside of me. I raise my knees up for him so that he can push himself deeper inside of me. He has placed one of his hands on the back of my head so that he can hold me tightly to him as I continue to drink his blood. He knows my body so well because I am now welling up inside. I release his skin from my mouth I notice that there is blood on his skin. I place my tongue upon him as I am now slowly licking his blood that has escaped from me as we continue to move together. I can feel that the both of us are now ready to come. This is the first time that we have released ourselves at the same moment.

As Marrick still lies upon me he places his hand in my hair as he looks at me once more and I cannot help myself, I am tightening the inside of myself around his shaft that is still hard inside of me.

He closes his eyes as I can feel him slightly move inside of me, once more I tighten the inside of myself around him.

“Renee, please allow us to save this one for another time.”

“Whenever you are ready just sweep me off my feet Marrick.”

I say to him as I watch him open his eyes to look at me.

“I promise that I will do just that.”

He replies to me as we continue to lie together.

Sarah and Damon are now dressed and they are both trying to quietly walk out of this room they both make their way to the door but they stop before they walk out.

“We will see you both upstairs, but please do not be too much longer we must be ready to leave.”

Damon says to the both of us.

“We will be upstairs in just a few minutes Damon.”

Marrick replies to him as they now leave the room.

“Renee we must put our clothes back on. Damon is right we must be ready to leave.”

“Yes Marrick I do agree with you. I promise that we will all be ready to leave when they arrive.”

As I continue to lie on the cot I watch Marrick as he quickly gets up he is moving so fast that he is now right in front of me but I was able to watch him as he moved so quickly. Marrick has his body bending toward me I am looking at him. He is now holding my pajama pants for me in his pale white skin hands.

“Renee please allow me to help you to put these back on your beautiful body.”

He says to me as I am moving myself to sit on the cot. I lift my legs so that I can place them into my pajama pants

"Marrick this is not fair because I want to be with you once more. Do we have time?"

I ask him as he moves his body to stand up straight while holding out his hand for me. I place my hand in his and I stand up in front of him. My pajama pants are now around me knees.

Marrick is now slowly kneeling down in front of me and he release my hand so that he can take hold of my pajama pants. Marrick is taking his time as he pulls them all them up. But he stops and as I watch him he is staring at the lower part of my body. He is moving his head toward me I close my eyes as he presses his beautiful pale lips against my pelvic area to kiss my skin. He moves his head away from me and he is now pulling my pajama pants all the way to my waist. He is standing in front of me once again.

"Marrick if my heart could still beat, it would be pounding inside of my chest at ninety miles per minute."

I say to him as I watch him walk over to grab his clothes so that he can put them back ok.

I am now making my way over to him.

He looks at me with such a beautiful smile upon his face.

"My beautiful Renee, please do not come any closer or we both will be in trouble because we will make everyone wait for us."

I stop walking and I just stand here in my place as I continue to watch him put his clothes back on his beautiful sculptured body.

As we walk up to each other now that we both have clothes on, I cannot help but say to him.

"I feel that I must say again that I am glad to be myself once more. And I need to say that somehow I am very proud of myself that I am able to be with you like this. I honestly thought that it would take a very long time for myself to heal from what I went through when I was a captive."

I say to Marrick as I look into his eyes.

"Once you had realized that you are safe and that you were no longer his captive, at that moment you said that you are NOT going to let what had happened destroy us and I promised you that it would not harm us in any way. It helped you to heal yourself, but I do know that you still have horrible memories but in time they will fade away. Renee you are so much stronger now emotionally and physically."

He explains to me as he is now holding onto my hand.

I look down at our hands touching and then I look back up into his eyes once more as I smile to him.

"We should go upstairs Marrick so that we can gather what we want to take with us. We must be ready to leave by the time Robert and the others arrive.""

"Yes Renee we should."

He replies to me as I can feel his thumb rubbing my skin.

As we are still holding hands we walk out of the safe room so we can make our way to the steps that lead upstairs. As we enter into the kitchen Keith looks very well rested and he is handing us a bag of warm human blood. I also notice that the brown leather bags that he gave to Sarah and I are now on the kitchen table next to the first aid items.

"I worked very hard to prepare this blood for you so you better enjoy it."

Keith says to us as we take hold of the bags of blood.

"I bet that you worked a whole two minutes."

I reply to him as I smile back at him.

"Renee I have your leather bag packed full of supplies and your wrist halter and cross bow are also inside of the bag."

"Thank you Keith, I will need to go upstairs and to get the belt out of our room."

"I hope that you do not mind Renee but I already have your belt packed and ready for you."

"Thank you Keith for doing that."

I reply to him.

We can hear Keith's cell phone ringing and he pulls it out of his pocket to answer it as he is walking out of the kitchen.

"Marrick it is Robert, I can hear his voice."

I say as I look up to him.

"Renee you correct I can hear him as well."

He replies to me as he raises the blood bag to his mouth.

I cannot help myself as I look over to Sarah.

I cannot believe what we had just done in the safe room! This is the first time that we have had sex in the same room at the same time. I must say that it was strange but a little exciting as well.

As I think to myself.

Sarah is looking back at me with such a big smile.

"I agree with you Renee."

She replies to me.

I do not know what to say so I am not going to say or think anything at this moment!

I look at Marrick and he has a smile upon his face also.

If I was still alive I know that my face would be very red right now.

I can now hear Damon laugh very softly; I now know that Sarah has told him what I was thinking. I am slightly embarrassed.

I raise my blood bag to my mouth and I begin to consume the blood.

Marrick places his hand on the back of my head I can feel his fingers gently rubbing my hair. I press my head against his hand I do enjoy when he does this.

"I think that while we are waiting for Robert and Michael along with the others we should gather up what we feel that we will want to take with us when we leave this evening."

I am so glad that he did not say anything to what I was just thinking of a moment ago about the four of us in the safe room.

I say to myself as I still feel embarrassed.

"Has anyone seen my cell phone? I do not know where it is."

I ask everyone.

"Renee, I have no idea where your phone is, I cannot find mine either the last time I saw my cell phone was here in the kitchen before we went walking in the woods a few weeks ago."

Sarah replies to me.

"I think that this is the first time we have ever lost our phones."

I say to her.

As we continue to stand in the kitchen I move my hand toward Marrick and I take hold of his empty bag and I make my way over to the trash can to place them in side of it and I walk back over to his side.

"We should go to our rooms and figure out what we will want to take with us."

Marrick says to us.

"Ok I am going to go upstairs and start packing some of my things."

I reply to him.

"We will do the same as well."

Damon also replies to his brother.

The four of us are walking out of the kitchen together as we are now entering the dining room to the staircase that leads to the second floor. As we walk up from the last step we are now entering our bed rooms. Marrick goes to his dresser he opens the drawers to gather some of his clothes. I turn to make my way into the bathroom. I grab my tooth brush, tooth paste and deodorant along with my body wash and other items that I feel that I want with me. I walk back out of our bathroom and as we are both placing our items together in a big zip up shoulder bag that Marrick had placed on the bed, I look over to him.

"Marrick, I am becoming very nervous."

"I know that you are nervous Renee and trust me I do understand because I am nervous as well."

He replies to me as he is now finished packing the items that he wants to take.

"How can I be brave when I feel this way? We are going to be facing David once again."

I say to him as I am trying to control myself.

"Renee, we are all in this together, but keep in mind that we are also on our way to getting our revenge for what he has done to us all."

He replies to me, as he tries to comfort me with the loving look in his eyes.

"Revenge I will make myself remember that Marrick when I start to feel myself becoming nervous."

I say to him as I walk away from him to go into the walk in closet to gather some clothes.

I do not say anything else to him about the matter. I have the clothes that I want to take. I leave the closet as I start walking toward Marrick as he continues to stand by the bed.

As I am standing by the bed I turn myself so that I can sit upon it and no sooner as I sit down I see Keith standing at the door way to our bedroom. I begin to place my clothes into the bag.

"Marrick I wanted to let you know that Robert and the others will be here in just a few minutes. I have already told Damon and Sarah and they are now down stairs waiting."

Keith says to him.

"Very well Keith we have finished gathering our things and we will be making our way down stairs in just a few minutes to join everyone."

Marrick replies to him as he continues to stand by the bed.

"Very well, we will be waiting for the both of you to join us."

Keith replies to Marrick then he turns away from our room and he makes his way down the stairs to meet Damon and Sarah.

As Marrick places his hand on the straps of the bag that now contains some of our belongings that we are going to take with us there is a very strange look at appears upon his face and I can feel from him that something is not right. I remove myself from sitting on the bed so that I can stand by his side. As he remains still the feeling that I am receiving from him has now turned into sadness.

As I look up into his eyes I can see that he is worried. I am waiting patiently for him to come back to me.

"Renee!"

He says as he moves his eyes to look back to me.

"Marrick is everything ok?"

"I am not sure Renee, it is Maryann."

He replies to me.

"Marrick is she ok? Please tell me that she is safe?"

I ask him hoping for him to tell me something good but I know that whatever it is will be bad news.

"Renee, Maryann said that she wants her existence to end! She wants to die."

"No Marrick that cannot not happen! I do not understand why would she say this to you?"

I ask him as I continue to stand in our bedroom with him as I am taking hold of his hand.

"She said that she is going to meet up with us and that we MUST destroy her. Renee she is not able to say anymore to us."

"Then David must have said something to her. But what has he commanded her to do? Marrick does Damon know what she has said to you?"

I ask him as I am now also concerned.

"Yes Renee, Damon does know what Maryann has said."

He replies to me as he picks up the bag from the bed.

"Renee we must now go downstairs."

"Ok Marrick."

I reply to him as we both walk out of our bedroom to join everyone.

As we are now walking down the stairs, Marrick stops and he turns to look at me with his completely back eyes.

"Renee, please promise me that you will keep your guard up and make sure that you have your weapons ready at all times!"

He says to me with great concern in his voice.

"Marrick I promise to you that I will."

I reply to him as I look at his beautiful pale white face.

He turns from me and we both continue to walk down the steps as we are now making our way into the living room to join Sarah, Damon and Keith.

As we walk into the living room Marrick looks over to him.

"Keith where is Logan and Richard?"

"Marrick they are out in the back yard getting everyone prepared to leave as soon as Robert and Michael and the others arrive. We have also placed what is to be used for first aid inside of one of the trucks."

Keith replies to him.

As we are remaining in the living room I am developing a strong feeling and I am now able to since what it is.

"Marrick they have arrived."

I say to him.

"Very well then, I trust that we are all ready to leave?"

Marrick says to us all.

"Yes Sarah and I are both ready."

His brother Damon replies to him.

"I am ready as well."

Keith replies.

"Then let us gather our things and close the house."

Damon says to us all.

"I will go and turn off the breaker box."

Keith says to both Marrick and Damon.

"Marrick, before we leave do you have a human in mind for us to give ownership of the house to?"

I ask him as we are still standing in the living room; I am hoping that he will suggest Keith.

"Renee that is yours and Sarah's decision but I will tell you that it will not stop the half turned human vampires from entering the house."

He replies to me.

"Renee, maybe we should wait for a while before we decide about this."

Sarah says to me.

"Ok."

I reply to her.

I turn my head and I am watching Damon as he bends down to pick up the bag that contains their belongings and as he stands up he places his arm around Sarah. I continue to watch them as Damon opens the door for both of them to walk out of the house and onto the front porch they have left the door opened for us.

The lights are now turned off it is completely dark inside of the house. I can see Marrick very clearly in the darkness.

As Marrick and I are the only ones now left in the house I can hear Keith's voice outside he is at the front of the house with the others.

I can feel myself becoming nervous once more, I can also feel that Marrick is also nervous. I do not have any words to say to him as I remain here in the living room with him. I can feel that he is thinking of his mother but he will not allow me to hear his thoughts. Or maybe I am just too scared to know what he is thinking.

"Renee."

Marrick says to me as I raise my head up to look at him, he bends down just slightly to place the zip up bag on the floor.

As he stands back up Marrick gently places both of his hands on each side of my face as I continue to look into his beautiful completely black eyes. I am looking at him as his he bends himself down toward me so that his lips can gently touch mine. I am kissing him back.

I am so frightened at this moment that after our kiss I grab hold of his body and I hold on to him as tightly as I possibly can. Marrick has wrapped his arms around me as well.

While we still hold onto each other I can feel that he is going to say something to me.

"We both must be strong Renee!"

He gently says to me.

"I will be as strong as I can be so that I can help to do whatever must be done."

I reply to him as we still hold onto each other.

"We must keep watch for Maryann we do not know what she is planning to do, but she wants to die."

"Marrick we can save her, can't we?"

Marrick continues to hold onto me but he does not reply but I do feel a heavy sadness within him and I have a very bad feeling about this.

"We must go outside and meet the others so that we can start our search."

Marrick replies to me as we release each other, he bends down so that he can take hold of the zip up bag once again. We begin walking as we make our way to the front door, he allows me to walk thru the door first and I stand on the front porch waiting for Marrick as he closes the door so that we can walk off the porch together.

I look up into the sky I gaze upon the stars that are shinning very brightly in the night. I can see a very thin bright white crescent moon.

In just a few nights the moon will be completely bright and full.

As I lower my head back down from gazing at the night sky I can see Keith walking toward us.

"Renee, I wanted to let you know that I have the keys to your S.U.V. I will be the one driving it while we are on our search."

He says to me as he smiles.

"If you put one ding in it I will be upset."

I say to him as I try to give him a very stern look.

"Oh whatever Renee you can never get upset with me because I am one of your favorite people."

He replies as he stands in front of me trying to give me a smile.

"Keith I must say that you look really cool with your eyes completely black and yes you are one of my favorite people."

"Thank you Renee, but I was hoping that you were going to say that my eyes make me look sexy."

Keith replies to me with a smile.

"Um ok Keith."

I reply to him as I giggle.

"Have you seen Luna and Beauty?"

I ask him as he continues to stand together.

"Yes Renee, they are both with Sarah and Damon. Is everything ok?"

"I am thinking that it may be a good idea if they both stay here, I do not want anything to happen to them. Do you think that is a good idea Keith?"

"Renee, there is no way that those two wolves are going to let you and Sarah leave without them. They will come searching for you both."

He replies to me.

"Keith I do know that you are right, they will come looking for us."

I cannot help but worry that something bad is going to happen, I really do not want Luna and Beauty to go with us.

I say to myself as I look around; I am now watching Paul as he is walking toward us.

He is now half human and vampire his eyes are completely black and he has a beautiful yellow glow with a hint of red surrounding him.

"Renee and Keith I hope that you both are doing well this evening."

He says to the both of us as he walks closer to us.

"Hello Paul, it is good to see you again."

I say to him.

"Thank you Renee, it is good to see you as well."

He replies to me as the three of us are now standing together.

"Hello Paul, I will answer your question later this evening if it is good evening or not."

Keith replies to him as they shake hands.

I look over and I notice that Sarah and Damon are now walking toward us, I raise my hand up and I gently touch Keith's arm as I walk away from the both of them as they continue talking. I begin to walk toward Sarah and Damon. Sarah turns her head toward me as I am coming closer to them. She is doing her best to give me one of her beautiful smiles but her blue eyes are showing how worried she really is.

"Renee, here is a plastic bottle for you, you must keep it with you at all times and make sure that you have human blood in it. You do not want any humans that cross our paths to know that you are drinking blood."

She says to me as I am now standing next to her.

I reach out my hand so that I can take hold of the bottle from her and by the weight of it I know that she has it ready for me it contains human blood.

"Thank you Sarah."

I reply to her as I lower my head slightly down to look at the bottle that I am now holding.

"Renee here is your bag that Keith has prepared for you as well."

Damon says as he hands it to me.

"Thank you; I will place my blood bottle inside of my bag."

I reply to him as I am placing my arm around it so that I open it up with my other hand to place my bottle of blood inside of the bag.

I also notice after I have opened my leather bag that there are several bags of blood inside as well.

As we continue to stand together we do not say anything else to each other but I am now looking around to see where Marrick is. I have found him; he is standing with Robert and Michael they are talking.

I know that Marrick will allow me to know what they are talking about, but I already know that he is telling them about what Maryann had said to him earlier with her thoughts.

I say to myself as Sarah is looking at me, she can hear my thoughts.

I can now feel that Keith is making his way over to us and as he now stands with Sarah, Damon and I he looks over to us with such sorrow in his eyes.

"Sarah and Renee, would you mind if we do a group hug in honor of Fred?"

He asks to both of us as he holds out both of his arms, we can also hear sadness in his voice as well.

Right away Sarah and I place our bags on the ground and move closer to him. We both hold out our arms as well so that we can take hold of each other. We are now in a three person hug in honor of Fred as we begin thinking of him.

"May we find this bastard and destroy him!"

Keith says to us while the three of us are still holding onto each other.

I can now feel great sadness from them including myself because we miss Fred very much. The three of us release our hold on each other and Sarah and I take hold of our leather bags once more. I can now feel Marrick as he is coming closer to us. I look over to Sarah and I can now see that Damon is standing right behind her with his hands gently holding her arms.

As we all stand here together, without thinking I find myself saying.

"Let the hunt for David begin!"

I say as I look into Keith's eyes.

"Yes let the hunt for that fucking monster to start so we can kill him!"

Sarah replies to what I have said.

Keith does not reply to us at all, he remains silent.

I turn to look behind me because I can hear another truck coming toward us I can see that it is another semi, I can also see two more trucks following behind it.

"I wonder if these trucks are for the half turned humans so that they are able to rest as well."

I say out loud to whoever maybe listening.

"You are correct Renee; these trucks are for us so that we can also rest during the search."

Keith replies as he pulls my keys out from his pocket.

Sarah and I both reach into our bags and we are taking out the waist belts and our wrist halters with the small cross bows still attached to them. I bend just slightly so that I can place my bag and my wrist halter on the ground. As I am standing back up, I am placing the belt around my waist I notice that it is already loaded with the wooden weapons that Keith has made. Now I bending down again as I take hold of my things. I place the wrist halter between my knees, now I am sliding my arm thru one of the shoulder straps and now I am doing the same with my other arm. My leather bag is now resting on my back. I take hold of the wrist halter from between my knees. I am placing my hand into it and I can smell Becky's dried blood is now embedded into the leather of the wrist halter. I now have it completely on my wrist I am reaching my hand onto my leather belt as I am now taking hold a small wooden arrow so that I can load it into the cross bow. As I slide the wooden arrow toward me I can feel it locking into place. Sarah is now armed and ready as well.

I can hear Keith moving I am now watching him as he turns from us making his way to my S.U.V. He is unlocking the door and after he opens it he places himself inside to sit on the driver side of my vehicle. As I continue to watch him move around inside of it I can now hear music playing. Keith has changed the station on my radio to country music as I am now making my way over to him I can hear the song "A Heart Beat Away" by Ray Bond and The Black Diamond Band.

As I am now standing by the opened door of my vehicle on the driver side Keith looks over to me.

"Renee, do you know that this is my favorite band?"

He asks me.

"No Keith I did not know. Please tell me the truth; are you going to be ok?"

I ask him as he is moving his eyes from me so that he can lower his head down.

"Renee I will be ok, I will do my best to be anyway."

He replies to me while he still has his head lowered. For some reason he will not look back up to me.

"May I please have a moment alone Renee?"

He asks me, he continues to keep his head lowered.

"Sure Keith, just please let me know if you need anything."

I reply to him as I walk away from him.

I still feel sad but I am also very worried about him.

I say to myself.

As I leave him I see Marrick and Damon are talking to Robert and Michael once again as I am now making my way over to them. As I am getting closer Marrick moves his head so that he can look at me as I am walking closer to where they are standing.

As I am now standing with them, Marrick turns and lowers his head to look at me.

"Renee, Sarah and Damon are going to be with us as we search for David and his people."

"Ok Marrick, I will say that I do like this idea."

I reply to him as I can feel myself becoming nervous once again.

"We must leave as soon as possible; we have already wasted enough time. Please gather everyone because it is now time for us to leave."

Robert says to Michael as we remain standing in the front yard.

Right away Michael turns from us so that he can do what Robert has requested.

I start looking around as everyone is preparing themselves before we leave. They are gathering their weapons. As I continue to look around I see Thomas and Sabrina they seem to have everything they need and as I am still watching them I see Thomas taking hold of Sabrina in his arms so that he can hold onto her before we have to leave. As he holds her to him Sabrina closes her eyes and she places her arms around him as well.

As I continue standing here with Marrick, I cannot make this horrible feeling about Keith go away.

I do hope that he will be ok.

I cannot help but say to myself once more as I stand here looking at my vehicle. Keith is still by himself as he listens to "Cherry Wine" by Ray Bond and The Black Diamond Band. I can hear the music playing from within my S.U.V.

I can smell animal blood in the air and as I turn myself in the direction that it is coming from I see both Luna and Beauty making their way to us as fast as they can run from out of the woods.

When they were with Sarah and Damon earlier the wolves must have decided to leave their side to go hunting.

I stand here waiting for Luna as I am watching her as she is slows herself down from her run. She is now walking toward me and I cannot help but smile as she is coming closer. I can also see Beauty making her way over to Sarah.

I continue to watch her as she sits down beside of me.

"My beautiful friend, I must carry you as I run because we must move very quickly. So I hope that you are ready for this."

I say to Luna as she looks up at me.

I can feel Marrick getting ready to say something to me and so I turn so that I can look at his beautiful pale white face.

"Renee, it is time, we must go."

He says to me as he takes hold of my hand.

"I am ready Marrick."

I reply to him as I tighten my grip on his hand.

As we continue to stand here he raises his other hand and he places it in my hair and I rest my head in his palm. When he removes his hand from my head I release my hand from holding onto his. I bend down and I take hold of Luna to hold her in my arms and I stand myself back up; I now realize that she has grown as I hold her close to me.

"Luna please bear with me, I know that you do not like this."

I say to her as I gently rest the side of my face in her black fur.

"Renee we need to go!"

I hear Marrick commanding me with his soft voice.

I listen to what he has said to me and we are now running as fast as we both can run. I continue holding onto Luna as tightly as I can. The poor wolf does not like this at all because I can hear her softly crying as I continue to carry her.

As we continue to move I look at the trees and the fields as we quickly pass by. I must say that it is such an amazing sight to see. It is like moving very quickly in a rollercoaster. But I can see everything and it looks so beautiful to me.

I can feel Sarah, she and Damon are not too far behind us. I have also come to realize that I am able to match my speed with Marrick's. I cannot help myself but to smile.

"Renee, we must slow down so that we can walk."

He says to me as we both start to slow ourselves down.

As we both have completely stopped I gently place Luna on the ground. The poor thing is not very happy but I can see that she is trying to control herself as she looks around while sniffing the ground.

"Renee we should split up as we continue to look around. I will not be very far from you."

He says to me as he looks into my completely black eyes.

"Ok Marrick."

I reply to him as I remove the bag off of my back. I place it in my arm and I open it up with my other hand then place it inside to pull out a blood bag and I hand it to Marrick so that he can take hold of it. I move my hand back into my bag and I take hold of the blood bottle I raise it up to my mouth and I place my lips upon it and I begin to consume the cold human blood.

I take a couple of drinks and I remove the bottle from my mouth and I look at him.

"Marrick I promise that you will know right away if I see or feel anything bad."

I reply to him as he finishes consuming his bag of human blood.

"Yes I will know Renee."

He replies to me as he smiles.

I move my hand toward Marrick so that I can grab onto his plastic empty blood bag. I place in into my leather bag as we both turn and walk away from each other. As I turn from him I begin watching Luna as she is walking around still sniffing the ground once again. So I am now making my way to her as I continue to drink my human blood.

I have now caught up with Luna and as we walk around together I cannot help but notice the beauty as we walk through the fields.

There are so many different colors of green grass.

I say to myself as we continue to walk.

I am now starting to feel very nervous, I am looking around trying to see if I can see anything or anyone but at the moment I do not. But this feeling still remains!

"Marrick, I am very nervous but I do not see anyone."

"I know Renee, I can feel you."

He replies to me with his thought.

As I continue to look around to see what I can find this feeling that I have inside of me is becoming worse, I do not know what to do about it. I still do not see anyone but I can feel that something is not right.

I place my bottle back into my bag and I close it up. I take hold of my back pack so that I can place my arms thru the shoulder straps; I have it resting on my back once again.

As I continue to keep Luna in my sight, I am now standing in the middle of this field that I have been walking in and I can feel a cool gentle breeze touching my skin. I am using this feeling to calm myself.

I can feel my nerves starting to settle but I still have the same feeling and as I continue to watch Luna I now understand why I feel so nervous.

"This feeling is coming from you and Sarah!"

I say right away to Marrick with my thoughts.

"Stay where you are Renee!"

Marrick demands to me as he sends his thoughts back to me.

"Sarah, are you and Damon ok?"

"No Renee, you must protect Luna, we have been set up!"

She replies to me with her thoughts.

Right away I turn so that I can look over to Luna.

"Please come and stand next to me."

I beg to her as she moves her head to look at me.

Luna is now making her way toward me.

I must be strong!

I cannot move from where I am at because Marrick has commanded me to stay here. I am slowly moving my hand to the belt on my waist so that I can take hold of a wooden dagger, and my cross bow is still ready to fire.

I can feel fear and anger coming from both Sarah and Marrick.

"Renee, you must be on your guard! Maryann is here, WE will be there with you as soon as we can. We are in a battle with David's half turned

creatures. You must know that Maryann has escaped from us. I am sure that she is making her way to you."

I hear Marrick say to me with his thoughts.

This feeling that I have is now completely worse.

I move my head so that I can look down at Luna as she stands next to me.

"I was told to protect you but I cannot move from where I am at. I cannot help but wonder, did something happen to Beauty?"

I say to Luna as she continues to stand here with me.

"Yes Renee, I killed the white wolf."

I hear a familiar female voice answer my question.

I turn around as quickly as I can and I am now looking at Maryann as she is moving toward me. She found me!

"You killed Beauty, but why did you do that?"

"Renee, I was commanded to kill both of the wolves and you as well and then I am to kill Sarah after I have destroyed you."

"Maryann you do not have to do this! I know that we can free you from David."

I say to her as I am also now scared because of what she has just said to me.

I stand here looking at her and I can see fresh blood on her clothes and she has bite imprints in her skin, it must be from Beauty.

"As long as David is still walking on this planet he will always be able to command me and he will also know exactly where Marrick and Damon are. Please Renee; YOU MUST KILL ME before I kill YOU and SARAH!"

She begs to me as she slowly begins to walk toward me.

"Can you tell me, where is David? Please tell me where he is so that we can save you!"

I say to her as I can see her blood tears forming in her eyes as she continues to move closer to me.

She is moving so slowly towards me, I cannot help but wonder if she trying to wait for Marrick and Damon. I can feel myself becoming upset because I have been commanded not to move from where I am standing.

I continue watching Maryann as she continues to move toward me, she is raising her hands and she places them at each side of her head and she looks so angry.

"DAVID, GET OUT OF MY HEAD!"

She yells out so loudly as she stops walking toward me.

Luna moves herself from my side she is taking a few steps to stand in front of me. She is watching Maryann's every move as she is growling very loudly and showing her teeth.

"Luna please stay here with me!"

I say begging to her as she is now moving toward Maryann.

Luna is not listening to what I am saying to her. I can now feel my blood tears starting to form in my eyes because I am frightened. Luna continues to slowly move toward her. I know that she is going to do whatever she can to protect me. Maryann is lowering her hands from her head and she has her eyes lock on my wolf.

As I stand here I am slowly raising my right arm up so that I can point my cross bow at her.

"Please Maryann do not do this! I do not want to hurt you."

I beg to her once more.

"I am sorry Renee, but I have no choice! David is commanding me to kill the black wolf along with you and Sarah. David also commanded me to kill my grandchildren and their mothers. The wolves are your children."

I hear her say to me as I have realized that the tears of blood that was forming in her eyes are gone.

Maryann is slowly making her way closer to me again and the sound of Luna's growling is becoming much stronger, she is now preparing herself to attack Maryann.

Maryann looks down to Luna and then she quickly moves toward the wolf as fast as she can move. Maryann quickly begins to kneel down in front of her. Luna is now running toward her at full force. Maryann is now completely kneeling on her knees directly in front of her, Luna continues running toward her and I am forced to stand in this spot I am watching as Maryann is moving her arm with her fingers straight out to use her long sharp nails as weapons. Luna is now attacking her. I am looking upon the two of them as they battle against each other.

"Luna stop! Maryann please do not hurt her!"

I yell to the both of them, but they continue on with their battle.

Luna is making such a horrible growling sound as she takes her mouth and clamps down on Maryann's arm. Luna pulls on her with such force that Maryann falls to the ground on her back. I can see that my wolf is bleeding but she continues to fight. I can see the blood falling on the ground as Luna is pulling on Maryann's arm as if she is trying to rip it off from her body. Luna is shaking her head and her body is moving from side to side as she continues to pull on her. She is dragging Maryann away from me. But she is not yelling or even making a sound as Luna continues pulling her body and digging her teeth deeper into Maryann's pale white flesh.

I must do something to help Luna!

I say to myself as I raise my right arm to aim my cross bow at Maryann. I am now moving my left hand over to place my left index finger on the trigger behind the track of the wooden arrow.

I need a clean shot to shoot Maryann but I do not want to hurt Luna!

I say to myself as I try not to panic.

Maryann moves herself as she takes hold of Luna to push her away. Luna is now out of the way, I am going to take my shot. I push down on the trigger of the cross bow and I can hear it as it flies thru the air followed by a thump sound. I look at Maryann; I have shot her in the shoulder.

"Renee you missed my heart!"

She yells to me as Luna is running toward her once again.

Maryann holds out her arm once more and Luna jumps up at her. Maryann has caught Luan by her neck with her hands buried in her blood soaked fur. I can hear Luna gasping for air. Maryann removes one hand from Luna's neck she raises it up. All at once I hear Luna make a very high pitch sound and as I continue watching Maryann, she gently lays Luna's lifeless body down upon the ground. Maryann moved her hand so quickly that I could not see what she was doing.

She killed Luna my wolf friend.

Because of their battle Maryann is now farther away from me. All I can do is take a wooden arrow from my belt I am now loading it into my cross bow.

As I stand here looking at Luna's body lying on the ground I can feel Marrick and Sarah and as I move my head toward their direction I can also see Damon, they are finally here. Sarah is carrying Beauty's body in her arms.

Sarah is coming toward me as she moves to the speed of light; she is now standing by my side. She bends down so that she can lay Beauty upon the ground then she stands straight up. Both Sarah and I have our arms straight out, our cross bows are pointed directly at Maryann with wooden arrows ready to fire.

"I love Luna and you are right she was my child. But it is not your fault for what just happened because that monster commands you to do what he wants YOU to do."

I say to her as she looks at me.

Maryann's clothes are torn and her vampire blood is slowly dripping from the wounds on her body from Beauty and Luna.

"Renee, are you also going to forgive me after I kill you and Sarah?"

She asks as she is coming closer to me once again.

"Mother, please stop! You will not harm them."

Marrick yells to her.

"Renee, you can now move."

Marrick says to me right away.

As she continues to slowly walk toward me, I begin to step backwards.

"I am so sorry my sons, but the only way I can be stopped is if you both kill me."

She says to Marrick and Damon as tears start to stream down her pale white face.

"Please I ask for your forgiveness for what I had done to your families so long ago."

Maryann begs to both of her sons.

"Mother we do forgive you."

Damon says to her as he is now moving to stand behind her.

"I forgive you as well. We have never stopped loving you."

Marrick replies to her as he is now moving to stand in front of Maryann.

"Thank you. I have always loved you both so very much even though I treated you so badly as you were growing up. I am now ready to die!"

Maryann says to the both of them as she continues to walk toward Marrick because Sarah and I standing behind him.

"I will tell your father that you both say hello."

She also says to them.

"Can you tell us where can we find David?"

"I am sorry but I cannot tell you but please keep looking because before this was just a game to him. Now it has become personal and he is planning to KILL all of YOU!"

She says to the both of them as she is placing her hands on both sides of her head once more.

"Now I must KILL YOU because he demands it from ME!"

She says to them with such a harsh sound in her voice.

As Sarah and I continue to stand behind Marrick we can hear her as she starts to move very quickly toward us. She has to attack Marrick to be able to get to the both of us. Right away we hear wooden daggers flying thru the air and there are several very loud thumps as they hit her body; Maryann is falling to the ground. Sarah and I are both watching Marrick and Damon as they move very quickly toward her so that they can catch her before she lands on the ground. They did what she had asked of them. They gave her peace and now she is truly dead.

Marrick and Damon are placing her body slowly upon the ground. Damon is gently moving her hair from her face and Marrick is holding onto her hand as they both sit beside her. We can see the wooden daggers in her chest where her heart used to beat. By the way her body is raised she also has daggers in her back.

As we stand here watching them, we can hear that there are more people coming toward us and by the sound of their movement we know that they are vampires. Right away Sarah and I turn to see who it is as we are both ready to fire our cross bows. We see that it is Thomas and Sabrina we watch as she walks toward us. Thomas walks over to Marrick and Damon.

"I am so sorry for what has just taken place."

Sabrina says to Sarah and I.

We do not reply to her but Sarah nods her head to Sabrina as to say thank you.

We watch her as she moves to take her place next to Thomas.

"We are very sorry for you loss."

Thomas says to the both of them as Marrick and Damon move themselves to stand up from Maryann's body.

Sarah and I do not know what to do to help them. But I am glad that Maryann was able to say that she has always loved the both of them.

I look back over to Luna's body and I walk over to her I lower myself to the ground so that I can sit beside of her. I move my hand toward her and I begin to pet her fur. I can feel Sarah, she is coming closer to me once more but as I look up to her I can see that she is carrying Beauty in her arms again. I lower my head to look at Luna once more as I continue to pet her. Sarah is now bending down and I watch as she is placing Beauty beside her sister.

"We should bury them together."

Sarah says to me as we both begin to cry.

I do not say anything to her as I continue to pet Luna's black fur one last time before we put them into the ground.

"Please allow Sabrina and I to help you burry your mother and both of the wolves."

Thomas says to us.

"No, we will take care of them."

Damon replies to him as he continues to look upon his mother's body.

"I understand."

Thomas says to him as he and Sabrina continues to stand close to them.

As Damon and Marrick continue to look upon their mother, Damon raises his head to look up at Sabrina.

"Sabrina may we please borrow your sword?"

Damon asks to her as she looks back to him.

I can hear her pulling the sword out and she hands it to Damon.

Damon moves his head toward Marrick.

"Brother."

Damon says to him as he continues to look at him.

Damon walks around Maryann's body so stand next to Marrick and offers part of the handle of the sword to him. Marrick and Damon both are holding the sword together; Sarah and I now understand what it is they are both going to do. We both take hold of each other as we listen to the sound of the sword as it moves very quickly whips through the air followed by the sound of Maryann's head being cut off from her body.

Right away Sarah and I release the hold on each other and we both start digging into the ground with our hands because this is the only thing that we know that we are able to do at this moment. We are digging a grave big enough to place Luna and Beauty's bodies together.

As we continue digging their grave we can hear Marrick's voice once more.

"Sabrina, I want to thank you for allowing us the use your sword."

Marrick says to her as he hands it back to her.

"You are welcome."

Sabrina replies to him as she puts her sword away.

"We have also taken care of all the bodies from the battle you had a while ago with David's creatures. We removed their heads from their bodies and we also placed them in a pile for the morning sun to burn them."

Thomas says to them.

"We will leave her body upon the ground so that when the first light touches her, her body will burn as well."

Marrick says to them.

As Sarah and I have finished digging the grave for the wolves we both continue to cry as our blood tears are streaming down our faces. We both move over to the wolves' bodies. Sarah gently takes Beauty in her arms for the last time and I am taking hold of Luna's lifeless body in my arms. I do not want to put her into the ground; I hold her close me as I press her head against my face. When I am somewhat calm I look over to Sarah as she continues to pet her wolf friend, Beauty. I look back to Luna and I notice that my blood tears are smeared on her nose, her mouth is also covered in blood. It must be from Maryann.

We know that the sun will be rising very soon as we are now placing them in their grave together. We both place our hands in the dirt pile; we are now pushing dirt upon them to fill their grave. We are no longer crying but we are both very sad from what has happened this evening. We are finally finished and as we stand up we begin to walk toward Marrick and Damon as we pass by Thomas and Sabrina.

I raise my hand up so that I can take hold of my leather bag, after I remove it from myself I open it up and I grab my blood bottle and the remaining bags of blood that I have. I hand one of the bags to Marrick and then I also give one to Sabrina and Thomas. Sarah hands one to Damon from her bag as well as one for herself.

"Thank you Renee."

Sabrina says to me.

"You are welcome."

I reply to her.

I raise my bottle to my lips and I start to consume all of the human blood that is left inside of it. When I am finished I open my bag up once again so that I can place my empty bottle inside of it.

"We need to head back to the rest of our group; the sun will be rising within an hour."

Thomas says to us.

I am extremely sad as I look upon Maryann's body I am trying not to look at her head; it is lying above her body. I turn back to look upon the grave of Beauty and Luna. I lower my head as I close my eyes. I am trying very hard to control myself. Damon and Sarah are holding onto each other as they try to comfort one another.

Maryann was right for what she had said to me, Luna and Beauty are our children. They will never be replaced. I now feel that a part of me is missing.

"Are you ready Renee to go back?"

He asks as I look up into his sad black eyes.

"Yes Marrick I am ready to go back with the others."

He does not say anything else to me he moves his hand so that he can take hold of mine. I cannot help to take comfort in his touch. We all begin to run as fast as we possibly can so that we can meet up with the rest of our group. We are moving so fast this time that everything looks like a blur as we pass by the trees and fields along with the different shades of green grass. As we pass through the night air I begin to worry about Keith once more.

"Please let Keith be safe."

I say to them as we continue to make out way back.

"I agree with you Renee, I am wishing for the same thing."

Sarah replies.

I am remembering Maryann's words that she had said to me.

"The wolves are our children."

I have a knot in the pit of my stomach.

If Marrick had not commanded me to stay where I was standing I could have helped Luna and maybe just maybe she would still be alive.

I think to myself as I am trying not to become angry from everything that has taken place this evening.

"Renee, I am truly sorry."

Marrick says to me with sorrow in his voice.

We are still far away from our group but we can see the trucks; they are traveling down a back road. I also have no idea as to where we are at.

I do not have a very good feeling at all about Keith! I am scared for him.

As I send my thought to Marrick but he does not reply to me.

We slow our speed down we are now walking toward everyone, they have stopped the vehicles after they have seen us. Some of them are now getting out of the trucks.

We see Richard and it seems like he is waiting for us, he looks very upset.

As we walk up to him Richard looks at me and then to Sarah.

"There was an ambush waiting for Paul, Lizzie and Keith. We were not able to get to them in time and we did everything that we could to save him but Keith did not want to complete his change to vampire. I am sorry to say this to you but he refused Logan's help, he has passed away from his injuries. He bled to death."

Richard explains to us.

"Where is he?"

Thomas asks him right away.

"Keith is laying on one of the cots with in our resting trailer."

Richard replies to him.

Right away we are making our way to the trailer as fast as we can possibly can run. As soon as we get to the back of it we see Logan kneeling beside of Keith and there is another female beside her. She is half turned; we can see her red glow with a hint of yellow mixed with it. We can see that she looks to be around 5'3 with long brown hair she also has brown eyes.

Without haste we all jump up inside of the trailer and as we walk toward them Logan looks up to us as she continues to stay by Keith's body.

"He would not allow me to complete his change."

Logan says to us as she continues to cry.

"David is killing everyone that we love."

Sarah says to us all with fear in her voice.

I cannot say nor do anything, all I feel is a very powerful anger growing inside of me.

"It was David's vampires; they trapped us like we were animals! It was just me, Paul and Keith. I would not be here if he had not saved me."

The female explains to Sarah as she looks upon Keith lying on the cot.

Her voice sounds so familiar, I look over to her.

"Are you Lizzie?"

I ask to her, I feel so badly for what she had gone through this evening.

"Yes, I am Lizzie."

She replies to me with such a great sadness in her voice.

Logan turns her head to look at Sarah and then she moves just slightly to look at me.

"Keith did not want to be saved because he did not want to continue his existence without Fred. But he had me promise that I would give you both a message. He said please forgive him for leaving you both."

Logan says to us, she turns her head back so that she can look upon his body once again.

No one says anything to what Logan has just said to us because we all knew how Keith felt.

I look over to Sarah and she is trying very hard to control herself but the tears of blood are escaping from her eyes once again. I feel such a heavy weight upon my chest again. I am trying so hard to keep my head up but my non-beating heart now has a very large hole in it. I give into myself and I lower my head as I close my eyes.

When I am able to raise my head back up I look over to Lizzie I can now see that she is in much need of medical attention.

"Lizzie is there anything that we can do to help you?"

I ask her.

"No I will be ok; I will heal as soon as I consume some blood."

She replies.

"I am so very sorry for what had happened to Keith."

Lizzie says to us with great sadness within her voice.

"There is nothing for you to be sorry about Lizzie."

Sarah replies to her as she tries to comfort her.

As I look back over to Keith's body, we are all now watching as Marrick gently picks him up from the cot and he slowly walks past us to the opening of the trailer. We are all very silent as we watch him carrying Keith. Marrick is lowering himself down so that some of Logan's people can take Keith from Marrick's arms.

As Marrick turns to walk back to us I begin to walk toward him so that I can place my arms around his body. He places his arms around my back to hold me tightly to him.

"It is time that we all rest. The Sun will be up within minutes."

Richard says to us all.

Marrick very quickly picks me up in his arms and he walks over to one of the cots and lowers himself so that I can stand and I remove the belt and my wrist halter. I remove the bag from resting on my back so that I can place the items back inside of it and I place it on the floor then I remove my shoes. Marrick takes hold of me once more in his arms as he lays me down upon the cot, he lies down with me. He gently places his head upon my chest and he wraps his arms around me and he moves his leg to rest it on top of me. I look over to Sarah and Damon as they lay together upon one cot as well. But Damon does not have her strapped to the cot with his body.

"In a moment Lizzie will be entering this trailer to place I.V's into our arms so that we are able to consume human blood while we are resting during the day. She will be remaining in here with all of us until the sun sets."

Logan says to us just right before our bodies shut down to rest for the day. I can also hear the door to the trailer being closed and locked.

Will she be well enough to take care of us during the day?

I can feel Marrick he is in my mind.

"Renee, I do not want you to think about anything as we rest. I command you to rest your mind until the sun goes completely down."

He says to me as I lay with him upon this cot as he continues to hold me to him.

I now want revenge more than I ever did before; I no longer want to wait for it! But why did Marrick command me not to move when I was in the field? I could have died tonight!

I say to myself as I am now starting to rest my mind.

Chapter Four

As I am waking up I have come to realized that I am able to move my body but there is a weight upon me. The sun must have set, but then Marrick commanded me not to wake until the sun has gone down. I now realize that Marrick still has his body completely on top of mine, he is also awake. It is as if he is waiting for me to open my eyes. I can feel the anger and revenge that I still have inside of me from what had happened last evening.

I open my eyes so that I can look at him

"Marrick may I ask you to please allow me to get up so that I can remove the I.V. needle from my arm."

I ask him hoping that he will accept my excuse and allow me to move.

I did not even say good evening to him.

I say to myself as I try to block my thought from him.

"No Renee you cannot but I will remove the needle for you."

Marrick replies to me as I can feel his hand sliding down the skin of my arm. I can feel the tips of his fingers nails taking hold of a corner. He is removing the tape from my skin and now he is pulling the I.V. needle out from my arm. He does not even move his eyes away from looking into mine. I am trying not to show that this does not bother me, but I can still feel the pain as he pulls the needle from out of my arm.

I am trying to keep my mind silent and my feelings to myself because he knows exactly what it is that I want to do and that I am also extremely angry with him.

"Marrick, why will you not allow me to get up?"

I ask him as I can feel myself becoming very inpatient with him for what he is doing.

"Because I can feel what you are feeling, I know what it is that you want to do Renee! I want you to realize that you cannot go after David alone."

He replies to me as he continues looking into my black eyes.

"I will not go after him alone Marrick, I promise you that I will not do that."

I say to him as I close my eyes and turn my head away from him.

"Then PLEASE tell me Renee why do I feel that you are only telling me what I want to hear?"

He asks as he is still lying on top of me.

"Because Marrick, I am very angry and sad from what had happened last night! But you are correct; I want so badly to go after him and I do not want to wait for anyone to go with me!"

I reply to him with anger in my voice as I am now looking into Marrick's beautiful completely black eyes with my completely black eyes filled with tears of blood.

Marrick brings his hand close to me and gently places his soft pale white hand upon my face and he uses his thumb to wipe a tear of blood that has escaped from me.

"Very well Renee, I will allow you to get up. But I command that you KEEP your promise to me."

Marrick says to me as he tries to keep his voice calm as he continues to look at me.

"Why did you command me last night not to move from where I was at? Maryann said that she was ordered to kill me and Sarah, she was also commanded to kill Luna and Beauty and she succeeded with killing our wolves!"

"Renee, if you would have tried to escape from her then she WOULD have tried to KILL you! It was safer for you that you did not move from where you were at. She was trying to buy time until we were able to come to you."

"You have never commanded me to do anything like that before Marrick. Both wolves and Maryann are DEAD!"

I say to him as I look over to Sarah and Damon as they are watching us.

"Renee please I want you to look at ME!"

He says to me with such a soft low whisper in his voice.

Marrick's voice sounds so different to me.

I can feel such a strong feeling from him, what is he going to say?

I turn my head so that I can look at him. He is moving himself from lying on top of me I can now finally move. I sit up on the cot and I have my body next to him. I position myself so that I can now face him. Marrick moves his hand toward me as he is taking hold of my hand; he locks his fingers with mine.

"I am going to tell you Renee why Damon and I have never turned anyone else into what we are."

He says to me as he now looks so sad once more.

I continue to sit upon the cot as I look into his eyes.

"Renee the reason why we have never turned anyone other than you and Sarah is because once we had fulfilled our promise to our father to destroy David. Damon and I had agreed after our father had passed away, to allow the first light of the sun to destroy us. But from the first moment when we looked into your eyes we knew right away that we wanted to be with the both of you, to spend the rest of our eternity with you!"

Marrick explains to me with such a soft look in his eyes.

"Why are you saying this to me, I do not want to hear that you both were planning on destroying yourselves!"

I say to him as I try very hard to remain calm.

"Because Renee, you should know what we WERE going to do, what we had wanted to do. But because of the both of you we do not want to end out existence any longer. We just want to destroy David more now than what we ever have wanted before. You and Sarah have showed us how to live and love once again and we WILL die if anything ever happens to the both of you!"

Marrick explains to me.

"I understand how you feel, I feel the same way about you Marrick I have never felt anything like this before. I love you with every part of me. I never want to be without you either. I will keep my promise to you. I will not go out looking for that monster without you."

I reply to him as we move our bodies closer to each other so that we can wrap our arms around one another. I have the side of my head against his chest and he has arm holding onto me while his other hand is placed on the back of my head. We are holding onto each other very tightly.

"Renee, I am not going to say good evening to you either."

Marrick says to me with a smile, I look up to him as I now remember what I was thinking of a while ago.

"We must now begin to prepare ourselves so that we can start our search once again."

Sarah says to us all.

I am a little surprised that she is the one to say this; I am use to Marrick and Damon telling us that we need to get ourselves ready.

I can feel the heavy sadness coming from all of us. We lost Keith last night along with Luna and Beauty and also Maryann.

I was warned not to trust her, but I could not help it, I really liked her and she did everything that she could to help me escape from David.

I know that Sarah would not go after something as dangerous as David by herself. I hope that she will not do that.

Marrick and Damon had to do what Maryann wanted in order to protect Sarah and myself. They had to kill their mother last evening. David is no longer able to know where we are at.

But I still cannot help but wonder if we could have prevented ending her existence.

I am trying so hard to hold back my tears but I am not sure if I will succeed at doing it.

As I look around I notice that Logan and Richard are no longer with us inside of this trailer.

I wonder where it is that Robert and the others are resting at?

I wonder to myself as I am trying to stop myself from thinking about last night.

I glance back over to Sarah and Damon as they are both starting to stand up from their cot. Damon has such a sadness showing in his eyes and Sarah is also trying to keep herself calm. I can also feel that Marrick is also trying to control his feeling as well. For what I wanted to do on MY own did not help, I have upset my family even more, the ones that I love and hold dear to my non-beating heart.

I bend over the cot while sitting on the cot so that I can put my shoes back on. Marrick and I both remove ourselves from the cot and I take hold of my brown leather bag that Keith had given to me and now the four of us are slowly making our way to the opening of the trailer.

Before Marrick and I go outside he looks at me as I watch Sarah and Damon jump to the ground.

"Renee you do realize Renee that I can hear everything that you are thinking? You must also know that you cannot hide your thoughts from me."

"I understand Marrick."

I reply to him as we jump out of the trailer.

Right away Marrick and Damon make their way to Michael and Robert. Sarah and I remain standing by the back of the trailer because we are not ready to talk to anyone about what had happened last night.

Sarah and I are reaching into our brown leather bags to pull out our items and we are both putting our belts back onto our waists. We are now placing the wrist halters on once again. The both of us are now placing a wooden arrow into the track of our cross bows.

I really do not like that Marrick only allows me to hear what he wants me to from his thoughts and yet he can hear every single thing in my mind. It must be because he has turned me into what I am now. A Vampire who he can command, but I do know that he is truly in love with me I can feel it from him.

Sarah and I are preparing ourselves for when Marrick and Damon are ready to leave. As I look around I noticed that Lizzie is making her way over to us.

"Good evening."

She says to us.

"Hello Lizzie."

We both say to her.

Before she can say anything else to us there is something that I want to say to her.

"I would like to thank you for taking care of us while we rest during the day."

I say to her as she continues to stand with us at the back of the semi-trailer.

"You are welcome. Renee I have the keys to your S.U.V, I wanted to make sure that you have them back."

She says to me as she is now holding them in her hand for me to take.

I stand here looking at my keys. I slowly move my hand over to hers as I take hold of them. As I stand here holding my keys in the palm of my hand, I close my fingers over them and I move my hand slowly back toward Lizzie as she continues to watch me.

I remember Keith from last night sitting in the driver side of my vehicle listening to his favorite band playing Ray Bond and The Black Diamond Band.

"Do me a favor and please take my keys, you are welcome to drive my vehicle. I do not think that I will need to drive it right anytime soon but I will let you know if anything changes."

I say to her as to takes hold of my keys with her hand.

"Renee, are you sure about this?"

"Yes Lizzie, I am sure. Maybe you can travel with us by following us in my vehicle."

"I can do that if that is what you would like for me to do."

She replies to me.

"Lizzie I would like that very much."

"Renee, I must check with Richard first to make sure that he does not have other plans for me."

She relies to me.

"Lizzie, what is your connection to Richard, if you do not mind me asking."

Sarah says to her.

As the three of us continue to stand together at the back of the semi-trailer, Lizzie begins to smile because of the question that was just asked to her.

"Not only did Richard turn me into half vampire and human but he is also my grandfather."

She replies to Sarah.

"Lizzie, I did not know that. Richard did not say anything about it the first time I met him. But there was not time to talk about family history we were rescuing Renee along with the others that David held captive. "

"Sarah, that is true because there was no time for conversation. But not too many people know that Richard is my grandfather. My mother passed away when I was just a few months old. Richard does not talk about what had happened to her, but he took great care of me. He only had people that he could really trust to make sure I had what I needed during the day as I was growing up and going to school. I was also taught how to fight and to protect myself."

She explains to Sarah.

"How long has Richard been a vampire?"

"Sarah he was turned when my mom was a teenager. But that is all I know because he does not like to talk about it."

Lizzie replies to her.

"Well maybe when he feels the time is right, he will talk more about what had happed."

I say to Lizzie.

"Maybe Renee, but I have become used to not knowing what had happened. Maybe the real reason is that I do not want to know."

Lizzie says to us with such a calm sound in her voice, she does not even look upset about it.

As she continues to stand with us at the back of the semi-trailer she looks at us.

"If you both will please excuse me, I am going to go and talk to Richard."

"Why do you not call him Grandfather?"

Sarah asks her.

"Because I think that it is a little weird to call him Grandfather when he looks just a few years older than what I do. But do not take it the wrong way, he is my family and I love him very much. Not only is he my Grandfather but he has taken the role of both of my parents as well while I was growing up."

Lizzie says to us as she explains her reasons.

"We understand what you are saying Lizzie."

I reply to her.

"Thank you and I will talk to the both of you again before we leave for our search."

Lizzie says to us as she turns and walks away from the both of us.

"Sarah we must go to the refrigerator truck so that we can supply ourselves with bags of blood."

"Yes Renee, I agree with you. Shall we go ahead and make our way over there to get what we need?"

Sarah asks me as we start walking toward the refrigerator truck.

As we continue to walk we are both silent I know that Sarah is running through her mind about what had happened last night. I can feel her sorrow. I am working on blocking my feelings and my thoughts but I am not sure if I will figure it out, as time goes by then maybe I will be able to.

Marrick had made me promise and he also commanded me not to go after David. But I feel that this is one thing that I must figure out how to break. I cannot help but feel so guilty about what it is that I must do or should I say WHAT I want to do. That is to Kill David!

We are approaching the refrigerator truck. The walls of the trailer are very thick it is also insulated. I look up and I can see the refrigeration system on the top of the roof. The door to enter the trailer is on the driver's side of the truck it is also open. Under the door of the trailer there are steps and as we are now standing in front of the door I can see that the steps can be pushed back under the door.

We are now making our way up the steps to go inside so we can gather bags of human blood to take with us. As we come inside Logan is gathering blood bags. Sarah and I can see that she has been crying her beautiful pale white face is stained from her blood tears.

She moves her head just slightly to look at us as.

"Good evening Sarah and Renee."

Logan says to us as she tries to keep herself under control.

"Hello Logan."

We both say to her, she turns her head away from us as she continues to gather blood bags.

"Logan, may we both gather some bags to take with us for our search this evening?"

Sarah asks to her.

"Of course please take as much as you need."

Logan replies to her.

Sarah and I both walk over so that we can stand next to her. She turns her head to look at us once more.

"I am so sorry for what happened last night. You both had lost Fred a few weeks ago. I feel so badly because you have lost so much in such a short amount of time."

She says to us as we continue to stand with her inside of the truck.

"Thank you Logan, We are sorry for what had happened as well, Marrick and Damon also lost their mother last night. You are the one who half turned Keith and the both of you were close for a very long time. We are sorry for your loss as well but I must say that we are very angry and we want revenge more than ever."

She replies to Logan.

"Sarah I know that the both of you do and I have to believe that we will have it! Robert and Michael are doing everything that they can to track him. But I feel so horrible for Robert because David is his brother."

She relies to Sarah.

"I agree with you Logan, we all feel that way for Robert. It is so horrible that David is the way he is. But what if he is now tracking us, now that Maryann's existence has ended?"

I reply to Logan as Sarah and I move farther into the truck so we can start to gather bags of blood.

"David was born evil as a human he was such a horrible person who enjoyed hurting so many people. But when he was turned into a vampire he became such a very powerful evil being that needs to be destroyed but he is too strong for us. We must have faith in ourselves that we will destroy him. We must hope that he is not going to track us because then WE will be the hunted! Our last encounter with him, we had badly injured David and we also rescued you and the others that he had captive. I do know that he wants his revenge as well. "

Logan says to the both of us.

"You are correct Logan; we must have faith in all of us!"

Sarah replies to her.

"Maryann said to me that this used to be a game to him, but now it is personal and he is planning to kill every one of us."

I say to them as I do what I can to stay brave.

"We are all in serious danger if he is now tracking us."

Sarah replies.

"Yes, we will be, but we must hunt him before he hunts us!"

Logan says to us, we can both hear in her voice that she is very terrified.

I do know that no matter how hard Logan tries to stay strong she will always be scared of him. I know exactly how she feels.

I am doing everything that I can to hide what I am feeling. I am becoming very angry once again for what has taken place. I must remain calm.

As we have finished gathering as many blood bags that will fit inside of our leather bags, I cannot help myself from asking Logan a question.

"Logan, where did they bury Keith's body?"

She lowers her head and before she answers my question she closes her eyes and then she raises her head to look back up at both us.

"Renee, I am so sorry but they did not burry Keith they burned his body as we were resting during the day."

Logan replies to me as tears of blood fills her eyes once again.

I do not know what to say because her words have put me in shock, but I can feel that her reply now has Sarah very upset.

"Logan, why did they burn his body?"

Sarah asks her, I can hear the anger in her voice.

"Sarah, his body was burned because that is what his wish was to be. Keith had said to us long ago that if anything happened to him, he made us promise that we would burn his body. Keith's ashes are being stored for the both of you. When you are ready to collect them all you have to do is let Richard know and he will give the ashes to the both of you."

Logan explains to us.

"Thank you Logan for letting us knows, and when we are ready we will ask Richard for his remains."

I say to her.

Sarah looks at me and I can feel from her that she is ready to walk out of the refrigerator truck.

I move my eyes back over to Logan.

"Logan if you do not mind we are going to go look for Marrick and Damon."

I say to her as we all turn to walk out of the truck.

We know exactly where they are, I needed to come up with an excuse for us to leave.

Logan does not reply to us, but she does walk out of the truck with us and after we all go outside she closes the door and walks away.

"Sarah please remember that Logan is just as upset as we are for what has happened."

I say to her without looking at her.

"I understand that Renee, if I had never taken you out for your birthday then maybe we would not be in the middle of this!"

"Sarah my existence would have ended! David was planning on taking me captive before we met Marrick and Damon. He would have taken you as well."

"What do you want to do Renee?"

"I want to Kill David!"

I reply to her.

"Then that is what we will do. How do we do this without Marrick and Damon knowing?"

She asks me.

"We must learn how to hide out thoughts and feelings from them as well as breaking their commands that they place upon us."

I reply to her.

"Renee, are you trying to block our discussion from them as we are speaking?"

"Yes Sarah I am trying really hard to and you must do the same."

"I am trying Renee."

She replies to me.

We slowly start walking toward the direction as to where Marrick and Damon are at.

I turn my head to look at Sarah because I have a strange feeling coming from her as if she has something that she must say to me.

"Renee, I want to tell you that Damon had made a command to me as well, I also had to promise that I will not go after David by myself."

"Sarah, are you positive that you want to do this with me? You must understand that we may also fail. We also do not know what

Marrick and Damon will do if they are to find out what we are planning.

I reply to her as we continue to walk.

We are trying so hard to speak in a very soft low voice that only the two of us can hear. We do not want the others to know as well.

I can feel Marrick as I try to keep myself calm.

"Renee, I understand that David will kill us the first chance he gets. I do not think that I would be able to face Damon if he were to find out."

She says to me.

"We cannot fail even if he dies with us. Sarah I want to see David's head removed from his neck and I want so much to see his body burn with the first light as the sun rays touch his skin."

I reply to her as we can now see Marrick and Damon they are making their way toward us.

"Renee are you honestly prepared to die especially after what Marrick had said to you this evening?"

"If I can destroy David as well then yes Sarah, I am prepared to end my existence."

"Renee, I will not leave your side. I am with you to the end. But how are you going to handle things with Marrick if he finds out?"

She replies to me as she tries so hard to be strong as she speaks her words.

"I am sorry Sarah but I am to full of rage to even worry about what to do if he finds out."

I reply to her as I try very hard not to let my feelings show.

We continue walking toward them as well to meet them; the four of us are now standing together.

"We are going to search together this evening, the four of us. Are you both ready to leave?"

Damon asks to the both of us.

"We are ready but we are waiting for Lizzie, I asked her if she would like to go with us. I also gave her my keys so that she can drive my vehicle."

I reply to the both of them.

"Richard wants to have Lizzie with him as well for what had happened last night, we were all set up. But we will meet up with them later this evening."

Marrick says to us.

"I understand."

Sarah replies to him.

I must do everything that I possibly can so that Marrick does pick up on anything.

As the four of us continue to stand together I can feel myself wanting to look for Luna and Beauty so that they can go with us. Sarah can feel that I want to call out for them.

"Renee, we can no longer call for them; the wolves cannot come with us anymore."

Sarah says to me as we both take hold of each other's hands.

I can feel that my non-beating heart along with Sarah's are both breaking into pieces because of the great loss that we are all suffering from.

Sarah and I release the hold that we have on each other's hands as I am now taking hold of Marrick and she is taking hold of Damon's hand.

We are all once again starting our hunt for David!

Sarah and I must figure out how we can break away from them.

The four of us are now moving as fast as we can run. Marrick's grip on my hand becomes tighter.

"Renee, I will NOT allow you to walk alone anymore! I will be by your side at all times during our search."

I am not going to reply to him. Does he know what we are planning? I continue to work very hard as to hide this feeling from him.

It was not Marrick's fault for what had happened to Luna it is that fucking monsters fault. I blame David for everything because he is the reason for all of the bad that has taken place!

As I think to myself knowing that Marrick and Sarah can hear this thought that I am thinking.

As we continue moving to the speed of light I find that I am enjoying how the cool breeze feel against my skin, the evenings are becoming much cooler.

I can see the beautiful colors of the trees as we pass by them. Different shades and textures of dark brown bark they are so pretty to look at. I can also see into the clear dark night sky and the moon is almost full. Just one more evening until we are able to gaze at her full beauty!

As we continue to move very quickly, we have come to a paved road and we begin to follow it. We can see lights up head of us, we are approaching a town. We are slowing down our speed so that we can walk the rest to the way.

"Damon, why are we headed in to this town?"

"Sarah the reason is that some of David's vampires have been seen here. Robert had sent a team here last night and they found out that two people were killed; they had no blood left in their bodies. That is why we are here."

Damon explains to her.

"I am going to admit that I am now very nervous. I will also do everything that I can to be brave."

I say to them as we continue walking toward town.

This is something that they did not allow us to know before we had left for our search. I know that we will be able to hide our thoughts from them. But it is going to take a lot of work to do so.

"I understand how you feel Renee, we feel the same way but we WILL stay together."

Marrick replies to me as we are now walking into town.

He does know! The fear that I have from this I am doing everything that I can to make him feel that I am scared of facing David again.

We are all now walking along the sidewalk and there are street lights just a few feet from each other. This town that we are now in must be a village because it does not seem to be very big.

As we continue walking we can see some buildings just a few feet from us and as we continue walking we find ourselves standing in front of a bar. There is a name on the front of the building and it is called "The Old Pub." There is also a small food market beside of it and also several houses on each side of the street as well as other small business farther up the street.

Sarah and I stop walking we are standing in front of the bar because we can hear music playing from inside of The Old Pub. As Marrick and Damon allow us to stand outside of the bar we find ourselves listening to the song "Santa Monica" by Theory of a Deadman. It is such a wonderful feeling as we listen to the music that is playing, allowing the sound of the music to surround us as the wind gently blows through our hair.

As we continue to listen we both begin to relax as the music plays.

"It is time for us to move on so that we can continue looking for signs as to where David's creatures have been."

Damon says to us, his words have brought us back as we remove ourselves from the music as it continues to play.

We are now walking away from the bar.

"I can tell you that they are not inside of The Old Pub because I did not feel anything evil in there. But I could hear a lot of people slurring their words as they spoke."

I say to Damon.

I cannot help but look at Sarah as we continue to walk through the village.

"Sarah did we sound that silly after we had been drinking alcohol?"

"Renee, I thought we sounded normal when we were drinking."

She replies to me with a smile.

"Well I can tell you both that you did not slur your words but you did make us smile."

Marrick says to us as Sarah and I both start to laugh.

As we continue on with our walk I can feel that Marrick is getting ready to speak.

"Renee, you must concentrate on what you feel around you."

He says to me as we continue on.

"Ok Marrick."

I reply to him as I am now paying close attention to what is around us.

We continue walking on the sidewalk and we can see a group of young men. There are four of them and they are walking toward us. As they see us they begin to laugh and they turn to walk down what seems to be an alley. They are completely human because their glow is a dark red, there is no yellow tint. They are clean looking but I can feel that something is not right.

"Marrick they are dangerous! I do not understand as to why they were laughing when they saw us. What did they do?"

I ask hoping as if someone knows.

"I can smell fresh human blood."

Damon says to us as we are walking closer to the alley that we saw those young men walk into.

"We should follow the scent of the blood to see where they came from. And by the sound of their laughter I bet anything that the blood is not theirs."

Marrick says to us as we now begin to walk faster.

"Marrick I do not have a good feeling."

I say to him as I take hold of his hand once again.

"We must find out what had happened!"

Sarah says to us all with great concern in her voice.

"How old do you think those young men are?"

I ask them.

"Renee, they looked maybe eighteen to twenty one years of age."

Sarah replies.

"Please be silent!"

Damon demands to the both of us as we all stopped moving.

We can hear a faint cry from what sounds like a young person begging for help.

"I do not like the sound of this voice, whoever it is they are in trouble!"

Sarah says to us all as we start moving as fast as we can to where the cry is coming from.

We are moving extremely fast, I cannot even see the buildings as we pass by them but it does not take us very long to find the person where these cries are coming from. It is a little boy and he looks to be around fourteen years of age.

As we are now standing beside of him the smell of his fresh blood is so strong and I can also see that his blood is coming thru his clothes. He has been severely beaten and we all know that this was done by those young men that we saw earlier this evening.

As Damon and Marrick slowly kneel down beside of him, they are looking at the damage that has been done to him. Sarah and I take a few steps so that we can move closer to them.

His eyes are swollen closed; he has blood coming from his nose and mouth. The dark red marks on his face and body are turning into a deep purple color. We can all hear that he is having trouble breathing. Because of the beating that they had done to him by those young men, his skin has broken open. He is lying in a small pool of his own blood.

"Is there anything that we can do for him?"

I ask to them.

"Renee, he needs to be taken to the hospital. His heart beat is starting to slow down."

Marrick replies to me as we look upon the young boy.

The poor boy has passed out from the pain that those men placed upon him and the blood that he has lost.

"Damon, can we help to heal his wounds by turning him into a half vampire?"

"No Sarah we cannot! It would be better for him if we take him to the hospital and we must have faith that they can save him. Sarah if we change him he will no longer continue to grow part of his body will die and he will be fourteen for the rest of his existence. His body may no longer continue to grow and the hunger for blood may be too strong for him to control. This is why some of us will not change a child into a half or a full vampire. They will eventually go insane because they will are trapped in a child's body and some of them can become just as dangerous as David."

Damon replies to her.

"If a child is changed they may be a child forever."

Sarah says with great sadness in her voice.

Damon moves himself closer to the boy and very gently places his arms under his body to pick him up.

"Sarah we must find him help right away."

He says to her as he stands up now holding the young boy close to him.

Looking at Damon holding onto this young boy tightly to him I cannot help but feel such a great sadness from him. I am not connected to Damon but I bet anything that Damon is remembering the evening when both of his sons were murdered by Maryann because David commanded her to kill them.

"I agree with you Damon, but what about those young men that had beaten him? He is very close to dying."

Sarah says to him as she looks into Damon's eyes.

"We will take care of them."

Marrick replies to her.

"Hopefully you will not have destroyed all of them by the time we return."

Damon says to Marrick.

"Then you better move as fast as you can!"

Marrick replies to him.

No sooner after those words are said to Damon while he is still holding the young boy in his arms Sarah and Damon are nowhere to be seen.

I can feel Marrick as he takes hold of my hand. I am becoming very nervous because I know what he is going to say to me as he moves to stand in front of me and he slowly raises his beautiful pale white hand and he places it on the side of my face. I close my eyes as he touches my skin, waiting to hear him speak his words to me.

"Renee, it is now time for you to hunt, we are going to find those young men and we are going to feed from their pathetic bodies. We are going to destroy them!"

"I am very nervous but I am ready Marrick! When I was held captive it seemed different I was doing what I could to escape, with the help from Cindy. But this group of young men must die."

"I understand how you feel Renee. Now let us give to them what they deserve!"

He says to me as I listen to his words.

"I am nervous about this Marrick, this is fresh human blood. Now that I am a full vampire, I am scared that I will lose control of myself."

"Remember you can control yourself. Renee, you will not lose yourself unless you allow yourself to do so."

He says to me as he removes his hand from the side of my face. He is now standing by my side and together we start walking once again.

We are now hunting for these young men following the scent that remains on them. The smell of the young boy's blood!

As we continue to walk in the village, we walk very slowly hoping to be noticed by them. We are coming closer to another alley way and we turn to walk into it.

"We need to set them up. Renee, you need to be the one to get their attention! I will be very close by, but you must make them believe that you are alone."

"Where are you going to be Marrick?"

"I will be on the roof tops. I will be watching for them as well. Renee, you will be safe I will not allow them to harm you, but you must remember that you are very strong and powerful and also very beautiful. The scent of blood is getting stronger so they are not very far away from us."

He says to me as he stops me from walking.

"Yes you are right; Marrick the scent is getting stronger."

"Renee, have you fed this evening? In just a few moments you will be served."

He says to me as he looks into my black eyes.

I do not reply to him, I am watching what he is doing.

He moves his hands towards me and he takes hold of my right hand, he pulls the wrist halter with the cross bow from my wrist and he hands it to me. He is now placing both of his hands on my waist so that he can also remove the belt from me that contains all of my wooden weapons and he also places it into my other hand. He is now taking two steps Marrick is standing directly in front of me and with both of his hands he takes hold of the shoulder straps to slide them down my arms to remove the leather bag from me. He opens the bag and takes my belt and wrist halter from my hands and he places my items inside of it.

"Renee, I do not think that you will need these as you attract their attention, your beauty will be what draws them to you."

He says to me as I give him such a wondering look.

He bend his head down to me and his lips touch mine and as he stands completely straight he turns from me and I watch him as he gracefully jumps up into the air as he lands on a roof top of one of the buildings along the alley.

I love to gaze upon him but I make myself look away from him and I continue to walk. I can feel Marrick as he is watching every move that I am making from the roof top. I have come to a field at the end of this alley. I am making my way toward it. I look up into the sky as I begin to slowly walk through the field and I am gazing up to the beautiful moon. The scent of the blood is now much stronger and so I change my direction in the field and I continue to walk very slowly. I now know that Marrick is not the only one who is watching me. I can feel their eyes upon me.

I am still looking up to the sky as I am now listening to these four men as they are now starting to walk toward me.

The scent of blood is making me very hungry. I want to drink the blood from their bodies!

"Hey are you lost?"

I hear one of them as he calls out to me.

I cannot let them see my face, not until it is time. I am worried that they may run from me because of all of the blood that my body has consumed I have not changed back to normal. My nails and fangs are still sharp and my eyes are still completely black.

For now I must keep my back toward them. But I feel that for some reason they may not be scared if they are to look at me.

"No I am not lost. I just wanted to take a walk."

I reply to them as I continue walking.

I can hear them as they are making their way closer to me. I can also feel that Marrick is also. I know that he no longer remains on the roof top of the building.

"Do you mind if we walk with you? I think that we can all have a good time together, if you know what I mean."

I now hear a different voice say to me.

"No I do not mind at all. The more there is the more fun it will be."

I reply to them as I can smell the blood on their clothes from the young boy.

I am craving the taste for fresh human blood!

They have finally caught up to me, I cannot help but close my eyes and my fangs are now thumping in my mouth.

I WANT TO FEED!

"You must stay patient Renee! Allow them to make the first move."

I hear Marrick say to me with his thought.

"Wait for us Renee; we are now making our way to you."

I hear Sarah say to me as she is also in my mind.

I do not reply to her because I am not sure if I can wait.

"So what's your name?"

Another one of them asks to me.

"Does it really matter as to what my name is?"

I reply to him.

"No, it doesn't matter to us one way or the other."

One of them says to me as I can feel one of their hands taking hold of my arm to stop me from walking.

I continue to keep my head lowered, looking at the ground.

"Look at her; she must be shy because she is looking down at her feet."

"Oh I am not shy; I just do not want to look at you."

I reply to them as I continue to stand here in the field with them as one of them still holds onto my arm.

Three of them are now walking around me to make a circle. I am moving my head around so that I can keep watch of them, my head is still lowered I am not ready yet to look at them.

"Renee, we are here with you."

I hear Sarah say to me as she sends her thoughts to me once more.

I do not reply to her because I am paying attention to what they continue to move around me.

These young men are now moving closer as they are making their circle smaller. I can feel another pair of hands taking hold of me as two of them are now pushing me down onto the ground. I allow them to take control because I am ready to feed.

I am now being held down on the ground on my back by the two that has a hold of me. I can hear Marrick, Sarah and Damon as they very quietly make their way toward me. One of these men are moving themselves to stand in between my feet, looking down at me. He is kneeling down to his knees as he positions himself between my legs lowering himself down upon my body. He is now completely lying on top of me. He places his hand under my shirt as he slides his hand up my skin so that he can touch one of my breasts. I can feel the anger growing inside of me as he is doing this to me, touching me.

Memories are starting to surface from when I was a captive. I want to destroy this man so he can never hurt anyone ever again!

I have my mouth and eyes closed so that he cannot see my black eyes or my fangs.

He rises himself up from me and he begins to unbutton my pants, he is forcing his hands inside of my jeans.

"Take him now Renee; his body is yours to feed from!"

I hear Marrick say to me as he sends his thoughts to me.

Right away I pull my arms away from the two men who are holding onto me and as I do this I immediately sit up facing the man who is trying to have his way with me. I place my arms around his body and I hold onto him very tightly, I cannot wait to kill him! I know that the other three men have been taken by Marrick, Sarah and Damon. I know each of them are now feeding because I can hear them as they consume the blood from their bodies. Those three men are screaming in pain. I cannot help but to feel joyful that they are going to die.

As I have him in my arms I force him on the ground so that I am now on top of him. I still have not allowed him to look into my eyes. He does not even realize that his friends are no longer with us. He is not paying any attention at all to their cries.

"Oh I like this, I take it that you like to be on top when you fuck?"

He asks to me as he presses himself up against me.

"Maybe I do like to be on top."

I say to him as I begin to turn my head very slowly so that he can look into my eyes, I smile to him just so he can see my very sharp fangs that are waiting to sink into his skin.

"I know what you are."

He says to me as he raises his head up from the ground to get a better look at me.

I can hear his heart beating inside of him, and I can also feel that he still has an erection and once again he raises his hips so that he can press himself against me.

I continue to look at him as he lays his head back onto the ground. He has a smile upon his face.

"I am your worst nightmare!"

I say to him as I glare into his eyes, I am allowing my anger to grow stronger inside of me.

I am now ready to sink my teeth into his neck I want to drain every last drop of blood that he has. I reach my hand up and I grab his hair with my fingers, I force his head to the side so that it is resting on his shoulder.

"Why did you harm the little boy?"

I ask him as I stare at the skin of his neck watching his flesh move with each beat from his heart.

"Why do you want to know about it?"

He asks to me as I am still lying on top of him not allowing HIM to move.

"Because I want to know why you did it and if you tell me I will give you a surprise."

I say to him as I lower my head so that I can whisper into his ear, I turn my head just slightly so that I can rub my nose against the skin of his neck.

"We did it because we wanted to! Are you going to be the one to change me? Let's take our clothes off and we can fuck as we exchange blood."

He says to me as he tries to looks back at me, but he is unable to move is head because I am still holding on to him by his hair with my other hand.

"Change you? I will NOT change you and I will not give you ANY pleasure!"

I reply to him with anger in my voice as I speak to him.

"We were promised that if we prove our loyalty we would be changed into vampires."

He replies to me, I can hear his heart as it is beating faster and his breathing is now heavy. I know that he is now starting to become worried about what I am going to do to him.

"You must understand I am not here to change you. I am here to feed on you!"

I reply back to him.

"I was promised!"

He yells to me as he is now trying to fight me.

"I am not the one who made that promise to you. You will not receive anything from me, but you will die and this is a promise that I will give to you!"

I say to him as I am now lowering my head down to his neck once more.

He continues to fight himself free from me but I am not going to let him win. I am now touching his skin with my lips as I am very slowly pushing my fangs into him. I want him to feel pain! I can taste the salt on him as I touch my tongue to his skin. I can hear him gasp from the pain as I my fangs are now completely buried in his neck. I remove my hand from his hair and I place my other arm around him. I am tightening my grip around his body that I can hear a crunching along with snapping sounds as I am breaking the bones in his arms as I squeeze my arms tighter around him. He has gone into shock.

I really do like the feeling of my fangs buried within his flesh as I close my eyes. I love the taste of his sweet fresh blood as it flows inside of my mouth. I swallow his blood into my body and I am very much enjoying as his blood fills my mouth once more. With each beat his heart makes it pumps delicious fresh warm human blood into me. It flows smoothly down my throat, I am now sucking very hard on his skin because I want every last drop that his body has within it!

His body still remains underneath mine. I continue to drink from him; my thirst for his blood has become stronger. I remove my mouth from his skin. I remove my arms from holding onto him and with my long sharp nails I place them on the side of his neck and I can feel his skin as it rips apart. I open his flesh with my fingers and I lower my face back down to him so that I can place my mouth upon his neck once again from where I removed his flesh. I continue to consume every last ounce of blood that he has left. I am drinking him dry, he is empty.

I can feel Marrick as he is coming closer to me.

"My beautiful Renee, are you finished with him?"

He asks me, I can feel him gently placing his hand in my hair as he bends down next to me.

As I remove myself from being on top of this now dead body, I stand up next to Marrick.

"Yes, he has no more blood left for me to take. Marrick I do not even feel bad for what I have just done. This person along with three of his friends badly injured a young boy and to top it off they were promised to be turned into vampires if they prove their loyalty."

I say to him, I can feel Marrick gently taking hold of my hand as I stand here looking down at the man I just killed.

"Renee, I am very proud of you. You did very well for your first hunt."

"Thank you Marrick, I must say that his fresh blood tasted much better than human blood from a plastic bag."

I reply to him as I am now looking up at him, I can feel that I have his blood all over my mouth and chin but I do not mind it at all. I can feel his blood coursing through me.

"We must destroy these bodies, all four of them."

As Marrick says these words to me I look over and I see Sarah and Damon bringing two dead bodies with them as they make their way toward us.

I cannot help but look to see where Marrick has laid the body of the young man he fed from. It is just a couple of feet from where we are standing. They are close to our age I am only twenty two and Sarah is twenty three so I really do not understand as to why I refer to them as young.

"How do we destroy these bodies?"

I ask to him, I look over to Damon and he looks at me after I have asked my question to Marrick but I cannot help but smile because I need to be honest with myself. I enjoyed what I had just done.

I turn myself back to look at Marrick but he has moved himself to make his way over to grab the body of the young man that he fed from and he is laying him beside of the other three bodies.

"My darling sister in law, this is how we destroy the bodies that we feed from."

Damon says to me, as I stand here looking at him I am now watching as he and Marrick moves very quickly as they tear apart all four bodies. They are moving so quickly, I can hear the sound of clothes being torn. Sarah continues to stand here with me as we both watch them rip apart the bodies. I can hear bones being broken and smashed as they take hold of it in their hands. The sound of their body organs being pulled apart is such a horrible squishing sound as they hold the insides in their hand and they are using their other hand to shred them with their long sharp nails. There are small pieces of their bodies all around Marrick and Damon. Their clothes and skin as well as their insides and including small parts of bones are scattered on the ground.

"Renee now, we must hurry to burry all of the parts and pieces!"

Sarah says to me as she walks away from me and takes her place next to Damon.

"Where do we burry this at?"

I ask to them, all I can do is stand here and look at these gross piles of what is left of the men.

"We can bury them right here. Someone will find them, and I bet it will be one of David's creatures. Once they pick up this scent, they will know right away what WE have done to them."

Damon says to us as we are all now bending down to the ground and we all start digging a grave for what is left of their bodies.

"We must keep our guard up; we do not want to find ourselves in another trap."

Sarah says as we all continue digging in the ground.

We are digging as fast as we can move and the hole is getting deeper very quickly. We are almost finished but as we all continue I begin to have a bad feeling.

I look over to Marrick.

"I know what you are feeling Renee, we must all hurry!"

He says to us as we are now finally finished. We are all taking hold of every piece of the shredded bodies as we put every part that is left of these four young men into the ground. We are now placing our hands into the dirt pushing it into the hole, covering them up as quickly as we can. We are now finally finished and we are all covered in blood and dirt and small pieces of skin.

"Marrick whatever or whoever this is, it is coming closer toward us at a very fast speed!"

"It is ok Renee, because we are now finished burring them. We must be ready for them!"

Marrick says to me as I look over at Sarah.

I see that Sarah now has hold of my leather bag, I watch her as she hands it to me but there is no time for me to arm myself because they are here. We are now looking at two females and they are both half vampire and human. They are not part of our group we know right away that they belong to David because we can see that they have been tortured! They have scars on their skin that is exposed. I cannot help but feel so badly for what they have been through.

Both of the females are thin, one of them has short blond hair and the other one has long red hair and part of her hair is pulled back from her face.

I can feel the blood that I have just consumed continues coursing through my body. I feel strong and very brave.

"What business do you have here in this village?"

I ask to the both of them without even thinking as they are now standing in the field with us.

"It is none of your concern why we are here!"

The blonde hair female replies.

"Are you looking for someone?"

Sarah asks them.

"We were but by the scent of their blood and the stains on your faces, we know that we no longer have to look for them."

The blonde replies to Sarah.

I cannot help but look at the red haired female because she will not stop looking at me.

"Oh I know who you are Renee, I recognize you from when David held you captive. I do know that he enjoyed fucking you even though your master had commanded you to sleep."

The female with the long red hair says to me.

I do not like the smirk on her face as she looks at me. I can feel a knot developing inside of my stomach from what she has just said to me. The rage inside of me growing once more; I can see his face in my mind. David's pale white face and his completely black eyes, and sharp fangs and his long white hair! I am going to kill her to.

"I have no master, but I will say to you that we will KILL YOURS!"

I reply to her with anger in my voice as I look at her directly into her eyes.

"Go ahead and try you stupid BITCH but he will find you before you can find him Renee."

I hate it when they say my name!

I say to myself as I look at her.

"Do whatever you want; you can take her blood Renee."

I hear Marrick speak to me with his thought.

As I continue to stand her in front of the red haired female, I slightly tilt my head to the side as I remain looking into her eyes.

"Will you give David a message for me, please?"

I say to the blonde haired female as I move my gaze to look at her.

"What message do you have and why should we let him know what it is?"

The blonde haired female replies to me.

"The message that I have for him will only come from you."

I reply to her.

"Sarah, hold her for me!"

I say as I send my thought to her trying to hide it from Marrick.

As they continue to stand here in the fields in front of us, I walk up the red haired female as I continue to look right into her eyes. As she is looking back at me, I can see Sarah as she moves very quickly she takes a very tight hold of the blonde haired female as she is now standing behind her. Sarah knows exactly what I am going to do. I very quickly take hold of the red haired female and I am not going to let go of her. Marrick and Damon are ready to help us if we need them.

I look over to the blonde haired female once more while I have the other female tightly in my grasp as she stands in front of me.

"You can tell that FUCKING PRICK that we are WAITING for HIM!"

I say to her as demanding as I can, then as quickly as I can move I place my mouth on her neck pushing my teeth into her skin. I begin to consume her blood. I have such a strong hold on her that she is unable to fight herself free from me as I remain standing in front of the red haired female holding on to her as tightly as I can.

Her blood tastes so good!

With each beat of her heart, sweet salty blood is pumped into my mouth. Sarah continues to hold the blonde haired female making her watch as I continue to consume her companion's blood. The more blood I consume from her body the weaker she becomes. She has passed out as I continue to drink from her I can hear her heart beat slower as she begins to die in my arms. Her heart has completely stopped beating and there is no more blood left to consume from her.

I remove my mouth from the skin of her neck and as I hold her lifeless body I look back over to the blonde haired female. There is blood dripping from my chin and my chest is now covered as well.

"Here is my gift to David. Do not forget to tell him my message!"

I say to her as I let the body of the red haired girl fall to the ground.

"You FUCKING BITCH you are going to DIE for this!"

She yells to me as Sarah releases her hold so the blonde haired female can now move.

I slowly turn from her so that I can make my way back to Marrick's side but I turn my head back so that I can look at the blonde haired female once more.

I smile to her.

I do not reply to the threat that she has just made I just continue to look at her. I do not want her to know how scared I am. Instead I continue to show how brave I am trying to be.

The image of David allowing the female to drop to the floor has just flashed in my mind. She cut her own neck and held my head to her skin so that I could consume her blood when I was a captive. She wanted to be free and death was her only way out.

The blonde haired female takes hold of the red haired female and she leaves with her lifeless body. We watch her until we no longer can see her.

The four of us turn and we begin to walk out of the field.

"I must say Renee, I am very proud of you."

Marrick says to me as he places his arm around my body to hold me close to him as we walk together.

With my face and chest still covered in blood, I look up to him.

"I am proud of myself as well. Marrick I am amazed with what I have done this evening."

I reply to him as we are walking back up through the alley.

"Renee, how did Sarah know what you were going to do?"

"Marrick, Sarah knows me very well. Maybe it was just instinct."

I reply to him.

I am doing everything that I can to hide my guilt for lying to him. I am not sure how long I can keep this up. I know that within a matter of time he will figure out what it is that I am doing. I am also allowing Sarah to be part of it. If anything happens to her I do not know what I will do.

As we continue walking in the alley once more I glance down to the pavement and I hear this very fast whoosh sound. I raise my head to look up Sarah and Damon are no longer with us. I am trying not to smile because I know what they are going to do. They are looking for a place so that they can make love to each other.

Marrick stops walking and he takes hold of me so that I am now facing him. He bends his body just slightly down and takes hold of me with his arms and picks me up. I wrap my legs around his waist and I have my arms around his neck holding tightly on to him. I let my leather bag drop to the ground. He moves us to the side of the building that is in the alley and he continues to hold me tightly in his arms as my back is now against the building.

He places his mouth on my skin and he is licking and sucking the blood from my pale white flesh.

"Marrick, I want to feel you inside of me!"

I whisper into his ear.

He lowers me so that I am now standing on the ground as we start to remove our clothes but we can hear a vehicle coming down the alley toward us. We both turn our heads as we look upon it.

"Renee, we are going to have to wait, Richard and Lizzie have finally found us."

He says to me as we release the hold that we have on each other.

"Marrick, I do hope that we do not have to wait too long so that we are able to finish what we just started!"

I reply to him, as Richard and Lizzie are driving closer to where we are standing.

As I look inside of my vehicle as it continues to come closer I can see that Logan is also with them, she is sitting in the back seat. Marrick and I start walking toward them and Lizzie stops the S.U.V. I can hear her as she puts the vehicle into park. We continue to stand her watching them move as they open the doors to get out making their way toward us.

"I can see that we have missed out on the hunt with you this evening."

Logan says to the both of us.

"Yes, sorry to say but you did miss out. We found four of David's people; they had badly beaten a young boy. Sarah and Damon found him some help hopefully he will survive. I must say that Renee did very well for her first time on a hunt as a full vampire. She was able to help set up a trap for them. But after we had destroyed the four men, two of David's females had found us after we had covered up their shredded bodies. Renee sent a message to him this evening and I am sure that we will be receiving a reply from David very shortly."

Marrick explains to Logan.

I am trying to feel what he is truly feeling and he does feel proud but he is also beginning to wonder what I am up to. I pull myself back to their conversation.

"Then we must make our way back to the others! It is hard to say what his reply will be. What was your message Renee?"

Richard asks me as he looks into my eyes while we all continue to stand in the alley.

"I killed one of his half turned females, and I told her friend to take the body back to David as a gift and to tell him that we are waiting for him."

I reply to Richard.

"Well then, I suggest that we leave at once, we must be ready for what is now coming our way. We have to prepare for his attack! I am proud of you for what you did Renee, but he will do everything that he can to destroy us all.

Logan says to us as she moves to walk back to the vehicle.

"I do understand what he will try to do."

I reply to her as I take hold of Marrick's hand.

Maybe this will be my chance to kill him.

As Marrick and I continue to stand here, we watch as they all get back into my vehicle and close the doors. Lizzie is now driving the three of them back to meet with the rest of the group.

"Marrick, did I do the wrong thing by killing that girl?"

"No Renee, you did not do anything wrong."

He replies to me as he turns to stand right in front of me.

Marrick places both of his hands upon my arms as I look up into his beautiful blood stained face. He gently pulls my body closer to his and he places both of his arms around my body, I wrap my arms around his and I hold onto him as tightly as I can. I cannot help that I now feel very fearful for us all. But I must continue to hide what I am going to do.

I can feel Sarah; I know that she and Damon are close by because I can since that she is coming closer to us.

As Marrick and I release the hold that we have on each other I can feel the change in the weather. The wind has pick up and as I look up into the night sky I can see dark black clouds moving above us, I can no longer see the moon. I walk over so that I can take hold of my leather bag, I open it up and I place my wrist halter back on and my belt as well.

I look up to Marrick and I smile as I look into his eyes.

"It is raining Marrick; I can hear the water as it drops onto the ground, it will reach us within seconds. I must say that I am happy about this because we are covered in blood and dirt, we are in need of a shower."

I say to him as we start walking out of the alley.

We are now walking along the sidewalk once again and I can smell the scent of roses within the rain. I take hold of Marrick's hand once again because the fragrance is reminding me of the beautiful bushes of red roses that Keith had planted around a marble birdbath in our back yard where Fred was murdered.

I will get our revenge as I can see the faces of Keith and Fred in my mind. I am missing both of the wolves as well. My non-beating heart aches so badly for Maryann.

I cannot help but remember the words that Logan had said to Sarah and myself.

"You both have lost so much in such a short amount of time."

"Marrick, Logan had said to Sarah and I that Richard is holding Keith's ashes for us, when we go back home I would like to sprinkle them upon the bushes in the back yard in honor of Keith."

"Renee, I think that is a wonderful idea."

Sarah replies to me; they have caught up with us.

We are now walking into the rain. I look over to her as we continue walking and I smile at her as I can see the blood being washed from her pale white face as the rain runs down her skin. I can see that the dirt in her hair has turned into mud. I raise my hand up so that I can run my fingers through my hair; I also have mud in mine as well. It is dripping off from all of us as it runs down our clothes as the rain continues to fall from the beautiful very dark night sky.

There are now great flashes of lightening. I realize that I am enjoying watching it as it lights up the night sky because with each flash we are able to get a glimpse of daylight.

The thunder is so loud I can hear as it echo's all around us. The rain is now pouring down and the wind is very strong that as the water falls from the sky is changes directions as it comes down upon us. The rain is coming down so hard that I can see the water droplets bounce from the ground as it hits.

We continue making our way out of town as we are now approaching the village limits. We are increasing our speed to a run and now we are moving as fast as we can go to make our way back to everyone.

"Marrick, I am worried or maybe I should say that I am scared! We do not know as to what his reply is going to be. I should have not killed the red haired female but I was so angry for what she had said to me!"

I say to him as I begin to question myself.

"Renee, you had done nothing wrong. If you had not been the one to kill her, I was going to be the one to do it for you!"

"Damon, how are we going to keep ourselves safe from him?"

Sarah asks as we continue to make our way to the others running as fast as we can go as it continues to rain.

"Sarah, I promise that I will not allow anything to harm you!"

Damon replies to her.

"Marrick, can we please go back home?"

"Renee, do you have any idea as to what you are asking?"

"Yes I do Marrick, and I also know that David will soon figure out where we are at. We will be much safer resting in the safe room in the basement. We are no longer safe, resting in the back of a semi-truck. But before we go home we must get Keith's ashes."

"I agree with Renee, please allow us to go back home."

Sarah says to Damon.

I can hear the fear in her voice.

If I do go through with breaking Marrick's command not to go after David alone then maybe I should not allow Sarah to be with me. I cannot lose her!

I think to myself as I do everything that I can to continue hiding my thoughts from the both of them.

"We must discuss this with Robert and Michael. But we do not have much time left. The sun will be rising soon. We will not be able to leave until tomorrow evening."

Damon replies to Sarah as we are now approaching the trucks.

As we are now coming closer to our group, I do not feel right at all. I am scared! I let go of Marrick's hand because I have stopped myself from running along with them.

Marrick and Sarah have realized that I have stopped moving and right away Sarah moves herself to be by my side.

"Renee, what is it? What do you feel around us?"

She asks to me as she places her hand upon my arm, I know that she is still very frightened.

I do not reply to her, but I look straight to Marrick and then Damon.

"There is a great evil presence here with us."

I say to them.

I am so scared I begin to shake. I move myself closer to Sarah and I wrap my arm around her arm. Marrick and Damon look to the side of them and we are all watching as David is making his way toward us.

"Evil, Is this what you are calling me now Renee?"

He asks as he is walking closer to us.

"His voice is calm. How I hate the sound of his voice!"

I think to myself as I send my thoughts to Sarah and Marrick.

"Sarah, please ask Damon to command you not to feel any pain that David may place upon you!"

"David you do not even want to know the other names that we call you."

I reply to him as I try to stay strong, he is now standing in front of Sarah and I.

I can see Marrick and Damon as they are moving themselves to stand behind him, waiting for the right moment to attack him.

"Do you really think that you can destroy me? I am sorry to say but you do not have much time the sun is starting to rise. I am here because I have received your message. I am here to give you my answer, my dear Renee."

"So tell us, what is your answer David?"

I ask him as he starts to smile.

Right away I can hear Sabrina's voice.

"Arm yourselves because they are here!"

I hear her yelling.

"How do you know where we would be at?"

"My dear Renee, this is happening because of you. This is my reply to your message so I wish you good luck because the sun has started rise. You better find a safe place to rest because I do hope that we are able to see each other again. Oh before I leave you I feel that there is something that you should know."

He replies to me as he smiles.

I do not want to ask but I am waiting for him to tell me.

"My dear Renee, I know where you are at all times. If you remember you also have my blood inside of you as well."

"What are you talking about David?"

I ask to him.

I am slowly raising my right arm straight out as he starts to walk away from us. Now I am moving my left arm over so that I can place my left index finger on the trigger behind the track of my cross bow.

"David, please wait!"

I find myself saying to him as I now know what he means that I have his blood inside of me.

My words have caused him to stop and he turns to look at me with his smile still upon his face. Right away I push done on trigger and I hear a high pitch whistle as the wooden arrow is released from my cross bow. I remain standing here looking at him as he is now holding onto the arrow with his hand. He caught it, he is holding in right in front of his chest where his heart used to beat. I can see him tightening his hand and I can hear the wooden arrow snap. He opens his hand up and I watch as the broken arrow is now falling to the ground.

David continues to stand where he stopped when I called for him to wait.

"Renee, I will give you credit for tying your best. But you will never get another chance!"

He says to me with his calm voice.

"I hate you David!"

"But I do not hate you my dear Renee. I do hope to see you again. Do try and stay safe I will be back for you, both of you! That is if you survive."

He says to both Sarah and I, before we can blink he is gone.

As we continue to stand here we are listening and watching as his half human vampires are making their way to attack our group, I cannot help but agree with his words.

"This is my fault!"

I say to everyone as we continue to stand here as it has finally stopped raining.

"No Renee, this is not your fault! David wants you to think that this is."

Sarah says to me.

"I have his blood inside of me because of what he did to me when he held me captive."

I say as I begin to remember.

Sarah looks over to the group as they are all now in a very bloody battle and she leaves my side as she starts moving toward them.

"I am going to do what I can to help them!"

She says to us all.

Right away Damon moves toward her and he grabs her very tightly in his arms, holding her close to him. Sarah is angry with him and she is trying to fight her way free from his hold.

"Sarah we have no choice, we must find a place to rest because our bodies are going to shut down!"

Damon yells to her as he keeps his tight hold on her.

"Damon let me go I must help them!"

She yells back at him with anger in her trembling voice as she cries.

"Sarah, I command that you listen to my words!"

Damon says to her.

Then right away I see her stop fighting him, but she continues to cry as he holds on to her, trying to comfort her in any way that he can.

I remain standing here as I turn my eyes to see so many people within our group fighting for their lives.

"Marrick please promise me that we will not lose everyone else after tonight."

I say to him as I can feel him gently taking hold of me in his arms as he is now picking me up from the ground.

"Renee, this is one promise that I cannot make to you."

He replies to me.

Marrick is moving so quickly that we are now caught up with Damon and Sarah. They are moving us away from the fight; they are looking for a safe place for us to rest. They have stopped running as they continue to carry us in their arms. We are in the woods. They come across a small area that they both have agreed on and right away they start moving their feet very fast, back and forth as they continue standing in the same place where they have stopped. They are using their feet to dig into the ground because they still hold us in their arms.

I look over to Sarah and Damon and I can see that they are slowly sinking into the ground. I cannot help but tighten my arms around Marrick's neck as I can feel that we are now going into the ground as well.

"I must stay CALM!"

I say to him as the earth is now starting to cover our heads.

"Rest your mind Renee."

I hear Marrick command to me as he sends his thoughts to me as we are now completely underground.

I am now slowly starting to shut down, body and mind as I still have a tight hold on Marrick.

Chapter Five

"Renee, wake up. I want you to open your beautiful eyes."

I hear Marrick say to me with his words as I do what he says.

As I wake I am looking up into the trees, I cannot see the sky because of the branches and the thickness of the leaves has created a celling. Marrick has taken us both out of the ground while I was still commanded to rest my mind.

As I realize that I am able to move my body, I can feel that I am resting in his arms. He is still holding me tightly to him as he sits up against a tree. I move my hands so that I can place them on his arms to hold on to him. I turn my head just slightly towards him so that I can look at his pale white face covered in dirt. I give him a smile.

"Damon we must go back to see who has survived the battle from last night."

I hear Sarah's words as she is trying to do what she can to make a demand to him.

Marrick removes his grip from me as I am moving myself from his loving arms so that I can stand up, he is now moving himself to stand next to me as I watch him.

"Sarah is right; we must go to them!"

I say as I turn my head to look at Damon as well.

"Sarah we are going to go back to them. But you must prepare yourselves because you are not going to like what you are going to see. I believe that the aftermath from last night is going to be a lot worse than the evening when we rescued you Renee."

Damon explains to us as we begin to make our way back.

"I am so sorry for everything that has happened."

I say to the three of them as I try to hold my blood tears back from escaping my eyes.

"Renee, this is not your fault, you must understand that!"

Sarah replies to me as we continue to move as fast as we can.

"But it is my fault! If I would have only listened to Marrick the night I was taken. If I would have ran back into the house and hid where he told me to go I would have not been captured. Then David would not know where to find us. Especially now, since he is no longer able to find out from Maryann! He is now using me. "

I say to them.

"Renee you must try to calm yourself!"

Damon says to me.

"I am trying but I do not think that I can."

I reply to him with anger in my voice.

"Renee, I can command you not to remember what had happened to you."

Marrick says to me, I can hear his concern for me.

"As much as I want to yes to that, I cannot allow you to do it. I need to remember. I need my hate and anger. I want to see him DEAD! David does not need to hunt for us because he knows exactly where we are! How can I do the same, how can I feel where he is at? He fed from me he placed his blood inside of me. Why did we not realize this sooner? My blood is inside of him as well."

I say to Marrick with such anger and fear in my voice as I allow my rage to grow stronger inside of me.

I hope that I can use this to my advantage against David.

I say to myself as I try to hide my thoughts.

As we continue to move very quickly, I can feel my eyes turning back to normal. I raise my hand so that I can hold it up in front of me and I am watching my nails become shorter. They are now even with the tips of my fingers. My fangs are no longer long and sharp. My speed is starting to slow down. I am not running as quickly as I was a moment ago. I look over to Sarah and she is going through the same thing, she is also changing back. We both immediately stop moving.

"What is happening to us?"

Sarah asks softly with great worry in her voice as she turns her head to look back at me.

Right away Marrick and Damon stop moving and they turn to look at the both of us. Damon's eyes are green once more and Marrick has his beautiful dark coal back eyes once again.

"This is because our bodies were unable to consume human blood while we were resting during the day. You must consume the blood from the bags that you both still have in your leather packs before the pain starts to develop within your bodies."

Damon says to the both of us.

"We are no longer evenly matched with them!"

I say as I can feel great fear within Sarah and myself.

Sarah and I are both removing the leather bags from our backs. I place my bag in my arm and I open it up and I reach my other hand in so that I can take out two bags of human blood. I hand one of them to Marrick so that he can feed.

Before we feed on our blood bags, I can feel my eyes and fangs changing my nails are growing long again. My body is very hungry and I can feel myself craving the blood. The four of us are holding onto our bags and we raise them up to our mouths, I am forcing my fangs into the soft thick plastic that contains the blood. I very much prefer the taste of fresh warm human blood from a living body.

I can see Sarah. She is removing the bag from her mouth.

"This bag of blood does not taste as delicious as the fresh blood from last night that we had consumed from David's people. I really did enjoy killing them!"

Sarah says to us, and then she places her mouth upon the bag so that she can continue consuming the blood that is cold and not fresh.

As we continue to stand here, we have finished feeding I take hold of my leather back pack and I place my arms through the straps so that I can place it on my back once again. Marrick takes hold of my empty bag and walks behind me and he places them in my back pack then he closes it back up.

Marrick moves himself to stand beside of me and I listen to his words as I start to feel better from feeding.

"We must hurry!"

He says to us as he takes a few steps so that he can now stand in front of me, I look down as I watch his hand take hold of mine. I slowly raise my head so that I am now looking into his beautiful coal black eyes. He takes his place at my side once again, we start moving as fast as Sarah and I can run. Marrick and Damon continue to run the same pace as us.

We are getting closer to our group and the smell of death and blood is very strong as the wind carries the scent within it.

We continue moving very quickly but as soon as we see what is up ahead we begin slowing ourselves down, we are now walking very lowly. There are bodies scattered everywhere laying upon the ground in pools of blood.

"Renee, we must be strong and we must do everything that we can to help the ones that are still alive."

I hear Sarah say to me with her words as we slowly walk around the dead bodies that remain on the ground.

"We must be ready for David; we do not know what his next move is or when he will strike again."

Marrick says to us as we continue to move slowly.

"We cannot allow this to happen again!"

I reply to him.

I see that Sarah has stopped walking and I am now making my way to be by her side. Marrick and Damon are now a few feet ahead of us. We know that they are looking for Robert and the others.

"I hope that Lizzie is safe."

I say to Sarah as I am looking at the bodies hoping that I do not see her.

"Renee, I am sure that Richard has kept her safe."

She replies to me as we carefully walk around the bodies.

"Renee, I miss Fred and Keith I wish that they were still here with us. I miss Beauty being by my side."

"Sarah I know how you feel, I also miss them very much. I miss the comfort that Luna gave to me. The wolves were so beautiful and very strong. I know that they loved us as much as we loved them. We will always carry Fred and Keith with us everywhere we go, their memories will live inside of us for as long as we continue to exist."

I reply to her as I place my arm around her back as I do what I can to comfort her.

"Renee, we must find the others and see what we can do."

"Yes Sarah I agree with you and we will do everything that we can."

I reply as we both start to listen for the slow heart beats of the ones that are still alive.

I move along beside her as we begin to walk again. I look down as we take our steps; our shoes and clothes are badly stained with blood and dirt.

I cannot help but close my eyes for a moment. I feel such a heavy weight upon my chest from what has taken place. I open my eyes and I am looking around at all the bodies that are lying dead upon the grass. They are either human or they have been half turned.

We can hear beating hearts from the survivors, we begin following the sounds.

As we continue on we see bodies with broken necks and some that had their throats cut open. There are also so many body parts on the ground as well, there are arms lying close to other bodies that still have arms. As we continue to move on we see heads that have been removed from their bodies as well. The grass is no longer green; it is now red completely soaked in blood. We have not found any bodies that have been burned by the sun from first light. That means that

Robert and the others are safe, that also means that David did not send his vampires to fight.

I can feel Sarah taking a strong hold of my hand. I move my fingers so that I can lock them with hers.

We both stop as we are now next to one of the semi-trucks that is still completely intact.

"Renee, I can hear voices coming from inside of this trailer."

"Sarah, I can hear them as well."

I reply to her.

Right away we can hear someone moving from the other side. We stay silent hoping that it is someone from our group. The sound of their movement lets us know that this person is in a hurry. We remain where we are at still listening to their every move. The footsteps are soft but also heavy, light but not quiet. We remain at the side of the trailer waiting as this person is extremely close getting ready to pass. We are waiting to see who it is as we are peering from where we are at. This person is coming closer and moving very quickly and I move as quietly as I can as I look to see who it is.

"Lizzie, we are so happy to see you."

I say to her right away, she stops to look at both Sarah and I.

"I am so glad that you are both safe! I have been waiting to see you."

She says to us.

"Lizzie, is there anything that we can do to help?"

"Yes Sarah, I am on my way to look for some blood bags. We have only a hand full who survived the attack. We need the blood so that those who are half vampires will be able to heal from their wounds. There are three people within our group who are now going through the complete transformation into vampires."

"Lizzie we are going to need the extra strength when we encounter that monster again. We will go with you to help gather the bags of blood."

I say to her as the three of us start walking toward the refrigerator truck.

As we continue walking with Lizzie I can feel Marrick.

"Renee, do you still want to go back home?"

"Marrick this needs to end and we have to do whatever we can to stop him."

"I agree with you Renee, we must continue the fight against him."

I hear him reply to me with his thoughts.

"Marrick it does not matter where we are because of me, he will find us."

I reply to him.

"We will destroy him Renee."

I hear his reply as I close my eyes to his words.

"Renee, I can hear someone digging in the ground. It is coming from that direction."

Sarah says to me as she points to her left.

"Who is it and what are they doing?"

I reply with my question.

"It is Thomas and Michael, they are burring those that we had lost."

Lizzie replies to the both of us as we continue walking toward the refrigerator truck to gather blood bags.

"We are extremely sorry for what has happened."

Sarah says to her.

"There is no need for you to apologize we have all lost friends and loved ones to him."

Lizzie replies to Sarah with sadness in her voice.

I am developing such a strange feeling inside of me. It is so familiar but it is also different, this is something that I have never felt before. The strong connection that I have with Sarah, I can feel that she has the same feeling as well.

"Renee, I do not understand this. What am I feeling?"

I hear her ask me with her thoughts.

"I am not sure Sarah, but I hope that we will find out soon as to what it is."

I reply to back to her.

We are now approaching the truck that contains the blood bags, it has been broken into. The door have been torn completely off and as we go inside we can see right away that there are no bags of human blood left.

"David's creatures have taken it all, there is nothing left for us. What are we going to do?"

Lizzie asks us.

"By any chance did you capture anyone from David's group?"

I ask her as she turns to look at me.

"Yes Renee, there are six of them."

"Then Lizzie I suggest that their blood should be used to heal the survivors. We shall feed on them and show them what real pain feels like."

Sarah says to her, I can see the anger in her eyes.

"Ok, then that is what we will do."

Lizzie replies back to her as we leave the refrigerator truck.

As the three of us walk back to the semi-trailer we do not speak, we remain quiet.

I still feel so responsible for what has taken place. I still have the heavy weight upon my chest. If I were still human I would be saying right now that I can't breathe!

As we continue walking back, I find myself starting to speak without even thinking as to what I am going to say.

"Sarah, I can feel anger developing inside of me it is becoming very strong. I am going to use this feeling that I have to destroy him. It will be my strength against David!"

"Renee, I will share my anger with you, it will help to make US strong and powerful."

She replies to me as we continue walking back to the semi-truck.

"Sarah, I still have bags of blood inside of my leather bag."

"Renee, I still have a few bags as well."

I hear her as she sends her thoughts to me.

"We must let Lizzie know that we have them."

I reply to Sarah.

"Lizzie, we have a few bags of human blood in our leather bags. We will give to you what we have so there will be more blood to feed on. You must take one for yourself so that you can keep your strength up."

Sarah says to her.

"Thank you so much!"

Lizzie replies to her, I can hear from the sound in her voice that she is still worried.

Once again we remove our bags from our backs and we open them up, we are handing her what we have left. I have four bags of blood and Sarah has three. Before I close my bag up I am taking hold of a wooden arrow and I am placing it in the track of my cross bow. As I now have my arrow locked into place, I slide my arms in to the shoulder straps to place it upon my back. I am being careful that I do not allow the straps to press against the trigger behind the arrow so it does not release. I do not want to shot anyone.

I turn my head to look over at Sarah.

"I will do everything that I possibly can this time not to miss David's evil non-beating heart!"

"Renee, we will kill that monster!"

She replies to me as she looks back into my eyes.

"Revenge Sarah, we must have it!"

"Renee, we must keep that thought in our minds but not in our hearts. Please do not let this change US. Do not let it change you."

She says to me as I watch her eyes begin to fill with tears of blood.

"I promise you Sarah that it will not change us, but we must have the strength and the courage to do what must be done! No longer will we show them how scared we are."

I reply to her as I try to keep my voice strong and steady.

"Renee you did not make a promise to me that it will not change YOU!"

Before I can reply to her, Lizzie gently places her hand upon Sarah's wrist.

"I want to make my promise to you both that I will do everything that I can to help you in this fight. But I must say that every one of us is in this together! We all want to see the death of David."

Lizzies replies to us as she removes her hand from Sarah.

We are now approaching the trailer where the wounded survivors from our group are being taken care of. It is the same trailer that we were at earlier this evening.

Sarah and I remain outside of the trailer while Lizzie places the blood bags that we gave to her on the floor at the opening. She bends her knees just slightly and we watch her as she jumps up into the trailer as her hair gently flows behind her. She lands inside upon the floor, she bends down to pick up the bags of blood and as we remain standing on the ground we watch as she walks over to Logan and Sabrina to hand them the bags.

I can see that they are using the items that we had gathered for bandages. The three of them cut open the bags with their sharp nails so that the survivors can feed. I have counted only five of them that are left from our group. But three people are being turned into full vampires. They must be resting in the ground as they make their transformations. Paul must be one of the three because I do not see him.

I can feel Marrick he is coming closer to us.

"We have something to show the both of you."

I hear his words as they continue making their way toward us.

We both turn to the direction that he is coming from. We see that they have someone with them. We recognize her right away. It is the blonde haired female from last night. Marrick and Damon are holding her very tightly in their grasp forcing her to walk with them. She survived the battle from last night and now she is a captive.

"We have a present for the two of you."

Damon says to us as they are now standing in front of us.

"I must say that this is the best gift that the both of you have given to us."

I reply to him.

As I look into her eyes, I can feel my eyes turning completely black and my fangs are growing long and sharp. I know that I am changing because of my emotions. The sight of her makes me angry.

As I continue to look at her, I smile and I place the tip of my tongue on my front teeth between my fangs and I slowly slide my tongue back into my mouth as I continue to look into her eyes. I find myself smiling as she looks back at me.

The Blonde haired female is beginning to struggle as she looks at us, she is trying to escape from the hold that they have on her. She knows that she is now the one who is now going to die.

I look over to Sarah her mouth is slightly opened and I can see her beautiful sharp fangs as they begin to grow. I can feel her hunger for the blonde haired female's blood.

"Renee I want to drink from her."

She says to me as she continues to stare at the female.

I walk closer to Sarah so that I can stand behind her. I raise my hand up so that I can brush the hair from the side of her face and then I move my face closer to her I gently kiss her cheek. I lower my head so that I can now rest my chin on her shoulder and I look at the blonde hair female once more as I smile again.

"Sarah my beautiful blood sister, she is all yours make sure that you drink every drop of blood that she has within her body."

I say to her as I whisper softly into her ear.

I remove my chin from her shoulder as she gently moves toward the female. I stand here watching the way that Sarah is moving toward the female as Marrick and Damon hold onto her, she looks as if she is floating through the air so gracefully.

When Sarah is directly in front of her she takes hold of the female as Marrick and Damon release their hold that they have on her. I can hear her slowly breathing very deeply as Sarah looks directly into her eyes. I can hear her half dead heart begin to beat slightly faster.

I move toward Marrick and Damon so that the three of us are standing together watching Sarah's every move. Sarah has one arm behind the blonde's haired females back as she tightly holds onto her.

Sarah gently places her other hand on the back of the females head. I can see that the girl is now scared and I am enjoying her fear. Sarah is showing how strong she can be.

Sarah is gently rubbing the back of the females head with her fingers as if she wants her to feel that she is being comforted.

"It is ok; I will take care of you. I promise that I will take my time as I slowly consume every ounce of blood that you have within your body."

Sarah whispers to her as her voice stays very calm and steady.

I can see Sarah gripping her arm tighter around her back. I can hear the bones cracking in her body. Sarah now takes hold of the female's hair with her fingers from her other hand as she forces her head to move exposing the naked skin of the blonde haired female's neck. Sarah lowers her head closer to the blonde haired female's flesh. Sarah opens her mouth as she places her tongue upon the skin of the female's neck. Sarah is now pushing her sharp fangs into the neck of David's half turned human vampire. The female is doing what she can to stay brave, but as soon as Sarah fangs are completely buried in the skin of her neck we can hear her gasp. I can hear the sound of her flesh ripping from Sarah's teeth.

"David is coming for all of you."

She says as Sarah begins to drink her blood.

No one replies to what she has just said to us.

I can see Sarah tightening her hold on the female as she continues to consume her blood. I can hear more bones breaking within the female's body as Sarah continues to tighten her hold. The female slowly begins to faint and her knees are starting to bend. Damon quickly moves over to Sarah and he helps her to lower the female down to the ground as she continues to drain her from every drop of blood that she has left in her body. Damon sits on the ground allowing Sarah to rest her body against his as she continues to feed from the female. Damon places his hand within Sarah's hair to pull it back so that he can watch her mouth as it moves sucking and drinking the female's blood.

I cannot help but feel so very proud of my beautiful pale white blood sister.

"Let that son of a bitch make his way back to us. He is going to die!"

I say as Marrick and I continue to stand together watching Sarah.

Marrick moves to stand behind me, I can feel him placing his arms around my body to hold me tightly to him as we continue to watch Sarah as she is now finished feeding from David's female.

Sarah releases her mouth from the skin of the blonde hair female she is now resting her head against Damon's arm as he continues to hold her. Sarah pushes the female's lifeless body away from her.

"I should have killed the bitch last night."

Sarah says as she continues to rest herself against Damon.

"My love, you must not think that. What is done is done."

Damon replies to her, he lowers his head close to her as he kisses her temple.

As I continue to stand in front of Marrick as he still has his arms wrapped around me, I can feel that the wind is becoming stronger as it touches my skin.

"It is going to rain again."

Marrick whispers into my ear.

"Then this time I would like to take a shower in the rain because I want to be clean for just a few minutes."

I reply to him.

"Then my beautiful Renee, shall we go collect our belongings?"

"Marrick yes please."

I reply to him.

"Renee, I would like to do the same. I want to take a shower."

Sarah says to me as she moves her head to look at me.

I look back over at the both of them and I am now watching as they stand up from the ground.

"Ladies our bags are in the semi-trailer where the survivors are resting as they heal."

Damon says to the both of us.

"Thank you for letting us know."

I reply to him.

He does not reply to me with his words but he does close his eyes as he slightly tilts his head to the side and nods to me. I understand that is his way to say to say to me "you're welcome".

Marrick releases his hold on me and we start walking toward Sarah and Damon as they begin to walk toward us. The four of us are now standing together, we turn in the direction of the trailer and we are now making our way back so that we can gather our things. As we continue to walk the wind is now a little stronger than what it was a moment ago. I can feel a drop of water that has landed on my shoulder.

As we are continuing on I have that feeling again that I had earlier. The familiar but strange feeling!

I am moving my hand away from my side and I can feel Luna. I am moving my hand as if I am petting her black fur on top of her head as I continue walking. I can smell the dried animal blood and mud that is imbedded in her fur. The scent is very strong. I continue to move my hand as she is by my side. I force myself to look down at her and she is not here.

I feel such an ache inside of me because I can truly feel her.

"Marrick please tell me, why is it that I can feel Luna as if she is here with me? Why do I not have this feeling about Fred or Keith?"

"Renee I do not understand how you are able to feel Luna so strongly. It is as if she is coming back to you but that would be impossible."

"I miss her so much."

I reply to him as I try to calm myself and not cry.

We arrive back at the semi-trailer and as we look inside I see that the survivors' wounds have started to heal. They are removing the bandages from themselves.

Damon has jumped up into the trailer and he makes his way to their bag that contains their belongings and then he looks over to his left. He is now moving toward our bag he bends down to take hold of the straps. Without saying a word to them as Logan and Sabrina are examining them to make sure that they are completely healing from the attack. Damon jumps out of the trailer and we walk away leaving them all inside. He hands our bag to Marrick.

The rain is now beginning to fall from the sky but it is not a heavy down pour as it was last night. We begin to look for somewhere to go so that we can take our showers in the rain. We begin to follow Marrick and Damon but we are not paying attention to where we are going because Sarah and I have become lost together within our thoughts.

We are remembering when we met Fred and Keith for lunch at our favorite restaurant. We had so much fun that day just being with them. We were laughing so much that the other customers we looking at the four of us. We are both remembering the feeling of all of us holding hands as we sat at the table. I can still feel their soft gentle touch.

I can now feel such a strong emotion from Sarah as we continue thinking about them.

She stops walking and I move very quickly to be by her side. I place both of my arms around her body as she falls to the ground on her knees. She has blood tears streaming down her face.

"Sarah I am right here with you."

I say to her as she lays her head against my shoulder.

I place my hand in her hair as I still hold on to her with my other arm. I allow my head to rest against hers as she continues to cry. I am doing everything that I possibly can to remain strong for the both of us. I do not say anything to her I remain here by her side as I continue to comfort her.

I can feel hands taking hold of Sarah. I look up as Damon picks her up in his arms. I watch him carry her over to the trees as the rain continues to fall to the ground.

Marrick is taking hold of my hand as I stand up. I do not even look up to him, but I can feel him looking at me.

"I promise that I am ok Marrick."

He takes hold of my hand and I lock my fingers with his as we continue to stand together watching as Damon steps under the trees as he continues to comfort her.

"Renee are you sure that you are ok?"

"Tell me Marrick, what do you feel from me?"

"I feel anger and hate. Renee I also believe that you are hiding something from me."

"You are right Marrick I am full of those feelings but why would I hide anything from you?"

I reply to him as I try so hard to lie because I cannot allow him to know that I am planning on leaving so that I can protect them.

"Yes Renee why would you hide anything from me?"

Marrick replies to me with such a very stern voice but I do what I do best and that is to change the subject.

"Can we please find somewhere to take a shower as the rain continues to fall?"

I say to him as I look up into his beautiful eyes.

"Yes Renee but then we will need to hunt."

"Ok Marrick."

I reply to him.

Marrick starts walking to a group of trees that in the opposite direction from where Damon and Sarah are at and I begin to follow him.

I can still feel the sadness from Sarah. I have anger!

Marrick bends down and he places our bag that has our belonging upon the ground under one of the trees and when he stands straight up he begins to remove his clothes. I watch him as he looks at me. He is now completely naked and he walks out from under the tree as the rain begins to run down him to wash away the dirt and blood from his beautiful sculptured body.

As I continue to stand under the tree I begin to remove my clothes. I am now naked I walk out from under the tree to join him. As the rain begins to wash over my body I have realized that I did not take out my shower gel or shampoo from the bag. But right now

I do not care I want to be with Marrick I may never get to see him again because of my plan to kill David.

I walk up to Marrick and I am standing behind him I raise my hand so that I can place it on the skin of his back. His soft beautiful pale white skin! As soon as Marrick feels my touch he turns around so quickly that I see my hand is now his stomach.

The rain is now pouring down as it hits our skin I can see the water bounce off from Marrick. The water is now racing down our naked bodies the dried blood and dirt is completely gone.

Marrick moves so quickly to take hold of me. My feet are off the ground as he now holds me tightly in his arms close to his pale white wet body. I place my arms around his neck and I raise my legs up so that I can wrap them around his waist.

At this moment I let go of all the hate and anger that I have allowed to build up inside of me. I only want to feel Marrick.

I move my head closer to him so that I can touch my lips to his.

I am enjoying how the water feels as it runs down our naked bodies.

Marrick carries me back under the tree while we are still embraced in our kiss. He slightly pulls his head away and looks into my eyes as he gently lowers us down to the ground as he continues to hold me to him.

He is now on his knees he bends his body forward so that he can place one hand upon the earth while he still holds me to him with his other arm. I still have my hold on him with my arms and legs. He lowers us down as he places me on the ground I can feel him as he now lies upon my body. I close my eyes as he places himself inside of me. I still have my arms around him. I remove my legs from his waist as we begin to move to each other making love.

He lowers his head down so that his lips can touch mine. He has one arm under my body holding me. He gently places his other hand on the side of my face. He removes his lips from mine and we look into each other's eyes as they begin to turn completely black.

As we continue to move together he opens his mouth slightly and I watch his fangs grow. I can feel mine growing.

Marrick slowly moves his hand from my face and he places it under my head as he lies completely on top of me he continues to move inside of me. He raises my head up to him I can feel his skin against my lips and I open my mouth. I place my sharp pointed fangs against his skin. I slowly force them into him and as my teeth go deeper into his flesh he thrusts himself deeper inside of me.

I can taste his blood on my tongue his thick sweet vampire blood as it begins to fill my mouth. I swallow his blood and I can feel as it flows through me.

I cannot help but to close my eyes once more as I move my body with his as I continue to drink his blood.

I feel him removing his hand from the back of my head and I release his skin from my mouth. I can feel a steam of his blood as it runs down the side of my face that has escaped from me. Marrick lowers his face closer to mine and with his tongue he slowly licks his blood from my face. He looks into my eyes as he places his mouth against mine. He places his tongue against mine. He slowly slides his hand down my side I can feel his touch going through me as it makes my body tingle with excitement. Marrick takes hold of my leg so that he can raise it up against his hip. He begins to thrust himself deep inside of me once again. I move myself up and down as I lay under him I can feel him sliding in and out of me. How I love to make him feel every part of me as I can completely feel Marrick.

I can feel myself starting to well up and as we continue to move. He is moving himself faster inside of me as he begins to come with his blood. I am melting all over him.

I have realized that he did not drink my blood.

We continue to lie on the ground together under the tree it is still raining I can feel water droplets fall from the leaves.

He continues to lay his body on top of mine Marrick moves his hips to pull himself out of me. He places his hand on the side of my head and he begins to plays with my hair.

"Do you realize how much I am in love with you and what you mean to me Renee?"

"Yes I do Marrick. I feel the same about you."

"I know that you do Renee."

He replies as he continues to look into my eyes.

I am not going to say anything because I am so worried that he will command me to tell him what I am hiding from him.

Marrick gently removes his body from mine and as he stands up he holds his hand down to me. As I continue to lay on the ground I reach my hand up and I take hold of his and I allow him to help me up. He walks over to take hold of our bag and he pulls out some clothes while I step out from under the tree into the gentle rain as the water removes the grass and leaves from my body.

My naked body is clean again and I walk back under the tree. Marrick is now dress and I walk over and I bend down next to him to pull my clothes out of the bag. I begin to put my clothes on and it feels so good to be clean again. I can feel Marrick watching me and I am enjoying it. I love it when he looks at me.

I am dressed and I look at my blood stained shoes.

"Marrick I am not going to put these back on because they are so gross. I will travel barefoot."

"I understand Renee."

He replies to me.

"Damon and Sarah will meet us here in a few minutes."

"Marrick I can feel that she is feeling a little better."

"That is good to hear Renee."

He replies to me.

"Marrick when we get back to the others I would like to have my vehicle for just a little while. I need to turn on the radio it will help to calm Sarah."

"Then you must listen to the music as well Renee."

"I will that I can assure you of."

I realize that he is being very short as he replies to me.

"Renee, tell me what it is that you CANNOT assure me of!"

He says to me.

Is this a demand from him?

I ask myself as I try to hide my thoughts from him.

If I do not answer then maybe I will not have to tell him. But I know that this was a demand because I now have a strong desire to tell him. Can I break this?

"Marrick."

I say to him.

I can see Damon and Sarah walking under the tree to join us. Marrick turns to look at them he walks away from me. I can feel that he is angry with me.

"It is time for us to go back."

Marrick says to us all.

I watch them walk out from under the tree but I remain where I am at.

Should I leave them now?

I ask to myself as I continue to watch them walking farther away.

I slowly turn around and I am now facing the other way. I am trying to gather as much courage as I can to leave so that I can protect them from David.

I am now running away from the tree where we were at. I am running as fast as I possibly can. I am moving through a field full of high thick grass and weeds.

David knows where I am at and it is time for me leave! To kill him!

I say to myself.

"RENEE!"

I hear Marrick yell very loudly his voice echoes through the sky like thunder.

The sound of his voice is so strong and powerful it immediately makes me stop running as my feet sliding on the ground. I bend my knees to lower myself so that I do not fall I also place one of my hands on the ground to balance myself.

"Renee what are you doing?"

I hear him as he sends his thoughts to me.

I stand back up and I have such a horrible sadness inside of me. I begin to walk in the direction that I am heading, away from them.

"Renee you must tell me!"

I hear him again as I begin to run as fast as I can once more.

"I am so sorry Marrick. I made a promise to you that I will do everything that I can to help protect you and this is what I am now doing."

I reply to him with my thoughts as I do everything that I can to hide where I am going.

"Renee, I am to protect you as well! I cannot do that if you are not with me."

"Please forgive me Marrick."

I reply to him.

I continue to run as fast as I can because all I want to do is destroy that monster so that we can all be free.

I am moving farther away from Marrick and Sarah. I can feel the bottom of my bare feet as I run over sticks and sharp rocks. I can feel the sting in the skin of my feet with each step my skin is being cut from the sharp objects that I place my feet upon. I can also feel my skin as it begins to heal.

Ahead of me I can see the woods it is very thick with trees as I continue to run through the high grass. I am pushing myself to run as fast as I can only to hope that Marrick is unable to feel where I am at.

I am entering the woods leaving the field. I am moving so quickly that I do not see the thin braches from the trees. I can feel cuts upon the skin of my arms and shoulders as I run past the trees. My skin is starting to hurt as I keep hitting these thin branches with my body. I have so many scratches I do not like this feeling as my skin rips. My body is not healing very well because I need to feed. My skin feels like it is on fire I need human blood.

I have tears of blood forming in my eyes.

Am I doing the right thing?

I ask to myself as I continue running through the woods.

I can feel Marrick as if he is right here with me. I begin to look around for him as I am running through the woods.

Does he know where I am?

I ask myself as I can see someone ahead of me as if this person is waiting for me.

"Renee Stop!"

Marrick yells his demand to me.

I cannot help it I stop running because he has commanded me to. I grab onto a tree to help me stop. My shoulder is now in great pain from taking hold of this tree.

As I look straight ahead I am watching Marrick as he moves toward me.

"Marrick."

I say to him as he moves closer.

"Renee do you remember hearing me say to you that you cannot hide your thoughts from me?"

He asks me as I continue to look at him.

"Tell me Marrick why do you still hide your thoughts from me? I do not hear everything that you are thinking or what it is that you are going to do!"

"Renee I had made a promise to you that I will no longer hide anything from you! All you have to do is listen to my thoughts and you can hear everything. But you do not!"

He replies to me as he is now standing in front of me.

Marrick moves his arms to place them both around me. He is holding me so tightly to him that I do not think I can break free even if I tried. My shoulder is in great pain.

"Renee I appreciate what you want to do and I am sure that there is a way that your plan may work. But you must go back with me and you need to feed. I can feel the pain that you have in your shoulder."

He says to me as he releases his hold on me.

He moves his hand so that he can take hold of mine.

Marrick and I begin to run back to Sarah and Damon.

"Marrick there is something that you must know. Sarah wanted to come with me but I could not let her do it."

"Renee your love for her is very strong and so is her love for you. I know that you also want to protect her as well."

He replies to me.

"Yes I do Marrick."

I say to him.

"Please tell me Marrick is there any way that I am able to learn how to feel where David is? He knows where I am at. There must be a way that I can do this. He fed from me and he also placed his blood inside of me as I asked you to command me to sleep. There has to be a way!

I can feel Sarah and hear her thoughts as she sends them to me, so why can I not do the same with that fucking monster? "

"Renee I believe that you can, but you must mentally prepare yourself he is evil as he is strong and powerful. Once you make your connection to him I am very certain that he will do his very best to mess with your mind. But he is older than us he can shield his thoughts from you. Maybe Logan can help you because David turned her for surviving his torture."

Marrick replies to me.

"How can I ask her to help me with that? David has does not allow Logan to know where he is. This must be his way of getting even with her since she has the ability to block David from her mind."

I reply to him as I grip my hand tighter to his because I am now scared once more.

"We will figure this out together."

He says to me as we continue running together.

We are now passing the tree where Marrick and I had made love under and where I had also tried to break his command to me. I can see that our bag along with our blood stained clothes are still there where we left them.

We continue to move very quickly through the grass. The rest of our group is just up ahead and I can see Sarah. She is standing there waiting with Damon and he is holding onto someone very tightly, it is a male.

As we approach them Damon and Sarah remain there standing with one of David's half turned human vampire.

"You must feed from him. The sun is going to be rising soon and we will need to find a place to rest."

He says to us.

I look over to Sarah and she is looking right at me. I can feel that she is upset with me because I tried to leave without her.

"We must share his blood because there are not enough of these captives to feed us all."

Damon says to us.

Marrick takes hold of the male and he holds his arm for me to feed from. I place my hands upon the male's arm as I move my head closer to place my mouth upon his skin and I push my teeth into his flesh. I begin to drink his warm delicious salty blood. My wounds are starting to heal along with my shoulder.

I can feel Sarah as I continue to drink from the captive's arm. She is taking hold of the other arm from Damon and she is now consuming this fresh blood.

This male is not fighting nor is he making threating remarks to us. He just continues to stand here as Damon and Marrick hold on to him so that we can feed on his blood.

I release his arm from my mouth so that Marrick can now feed from him. I back away out of Marrick way but before he feeds he looks at me.

"Renee, do I need to command you not to leave my side?"

"No Marrick there is no need for you to do so."

I reply to him.

He removes his eyes from me and takes hold of the male from behind. He places his mouth upon the male captive's neck and I can hear his teeth being forced into the male's neck. I look over to Sarah and she has moved so that Damon can feed as well.

Sarah moves so quickly toward me that right away I feel her arms around my neck as she hugs me very tightly. I place my arms around her and I hold her tightly as well. Without speaking a word or without sending her a thought as I hold on to her this is my way saying that I am very sorry for what I have just tried to do this evening.

"Renee, please do not do this again."

"Sarah I will not."

I reply to her.

As we release each other we notice that the male is now dead and we have drained him of all the blood from his body.

Damon and Marrick release the hold on him and he falls to the ground.

"We will leave this body where it lies for the moment. Renee let's make our way to your vehicle so that you and Sarah can listen to music so that you both may feel better."

I hear Marrick speak his words.

"Yes please Marrick."

I reply to him with excitement in my voice.

I look back over to Sarah and I can see in her eyes that she is ready to listen to the music as well.

This is the first time that we do not wait for them to lead the way. Within a blink of an eye Sarah and I are moving as quickly as we can run to my Dodge Journey. We do not stop to talk to anyone we keep moving making our way to it. I can see my beautiful S.U.V. and I stop immediately and I find myself sliding my feet on the ground toward the driver's door. I am now standing next to it and I raise my hand up to take hold of the door handle to open it I move myself to sit in the driver's seat. Lizzie has left my keys in the ignition. Once again I raise my hand this time I place it upon the key and I slightly move it to the right and the soft purring sound of my vehicle starts up. Sarah opens the door to the passenger side and she quickly sits down in the seat next to me. I place my index finger on the knob to push it in and immediately the radio turns on. I am adjusting the knob listening for a song that we know finally I found one as now we are both listening to the song "Comeback" by Redlight King.

As we listen to the music we make ourselves comfortable in our seats and I close my eyes and I let myself become lost in the music.

"Sarah this is now our song because we are going to make our comeback. We are going to defeat him."

I say to her as we both continue to listen to the music playing.

She does not reply to me because she is completely at ease now.

We remain sitting and now we are listening to the song "Crawling" as I become more relaxed. I allow the music surround me. I am listening to every word of the song and every note that is being played by the instruments I can feel it as it flows from the speakers.

As we begin to relax even more someone has opened up the back of my Dodge. I sit up in my driver's seat and I turn my head to the right of me to see what is going on. I am now watching as Robert and Damon are putting the back seats down so that everything in the back is flat and level. I continue to watch them as they get out of the back of my S.U.V. I am now watching as they are sliding in a very large wooden box and it is taking up the entire space in the back. This has also gotten Sarah's attention as well because as they are doing this my vehicle is rocking back and forth. We continue watching them as they push this huge box inside.

"What is it that they are planning?"

Sarah asks as she continues to watch them.

I do not reply because I do not know.

The box is completely inside they leave the back of my vehicle opened they do not close it. I am watching Damon as he is now walking toward the passenger side and he bends down to look at Sarah. He holds his hand out to her and she takes hold of it as she gets out.

"Renee."

I hear Marrick say to me as I now turn my head to the left to look at him.

I can see standing behind him Sabrina and Logan along with Lizzie. They look as if they are waiting for something.

"Marrick what is going on?"

I ask him as I get out of my driver's side.

"Renee I strongly suggest that you do NOT try to find where David is at. You have a small amount of his blood inside of you and it is enough for you to connect yourself to him. But if you do attempt it he will destroy your mind."

Robert says to me as he walks closer to us.

"Then tell me what shall I do?"

I ask to him.

"Renee you do not need to do anything. We are going to use this to our advantage. You are going to be the bait to drawl him out to you. He wants his revenge against us as well. But you will not be alone."

"What do you mean I will not be alone? Where am I going? Robert please tell me."

"Renee, I will not give you the answers to your questions."

He replies to me.

Marrick places his arm around my back to force me to walk toward the back of my vehicle. I turn my head to look at the wooden box that is inside.

"Marrick what do I do?"

I ask him as I turn to look at him.

"Renee you are going to get inside of it. Just as Robert has said to you, you will not be alone."

He replies to me as he gently places his hand on the side of my face.

"Renee we will be with you the entire time."

Sabrina says to me as she is now standing beside of me as Marrick removes his hand from me.

I look over to her and just like a few minutes ago Logan and Lizzie are with her.

"Renee I am going to be with you also."

Sarah says to me as she takes my hand.

"The four of you will be resting inside of this wooden box until you arrive at your destination. It may be a little cramped but I assure you that you will be safe."

Michael says to us as he makes his way toward us. Thomas is with him.

There is also another person with them and I can see that by his glow he is half human and vampire.

He seems to be about six foot tall. He is fit but not muscular. His head is shaved on both sides but he has a strip of hair running down the middle of his head. He has a short blonde mohawk.

"Hello my name is Stu Van Helsing."

He says to us as he stands here looking at us.

"Hello my name is Renee."

I reply to him.

Did he really say his last name is Van Helsing?

I hear Sarah say to me as she sends me her thoughts.

Yes he did.

I reply to her as I try to keep a straight face.

I lower my head down because I am trying really hard to go giggle at his name.

"He likes to say that his name is Stu Van Helsing because he is a vampire hunter."

Lizzie explains to us as she smiles.

"Ok that is cool."

I reply to her as I keep my head lowered trying really hard to control myself so that I do not laugh out loud.

"You can call me Stu. I will be going with you to help Lizzie with the driving. We will be taking shifts as you rest for the entire trip."

He explains to us.

I no longer have the desire to laugh.

"Marrick what does he mean that we will be resting the entire trip?"

"Renee you are not to know as to where it is that you are going. I am going to command you to rest your mind and your body until you hear Lizzie saying to you it is time to wake up. Do not try to reach out to me."

Marrick explains to me.

"I do not like this!"

I reply to him as I become worried.

"Marrick how long will we be completely resting?"

"If they continue to keep driving and only stop to fill up your vehicle for fuel then you should arrive to your destination within three days. Renee, do you understand?"

"I do understand but I still do not like this! You had said to me that you will not leave my side."

I say to him as I try not to panic.

"Renee you must understand that YOU will not be alone."

"Marrick!"

"Renee I am sorry but I cannot give you any more information."

"When do we leave?"

I ask to him as he takes hold of my hand.

I turn my head away from him and as I look around I see Robert.

"Renee you are all going to leave this evening."

Marrick replies to me.

I am not going to ask any more questions because I know that I am not going to like what his answers will be.

I stand here watching everyone around me and I am trying so hard to be brave. I am watching as Thomas holds Sabrina in his arms, is this going to be the last time that they will see each other? I continue watching them as she removes herself from his arms and she takes a few steps toward the box. Sabrina is now going inside head first; once she is somewhat comfortable we can see that her feet are now resting at the opening in front of us.

"Sabrina I command you to completely rest your mind and your body. You will awaken when Lizzie speaks her words to you that it is time to wake up."

"Good night Thomas I will see you soon."

She replies to him.

Stu is now making his way to the passenger side of the car he is getting inside once he is seated he is closes the door.

Richard walks toward Lizzie and he places his arms around her. He holds her gently to him. She places her arms around him as well.

"Grandfather I promise that I will be very careful."

"I know that you will."

Richard replies to her.

"I will see you soon."

He says to Lizzie as he releases his hold on her.

"We will not stop for anything except for fuel."

She replies to him as she gets into the driver's side of the vehicle.

"Lizzie, please continue to keep the music playing on the radio."

Damon asks to her before she closes the door.

"I promise that I will."

She replies to him as the door closes.

I continue watching as Richard is now making is way toward Logan. And the look in his eyes you can really see that he is truly in love with her. He quickly takes hold of her. Richard does not give Logan a chance to respond to him. He bends himself just slightly and as quickly as he can he moves his face towards her so that he can press his lips to her lips. Logan does not back away from him. She places her arms around his neck as she is now kissing him back. They release their hold on each other and Richard watches as she moves away from him to make her way toward the wooden box.

"Logan I wish that I could command you to rest."

Richard says to her with such sadness and worry in his voice.

"I will be ok."

She replies to him.

She looks over to him and she smiles such a beautiful smile as if it is her way to reassure him that he has nothing to worry about. Logan turns her head back as she is now looking inside of the box. She makes her way inside as she is positions herself to rest next to Sabrina.

This is the first time that we have seen Logan respond back to Richard in this manner.

I am still trying to remain calm because now it is our turn to get into the box to lay with them.

I look up to Marrick I raise my arms up so that I can place my hands on his shoulders and I pull on him. He places his arms around my body as I rest my head against his chest.

"Renee it is time for you to go."

He says to me as I look up at him.

"Ok."

I reply to him.

He places his beautiful pale white index finger under my chin. He moves his head closer to me and I close my eyes as I feel his soft lips press against mine. After his kiss he places his hand on my lower back and he walks next to me as we move closer to the back of the vehicle. I look over at Sarah and she is also making her way toward us with Damon right next to her.

"I will go in first Renee."

She says to me so bravely.

I watch her as she is now getting inside next to Logan.

As soon as she is lying on her back and we can see her feet as well. I hear Damon speak his words to her.

"Sarah I command you to completely rest your mind and body. You will wake up when Lizzie tells you to. I love you my lovely Sarah."

As I continue to stand here next to Marrick I can feel from Sarah that she is doing what Damon had commanded to her. She is now completely at rest.

As I continue to stand here I look around at everyone. I glance at Michael and I notice that he has a black canvas bag hanging from his shoulder. On the front of it there is a pocket and I can see that there is a plastic case inside of it. So I am going to distract myself.

"Michael may I ask what is in the pocket of your bag?"

He looks over to me and he smiles as if he knows what it is that I am doing.

"Renee it is a music cd of a country music group Ray Bond and The Black Diamond Band. It belonged to Keith I hope that you do not mind that I now have it."

He replies to me but his voice sounds somewhat gentle for some reason.

"Michael I do not mind at all. I know that you were good friends with Fred and Keith."

"Thank you Renee."

"You are welcome."

I reply to Michael.

"Renee it is time."

Marrick says to me.

If I could still breathe I would be inhaling very deeply to prepare for this. But instead I close my eyes once more. As I open them back up again I take a step toward the wooden box that is in my car. I can feel Marrick's hand sliding away from my back. I lift my leg up so that I can place my knee on the floor of the back of my Dodge Journey. I place my hands in front of me and I am now making my way to lie down next to Sarah. Once I am positioned on my back I hear Marrick as he speaks to me with his words.

"Renee love of my life I command you to completely rest your beautiful mind and body. You will continue to rest until Lizzie tells you to awaken."

I feel them closing up the opening to the end of the wooden box. I can feel the strong vibration as they hammer a very large piece of wood just a couple of inches away from our feet so that we are protected from the sun. Now I can hear them closing the back door to my vehicle. As I am now starting to completely rest my mind and body just as Marrick has commanded for me to do I can hear the music playing as Lizzie is now starting to drive away. I can hear the song "What I've Done" by Linkin Park.

I am now at rest mind and body.

Chapter Six

"Renee it is time for you to wake up!"

Lizzie says to me with her words as I can hear her slowly walking away. I can immediately feel that something is wrong.

I open my eyes there is a very strong and horrible stench around me. I realize right away that this smell is from the four of us it is the scent of death. I want out of this wooden box! I can feel someone placing their hands upon me and fingers wrapping around my ankles. I am slowly being pulled out. I know that it is Sarah she is helping me.

"Renee I am going to let go of you."

She says to me as she releases me.

I can feel my bare feet land gently upon the ground my legs are bent and I make the rest of the way out from the box that we were all resting inside of. I stand myself up and as I begin to look around to see where we are at. It is pitch black but with my vampire eyes I can see very clearly. I realize that we are back at the house that Marrick and Damon had built. We are home!

Sarah and I start walking toward the front porch I notice that the door is open and the lights are on.

I can feel that I am hungry for human blood but I realize that I am not in any pain.

I stop walking and I look at Sarah I decide to move my gaze to look farther back at my vehicle. There are scrapes in the paint and there are huge dents on the side that I am looking at.

"Oh my Stars, what HAPPENED?"

I ask with great concern in my voice as I look back to Sarah.

"Renee, Lizzie and Stu explained it to me after I was asked to wake up."

She replies to me as we continue walking toward the house.

"Sarah I take it that this is their plan for us to come back here? Is this where we are going to face David again?"

"Yes Renee it is their plan."

"I do not understand Sarah, why here?"

"I am not sure as to why Renee."

She replies to me as we walk up the steps to the porch.

"Sarah, are you in any pain from not feeding? We have been resting for a three nights."

I ask to her as I am waiting for her to tell me what had happened.

"Renee the reason why we are not in pain is because I was told that Logan had taken care of us while we were resting. She fed us blood from the followers that were badly injured from David's group. We were attacked on our way here. Marrick commanded you to rest but David was still able to know where we were at and he sent his half turned human vampires after us during the day and at night we are attacked by his demon vampires."

"Oh my stars Sarah how did we survive through that?"

"Lizzie and Stu asked Logan for her help because no one was able to command her to rest and we would not be here if it was not for her. That is all that I know right now but the three of them are seriously hurt. Sabrina helped Logan to the safe room in the basement so that she can feed on the human blood that is in the cold storage."

Sarah explains to me as we begin to walk inside of the house, we are standing in the living room.

I can hear Lizzie and Stu walking through the house, they are making their way toward us and I can smell fresh human blood. I can now see them they have severe injuries upon their bodies.

"We just turned the circuit box on so that we can have electric."

Stu says to us as they continue to slowly walk together toward us.

As I continue to look upon them I can see that Lizzie's chest has very deep slash marks and her left arm is very swollen. Her face is badly bruised and she has a very deep cut above her right eye, her top lip is also swollen. She is having trouble walking Stu has his arms around her he is helping her to walk. I can see and smell that she has dried blood under the fresh blood that is escaping from her wounds. I am trying very hard to control myself. I am trying not to allow my fangs and eyes to change because of my emotions.

As I now look at Stu I can see his injuries as well. He is bleeding from the inside of his left ear and there is a very deep gash going straight down the top of his nose. He also has dry blood on the tip of his nose. He has scratches on the right side of his face from his eye down to his neck. I can see that he has been very badly injured on his left side just right under his rib cage because his clothes are soaked in his blood.

The scent of their blood smells so sweet. I cannot allow myself to change!

Sarah and I go to them right away. Sarah gently takes hold of Stu and I gently place my arms around Lizzie so that we can help them to the black leather couch in the living room. I look over to Sarah she continues to hold onto Stu as he slowly lowers himself to sit upon the other side of the couch.

As we stand back up from helping them I look at both Lizzie and Stu they need to heal. I now have Lizzie's blood on my hands from helping her to the couch.

"I will be right back I am going to go collect some blood for the both of you."

I say to them as I walk away. I am making my way into the dining room I pass the beautiful wooden table and now I am walking into the kitchen toward the double doors that lead down into the basement. I am moving as fast as I can down the steps but I am licking her blood from my hands.

I hope that no one finds out that I am doing this!

I say to myself as I now feel so badly for tasting Lizzie's blood.

I walk off of the bottom step and I turn to make my way down the hall way toward the safe room. I walk in and I see Logan resting her body upon one of the cots. Sabrina is holding a bag of human blood for her as Logan feeds from it she is so weak that she cannot hold the bag of blood herself.

"How is she doing?"

I ask as I stop next to Sabrina as I look upon Logan.

"She is doing much better and her body is starting to heal itself."

Sabrina replies to me.

"Logan I cannot thank you enough for what you have done to protect us."

She does not reply to me because she is feeding but she raises her hand up to me and I take hold of it with both of my hands. As I hold her I bend my body just slightly and I kiss her fingers then I release her hand back to her as I stand straight up. I move my hand toward Sabrina's shoulder and I gently touch her as she continues to look at me.

"Are you ok?"

I ask to her knowing that she can smell the scent of Lizzie's blood upon my hand.

"Yes Renee. But we must be prepared because David will be coming soon."

"I know Sabrina."

I reply to her as I remove my hand from her shoulder.

I walk away from her so that she can continue to help Logan. I am now heading toward the cold storage unit. I place my hand on the handle and I open it up I reach both of my hands inside and I take hold of several bags of blood.

How can the blood still be cold after Keith had turned off the electric box before we left?

I ask myself as I hold them in my hands.

Before I close the door I can see that there are only a couple of bags left. I close the door.

I am now walking past Logan and Sabrina so that I can go back upstairs to the others.

I am doing what I can to remain calm. I do not know how much time we have left until David and what is left of his demons will return. I want to see if I can make some sort of connection to him just to know if I can feel as to where he is at. He fed from me while I was his captive and he also forcefully placed his blood inside of me against my will. I had been warned a few nights ago not to do it. David will destroy my mind leaving me with nothing if I try to do this!

I am now at the top of the steps I walk through the double doors to enter back into the kitchen. For some reason I feel drawn to the sliding glass doors. I close my eyes this feeling that I have is so strong. I slowly open my eyes and as I gaze out into the back yard I can see something looking back at me from the trees.

"LUNA!"

I say in a loud whisper.

I drop the bags of blood onto the floor and I place both of my palms upon the glass of the door.

I can see that she is alone. I want so badly to go to her but I am also needed inside. I feel torn I do not know what to do.

As I continue to look at Luna I cannot help but to say.

"Where is Beauty?"

I ask to her as I remain standing behind the closed sliding glass door.

Right after I ask her my question Luna turns to her left and she runs into the woods.

"No do not leave!"

I beg to her.

As I stand here I place my head upon my hands that I still have against the glass. I can feel Luna as if she is right next to me.

How is this possible for her to come back? Can she feel me as well?

I think to myself.

I open my eyes and I am looking down at the floor staring at the bags of blood that I dropped. I bend down so that I can pick them up I stand myself back up and I am now making my way out of the kitchen and into the dining room. I am moving as fast as I can.

I quickly stop myself and I am now standing next to Sarah, she is waiting for me to return. I notice right away that she had gone upstairs to grab a bed sheet. She is ripping it apart so that she can bandage up their wounds. Their blood in soaking into the torn material that Sarah is using to help stop their bleeding.

Sarah moves her hands toward me so that she can take hold of two bags. She cuts one corner of each of the bags with her finger nail. Stu takes one of them and he begins to feed right away.

I cut open two bags open for Lizzie so that she can feed as well.

"Renee I know that you have just seen Luna, I could feel it from you."

Before I look back over to her I lower my head to prepare myself but this time I cannot because I can't breathe!

"Where is Beauty, Sarah?"

"I do not know Renee. I can no longer feel her! I am worried that something has happened."

She replies to me as I can feel great sorrow from her.

"May I ask was Beauty the white wolf? I am sorry but I do not know their names."

Stu asks after he has finished feeding from his first bag of blood.

"Yes she is MY Beauty!"

Sarah replies to him as she turns her head to look back at Stu.

I can hear him take a very slow deep raspy inhale. He only has a partial of his lung that is still alive because he is half human and vampire.

As Sarah waits for him to speak Stu moves his eyes to look at her.

"Both of the wolves have been following us as we made our journey back to this house. I have never seen anything like these two wolves! What they have become I never knew that anything like this was possible. They are extremely fast and so strong and very powerful."

Stu tries to explain to us.

"Please tell me what happened to Beauty!"

Sarah begs to him to tell her as she stops him.

"David attacked us last night he had four others with him. They were running behind us while Lizzie was driving. AS soon as she realized that they were following us she was able to slow down just enough so that I could open the passenger door and jump out of the vehicle I was armed and ready to fight. As soon as she was able to finally stop she gets out as quickly as she can, but I was already involved in the fight. Logan was up a head of us but she came to help us within a blink of an eye. David is so powerful! Before we knew it both of the wolves were fighting along our side. We knew that they were protecting the both of you."

Stu replies to Sarah as he continues to explain.

"Where is Beauty?"

Sarah asks once more as she becomes angry.

Lizzie removes the blood bag from her mouth and she looks over to Sarah.

"Beauty went straight for David I saw her running toward him. It was as if he was waiting for her. He took hold of her and slammed her upon the ground. Beauty was doing everything that she could to fight him back and to free herself from his hold. As David had the white wolf on the ground he sat upon her as he placed Beauty between his legs. She no longer could claw at him but she was able to bite the inside of his leg. Beauty injured him and David became very angry he was no longer calm. He placed both of his hands upon her neck he dug his sharp nails into her flesh she did not scream out Beauty was able to move her hear to look at David directly into his eyes. He used his strength and pulled Beauty's head from her body you could hear the sound of her skin ripping apart. He held Beauty's head in his hands and he kissed the tip of her nose then he threw the white wolf's head directly at Luna so that she could see that the other wolf was dead and this time she is not coming back. I was in complete shock as I witnessed this. Stu and Logan were engaged in fighting. They did not realize what was happening to Beauty until everyone heard that horrible sound from her head being removed. It was like everyone was frozen in time as they began to watch what he was doing to Beauty. I have never heard such a horrible scream come from any animal as what we had heard from Luna as she looked at Beauty's head laying at her front paws. Sarah I am so sorry."

Lizzie says to her, but then she continues to explain.

"I turned my head to look back over at David right away he was still sitting upon her body with Beauty's blood all over him. You could see the look of revenge in Luna's black eyes. She was going after David but Logan yelled her name and Luna stopped, but she left us. David stood up from Beauty's body he was limping from what Beauty had done to him. He went directly over to Stu. David took hold of him with his hand firmly behind Stu's head and with his sharp nails he forced his other hand into Stu's side the same way that Renee forced her hand in Richard's stomach. After David pulled his hand out of his side Stu fell to his knees as blood started to escape out of his body. Logan was running toward David."

Lizzie explains to Sarah.

I can hear Stu taking another slow deep breathe.

"Sarah that son of a BITCH placed his hand against his mouth he licked my blood from his fingers. I would be dead right now if it was not for Logan. She went right for him with her sword by her side. She put a slit in that bastard's neck. But you could see him starting to heal right away. He placed his fingers on his neck to wipe his own blood from his skin. He looked at his fingers then he flipped blood all over Logan's face. She was standing right in front of him as she watched his wound completely heal. He began to laugh at her for what he had done. Logan stayed calm as she glared into his evil face."

He finishes explaining to her.

Sarah does not say or ask any more questions she hands Stu the other bag of blood then she stands up from sitting next to him. Sarah walks over to the small black leather couch and sits down with her legs drawn up in front of her. She is resting her chin upon her knees as she holds on to her legs that are now in front of her body. I walk over to sit next to her. She is doing everything that she can to keep control of her feelings but I can see her blood tears forming in her eyes. I can feel from her that she cannot wait for Damon to come back to her. I know exactly how she feels I wish that Marrick was here with me as well.

As I continue to sit next to her I can hear light footsteps making their way toward us from the kitchen.

"Sarah we are so very sorry for what has happened to Beauty. If there were some way that we could have saved her from David we would have done so."

Logan says to her as she and Sabrina are now standing behind Stu and Lizzie as they still remain sitting on the other couch as their bodies continue to heal.

I move my hand toward Sarah.

"Renee, please give me a few minutes."

She says to me before I touch her.

I do not make any more movements toward her but I move my hand back to and I place it upon my leg. I am in shock because this is something that she has never said to me. I am not sure as to how I am to handle this. She will not allow me to comfort her!

"I am going to go outside I will be in the back if you need me."

I say to Sarah.

I am trying to keep my composure as I remove myself from her side. I begin to walk away from them as I leave the living room. I am trying to walk at a normal pace as I make my way into the kitchen. As I stand here at the sliding glass doors once again I raise my hand up so that I can place it on the handle and I open the door. I walk outside but I do not close the door behind me I leave it open.

As I now stand outside I am listening to the sounds of the bugs making their music. I tilt my head back to look up to the sky and I cannot see any stars or the moon because it is so cloudy.

I am in need of some sort of comfort.

Marrick where are you?

I say as I try to send my thought to him.

I walk away from the house I realize that I am making my way toward the marble birdbath that Keith had place for Fred. I look down at the beautiful red fully bloomed roses. I lower myself so that I can sit next to them. I can smell their light fragrance as I continue to sit next them on the ground.

I miss Fred and Keith so much.

I say to myself.

I look down on the ground beside of me I see a rose petal I move my hand to pick it up and I hold it in the palm of my hand touching it with my finger from my other hand. The rose petal is so soft. I then raise the petal to my lips as I kiss it then I press it against my cheek. I lower my hand away from my face I place the rose petal back on the ground where I had found it. I move myself to stand up.

I start to walk back toward the house.

Since Logan has her swords with her then hopefully our weapons are in the S.U.V as well.

I think to myself as I am now walking beside the house.

I realize that I am moving very quickly because I am becoming nervous. I do not know when his next attack will be. I am now at my vehicle. I do not want to see the complete damage that has been done to it.

I open the back door on the driver's side and I can see right away our bags that Keith had made for us. I move closer and I bend down just slightly and I take hold of them, they are on the floor tucked under the folded back seat. As I pick them up I see a small handmade wooden box. I place the bags upon the ground and I bend inside my vehicle once more so that I can take hold of the small box.

I open it as my mouth opens slightly I realize right away what it is that I am holding.

"Sarah I have found Keith's ashes."

I say to her with my thoughts as I tightly close my eyes and mouth.

I open my eyes up and I move my head to look down. I close the lid I move the box now holding it next to my non-beating heart. I feel such a great pressure inside of my chest. My broken heart is breaking even more as I miss them both along with Beauty. The name that Sarah gave to her was perfect.

I close my eyes once more I can see the memories of the night when David murdered Fred in front of us all. I remember that night that Maryann killed Beauty and Luna. Marrick and Damon full filling their mother's request but she made them kill her because she was ordered to KILL Sarah and I as well as the wolves. That was such a horrible night. I feel such guilt and sorrow because Beauty's existence is no more. Luna is still here. I am doing everything that I can so that I do not have flash backs from when I became David's captive.

How did Maryann change the wolves? How is it possible that they came back?

I ask myself

I move the box away from my chest and I open my eyes. I can feel Sarah and I look up toward the house I can see her standing in the door way. She is holding a bag of blood.

"Sarah I have his ashes here in this wooden box that I am holding."

I say softly to her as she stands in the door way of the house.

She does not reply to me but I watch her move toward me within a blink of my eyes she is standing beside of me. I move myself so that we are now standing face to face. Sarah is looking at the box I move my hand toward her and she raises both of hands to move them toward me. I take the blood as she is now taking hold of the box she holds it close to her chest. As I begin to feed on the blood I can feel a change within her. She seems different.

We do not say a word to each other but we start walking toward the back of the house. We are moving very quickly and at the same speed. We are now at the side of the house we are making our way to the marble birdbath. We both stop at the same time. I am now standing once again next to it but this time I am standing alongside of Sarah.

Sarah opens it and she looks inside. I let my empty bag that I just fed from drop to the ground. She moves the box toward me and I hold both of my hands together as she begins to pour some of Keith's ashes into my cupped hands. When my hands are completely full of his ashes she tilts the box upright and she moves her hands back to her chest holding the box close to herself once more. I slightly bend over and I begin to walk as I pour out the ashes of my hands on the ground behind the rose bushes that were planted in honor of Fred. The ashes trickle out from between my fingers as I slowly begin to walk. I feel the ashes smoothly flowing from my fingers. I have made it half way around the birdbath. I have no more left in my hands I look at Sarah as I walk toward her. I do not rub my hands together I allow the dust from his ashes to remain on my skin. Without saying a word or a thought I take hold of the box and she cups her hands together as I pour the remaining ashes for her.

She begins to slowly walk around as his ashes gently pour from her hands onto the ground from where I stopped. I continue to watch her but I begin to have a very bad feeling. David is close I can feel his evil. I am trying to stay calm so that Sarah can finish pouring Keith's ashes. She is almost finished and this feeling is getting stronger. I am looking into the woods between the trees and I do not see him but I can feel him.

Is this his way of tormenting me? Where is he?

I say to myself as Sarah has finally finished.

"Renee, somehow it feels like they are both together once again."

She says to me as she looks down at the ground.

"I can also feel that you are very nervous and scared. Renee, David is here isn't he?"

"Sarah I cannot find him!"

I reply to her as I continue to look into the woods searching for him.

"Renee I want you to come into the house with me. We must let the others know."

"No Sarah I will remain out here. Just please let Damon know so that he can let the others know as well."

I say to her as she quickly makes her way into the house.

I begin to walk slowly in the back yard trying not to show that I am scared. I can feel him, David is so very close but I still do not see him.

Where are you Marrick?

I ask as I can feel my fangs forming, my eyes are completely black and my nails are long and sharp. I have changed because my emotions have taken over.

"Oh you have every right to be nervous my Dear Renee?"

I hear David say me.

"What is it that you honestly want and why are you here?"

I ask to him as I force myself to turn around and face him.

There he is now standing in front of me. His very tall figure his long white hair and his completely black eyes and pale white skin. There is no way that with all of our strength combined as we all fight him together that we will be able to defeat him. But we WILL do everything that we possibly can to KILL him.

David takes a step toward me and before he can move his other foot everyone that was inside of the house is now in the back yard surrounding the both of us.

Logan is standing to my left and David looks at her and smiles. As quickly as he can move he is now standing in front of her. He moves his hand and places it gently along the side of her face. He gazes at her for a moment as his smile fades away. He is now moving his hand down to her neck and with the palm of his hand places in the front as he quickly put his fingers tips upon her skin. He is slowly pushing his long sharp nails into the skin of her neck.

"You will never get another chance to slice my throat again you little BITCH!"

David says to her with his voice so calm as he continues digging his nails into her.

He is moving his fingers around making his nails go deeper into the skin of her flesh. She immediately places both of her hands on his wrist trying to pull his hand away from her but he is just too strong he will not let go of her. I can see that by the look in his eyes he is really enjoying this.

"I suggest that you release her NOW!"

Sarah demands to him.

David still has his hold on Logan. He turns his head to look at Sarah and she is armed with her cross bow and arrow. She has it pointed right at him. I look around at the others and they are armed and ready to fight David as well. I am not armed with my weapons all I have at the moment are my long sharp nails.

He slowly pulls his fingers out of Logan's neck as he continues making her feel the pain that he has inflected upon her. Her thick blood is now slowly flowing from the wounds. I know that what he has just done to Logan has also made her scared once more as well as weak because she is losing blood.

David takes a few steps back but as he does this he raises his hand and places a finger inside of his mouth one after the other sucking her blood from his skin.

I know that I need blood so that I can continue to exist but the sight of him makes me sick to my stomach as he removes her blood from his skin. But I did the same thing when Lizzie's blood was on my hand.

"Where are your followers David? I hope that you realize that Marrick and the others will be here soon."

I find myself saying to him.

"My dear Renee I am here by myself. Your precious Marrick and his brother succeeded in killing what was left of my… what is it that you call them, my demons!"

He replies to me.

"David I cannot express how happy that makes me to hear that."

I reply to him as I force a smile at him.

"So tell me Renee can you feel Marrick? Why is it that they are not here to help you to protect you from ME?"

He replies back to me.

"They will be here soon David."

"Are you positive about that my Dear? There was such a horrible battle and may I add that my brother's existence has finally ended."

He says to us as he now looks at Sabrina.

"I do not believe that Robert is dead! I am not going to listen to your lies David."

She says to him with great anger in her voice.

I know that Sabina is greatly concerned about then as well.

"Now Sabrina, what reason do I have to tell you such lies?"

"David you bastard every word that you speak is false!"

"Well then, I guess time will only tell you. Robert is dead and so is your precious Thomas."

He replies to Sabrina as he now smiles.

Logan, Sarah and Sabrina along with Stu and Lizzie and myself are starting to form a circle around him. They are standing fast while holding tightly onto their weapons. I am going to do everything that I can do to use my long sharp nails on my fingers and toes as weapons. They are the only thing that I have to use at this moment.

I am so scared! Are Marrick and the others really dead?

I ask to myself

We are all focused on David he is making his way into the middle of our circle. He is turning himself around looking at us one by one. It is like he is going to decide who is going to take him on first. He has is gaze set upon Logan. He is tilting his head to his right side as he smiles to her once more. I can see her hands gripping her weapons tighter as he continues to gaze into her eyes with his sick and twisted smile.

"Logan would you like to be the first do die?"

He asks to her in his very calm voice.

"David you are stronger than I am but I will not allow you to end my existence."

She replies to him as she becomes ready for his attack.

"Little Logan you keep telling yourself that as I open your chest and crush your non-beating heart with my hand."

David replies to her as he starts to move toward her.

He is torturing Logan and he will never stop doing this to her or anyone of us as long as he is still existing.

Before my eyes can blink Sarah is standing directly in front of Logan. I do not know what she is planning on doing. She must be following her instincts to do what she can to protect Logan.

"Do you honestly think that we are going to believe that we are only to fight you one on one? Oh David you are a FUCKING fool!"

Sarah says to him as she looks directly into his eyes.

"Oh Sarah I believe that I would not have it any other way. I remember the damage that you and your little friends caused me not so long ago. I will give to you such great pain that you will be begging me to end your existence!"

David replies to her as he moves his arm back.

I move as quickly as I can and with every ounce of strength that I have I take hold of his arm before he can strike my blood sister. I am wrapping my fingers around his arm and this time I am pushing my long sharp nails into his skin. I am moving my fingers back and forth hoping that I am causing him pain. I can feel his bone as my middle and ring fingers are embedded into his arm. He is raising his arm up to his face so that he can look at what I have just done to him. His movement is causing me to raise my arm up my fingers are stuck in his skin! The look on his face does not change at all. David is moving his head just slightly to his right so that he can look into my eyes. I cannot help but look back at him.

How does he remain looking and sounding so calm?

All of a sudden I feel such a terrible force against my chest. I can feel the wind blowing thru my hair as it surrounds my face. I am in pain my body is hitting the back of the house with such a great force. I am in shock and I cannot move.

"What just happened?"

I ask to myself as I try to sit up but I am having trouble I fall down upon the ground again.

I am in so much pain I move my hands to place them on my chest just right below my neck as I am still lying on the ground. I can feel something sticking out of my skin I move my head so that I can see what it is. It is my collar bone! With both of my hands still on my chest I tilt my head all the way back as I lay on the ground and I gaze up to the night sky. I close my eyes and I begin to push my collar bone back inside of my body. Not only can I hear the cracking and popping sound as I do this but I feel the other part of my broken bone as I force it back inside of me. The pain too great to bear I refuse to yell out. I need to continue doing this so that I can heal. The bone is now inside of me and I can feel the flesh of my chest is closing.

I need more blood!

I move my arms so that I can raise my hands up in front of my eyes. I have my blood along with David's blood on my fingers and under my nails. I close both of my hands to make a fist and I force myself to sit up. The pain in my chest is not as bad as what it was a few minutes ago. I am slowly moving myself to stand up I am placing my hands upon the house to help steady myself.

I must try very hard to stable myself I cannot allow myself to fall to the ground again because that will show weakness. I have to be strong!

I demand to myself as I am now completely standing straight up.

My chest still hurts.

Without a thought I am walking back toward them as they continue fighting with David. I am no longer scared the closer I get to David I am becoming angry. I am going to use what I am feeling. I am going to allow this hate and anger to grow inside of me. I am going to use this so that we can defeat him, to KILL HIM!

"David I am going to make a promise to you. I promise that we are going to destroy you."

I say to him as loudly as I possibly can while I do everything to keep MY voice calm.

I am raising the hand that has his blood upon my fingers I am placing one finger at a time in my mouth as I suck his thick vampire blood along with mine from my skin, why am I doing this? Because I need BLOOD!

David turns his head to look at me he is watching as I continue to move toward them. I am placing my pinkie inside of my mouth it is the last finger that I have left that still has his blood.

"Well my Dear Renee I want you to show me just how strong you have become since the last time that we saw each other. Tell me how does our blood taste together as you suck it from your fingers?"

He asks to me.

"You David taste like shit!"

I reply to him as I look back into his eyes.

"Oh my Dear you look so beautiful with my blood upon your fangs."

He says to me as I now feel sick for what he has just said to me.

I know that the sun is going to rise soon and I have no idea as to how I am to help defeat him but I am going to do everything thing that I possibly can.

Marrick please hurry!

I say as I send my thought to him hoping that he can hear my words.

As I am getting closer David moves toward Sarah once more. He knows how I feel about her!

"Oh Renee I am going to give you a choice. Who among your friends should I kill first?"

He asks me as he is moving closer to her.

"If you are going to make me choose one of them then David I will be the one and only that you will destroy."

I reply to him.

"I will destroy you Renee but I will save YOU for last."

He says as he stops, he is smiling.

I have a horrible feeling in the pit of my stomach I feel sick again.

"Sarah we must stab him as many times as we possibly can to make him bleed, we must make him weak! If Beauty was able to do it then so can we. We need to rip his flesh and remove his head."

I say to as I send my thoughts to her.

She does not reply to me but as David continues to make his way toward her Sarah is moving her hand behind her as quickly as she can. She takes hold of a wooden dagger that she has hidden behind her tucked in the back of her pants. She is now making her way toward David she is raising her hand up and as they are now standing in front of each other she moves very quickly to stab him. David blocks her by taking hold of her arm with his hand to hold onto her. David very quickly moves his other hand he hits the bottom of her elbow. David just broke Sarah's arm her bone has been pushed upward sticking out of her skin. She is losing blood. As David still has ahold of Sarah's arm he straightens out his fingers and with a quick movement he cuts open her chest with his long sharp nails leaving a very deep gash in her skin. Sarah's shirt is turning red from the blood that is now escaping from her body.

"I hope that you do understand that vampire blood will not give me the life force that I need but it will sustain me for just a little while. I will drain every one of you as I feed from your bodies."

David says as he lets go of her as he watches Sarah fall to the ground from what he has just done to her. Sarah has her broken arm lying against her as she places her other hand firmly upon her chest as she tries to stop the bleeding. But I can see that the look on her face is pure anger. I cannot help but to smile because once again I can feel a change within her. I can feel her hate and it is very strong!

As David continues to stand in front of Sarah I hear a whip sound. As I continue to look at him as I am now moving closer to help Sarah I see David's head go back as his chest lunges forward. The blade of Logan's sword is sticking out the front of David's chest the handle is in his back. Logan is standing behind him. David lowers his head to look at the blade sticking out of him. His this blood is smeared on the blade.

I take hold of Sarah as she now rests her body against me. Sabrina moves very quickly toward us and as she now stands in front of Sarah she bends down and takes hold of Sarah's arm with both of her hands. She does not say a word to her but instead she pulls immediately to reset Sarah's arm. Sarah cannot help but to yell out in pain.

"Oh you little BITCH you will not survive this evening! I will remove your heart from your chest."

David says to Logan with such anger in his voice.

"Logan you should really try using a wooden sword you will see that it can be more effective."

Stu says to her as he is now moving very quickly to David.

Stu has both of his elbows bent and the handle of his wooden sword is next to his face. David remains standing where he is at. As Stu is getting closer I can see him moving his sword as he begins to straighten out his arms. David has his head still lowered as if he is looking at the ground but as Stu is now is coming towards him David quickly lowers himself to the ground. Stu has missed David's neck by just less of an inch. As Stu begins to move past David, he quickly stands up as he turns himself toward Stu David is moving at the speed of light right behind him and with his long sharp nails David cuts open the back of Stu's neck exposing his neck bone. Blood begins to pour from his skin. David still has Logan's sword in his chest, he stops and turns with a chunk of Stu's skin in his hand. David raises it up to his face he opens his mouth to place his tongue on the skin that he removed from the back of Stu's neck. David is licking the blood from it. David has the skin place right up against his face. He is truly a disgusting evil being! He removes the skin David's face from his nose down to his chin is cover in Stu's blood. David opens his mouth just slightly it is enough for him to lick his lips removing the blood.

We cannot allow him to defeat us!

I say to Sarah as I send my though to her.

Sabrina removes herself from us she is running moving as quickly as she can toward David she takes hold of the handle. She is forcing the sword upward thru David's body. You can hear the metal slicing his skin and the loud popping sound as she forces the sword through his bones. Finally we can see that David in now the one in pain as the sword comes out thru the top of his shoulder. His blood is splattering everywhere including on Sabrina.

As she still has hold of the sword she is also prepared for David not knowing what he is going to do. David falls on his knees to the ground. Once again he lowers his head his arms are at his sides.

"CUT HIS FUCKING HEAD OFF!"

Lizzie yells out to her.

I help Sarah to stand up and we both begin to move toward him. Sabrina is moving herself to stand behind him with the blade of the sword against David's neck. The blade of the sword is coated with his blood as there is a steady stream dripping of the blade. There are also pieces of bone and muscle on the blade of the sword as well. Logan, Stu and Lizzie are also moving toward him.

Stu's neck is slowly starting to heal the bleeding has stopped flowing from the hole that David gave him when he removed a chuck of Stu's skin.

We are making a circle around him once more. Stu has become very weak from the amount of blood that he has lost. We are all weak except for Sabrina and Lizzie because they are the only ones who have not had their bodies injured. But I can see that they do need to feed, we all need to.

"Lizzie you must take Stu into the house and make your way into the safe room in the basement. The both of you must feed on the two bags of blood that is left in the cold storage."

I say to her as I move myself to stand next to her.

Lizzie moves so that she can take hold of Stu.

"We will come back and help once he is healed."

She replies to me.

"No Lizzie you both must stay in the basement!"

I say to her with great concern for them.

Lizzie helps Stu toward the house but as she begins to move David is softly starting to laugh.

"Go now, run to the house!"

I yell to them with panic in my voice.

As they begin to move as quickly as they can toward the sliding glass door Sarah and I place ourselves between them and David.

David begins to stand himself up as he continues to laugh. As we look at him we can see that his body is starting to heal. He has lost a lot of blood as well and I am hoping that this will cause him to be very weak.

"You ladies do not have much time because the sun is beginning to rise."

He says to us.

"What are we going to do?"

I ask Sarah as I sent my thought to her.

I can hear a click sound as I hear the sliding glass door close. I cannot help but look over at the pool as I hear the sound of concrete rubbing together. One of them pushed the button for the concrete slabs to open over the swimming pool.

Right away Sarah and I look at each other we know what we must try to do. I look over to Sabrina and then I move my eyes back to the pool once more.

"We do not have much time!"

Logan says to us as the sky turns to a very dark blue color.

I need to do whatever I can to distract him!

I think to myself as I can now see light pink within the sky.

"Oh my Dear Renee I cannot help but wonder what it is that you are going to do."

David says to me with his calm voice once again.

How I hate the sound of his voice!

"Why are you doing this David and for what reason do you have?"

I ask him as I move myself closer to him.

He looks at me and he slightly tilts his head to the right.

"Renee have you not learned by now that this is my nature? I can show you how to endure pleasure with pain. Oh the enjoyment of reaching my hand into someone's body and pulling their insides out of them and ripping their bodies apart with just my hands. The smell and taste of their fear mixed with blood is like a bee making honey from the sweet nectar of a flower. How I enjoy fucking women with fear for their lives within their eyes and ripping their flesh with my teeth. I was not able to look into your eyes but that did not stop me."

David explains to me as I feel as if I am going to vomit the blood out of my body.

"You are going to die David I hope that you understand this."

I reply to him as I try to keep control of myself.

"Oh I do understand that you will give me your best as you try to kill me."

He says to me as he now beings to make his way toward me. I stop moving toward him and begin moving toward to pool.

I honestly do not have a plan as to what to do. I am now standing at the pool I close my eyes and not only can I feel how strong and powerful the evil within him is I can also hear him as he gently places his feet upon the ground walking toward me.

I can still feel the anger and hate that I have for him inside of me but I can feel the fear inside of me as well.

I open my eyes and I have my right hand which is my strongest ready to burry deep inside of his body I want to pull his non-beating heart out of his chest. I hope that I can bring him to his knees so that I can also rip his head off. But I must hurry I can feel my body becoming weak my body is going to shut down because the sun is almost above is. I do not want my existence to end today!

As soon as David is behind me I turn around very quickly and I look up into his eyes hoping that he does not realize what I am going to try to do. He is looking back into my eyes. I raise my right hand up as quickly as I can as I am reaching for his chest. Before I know it has hold of my wrist. Davie raises my hand closer to his face placing the inside of my wrist against his lips. He is kissing my skin.

Why is he doing this?

I ask to myself.

As he continues to look down at me gazing into my eyes I feel such a horrible pressure in my right side. I lower my head down his hand is inside of me I can feel him placing his fingers around the bones of my rib cage. I am doing everything that I can to brace myself. I close my eyes as his grip upon my bones tightens I can feel and hear them breaking. He is taking his time as he does this to me. I am in such great pain but once again I refuse to yell out.

David finally releases my wrist but he quickly moves his arm around me to hold me close to him as he continues to crush my rib cage. I close my eyes I cannot take much more of this. I can feel David's body moving against mine. He is pressing his lips against my forehead.

I must be strong!

"David the sun is rising."

I whisper to him with every ounce of strength that I have left.

"My Dear Renee I want to see if you can escape from the sun. Say goodbye to your friends because this evening will be the last time that you will spend together."

He says to me as he lowers his head to whisper into my ear.

I can feel him pulling his hand out of my side.

"I am taking a memento from you so that I can always remember this evening."

He says to me as his hand is now completely out of my body.

He lets go of me and I fall to my knees I force myself to look at him. He is holding a small piece of bone from one of my ribs. I know this because he is allowing me to see it.

"I am going to leave you know but I do hope to see you this evening my Dear. Good luck!"

He says to me as he pushes me into the swimming pool.

I do not think that I am going to survive this! The sun is rising higher and Marrick and Damon are not here with us. I AM going to die!

I think to myself as I now lay at the bottom of the pool.

I can hear the muffled sound of concrete rubbing together. I open my eyes and I am watching as the concrete slabs are now covering the pool blocking the sun from destroying me.

As I lay here in darkness inside of the water my body has completely shut itself down.

I am so weak and hungry for blood the only thing that I can think to do is quite my mind. I am not allowing myself to think of anything or anyone. I can feel my mind slowly starting to rest.

I am thankful that I am a vampire because I CAN'T BREATHE!

Chapter Seven

My body is waking up and I can taste warm fresh blood as it slowly flows into my mouth and down my throat. I realize that I am no longer lying at the bottom of the pool my body is lying upon the ground. As the blood continues to flow slowly into my mouth I need to open my eyes. I want to gaze upon him. He is finally here!

I can no longer keep them closed for I am now looking directly into Marrick eyes! He is holding a human wrist above my mouth feeding me.

I want to say something to him. I am so glad that you have come back.

I say to myself knowing that he can hear what I am thinking.

"Renee, do not speak. You must take hold of this wrist I want you to continue consuming this blood you need to regain your strength. Your body needs to heal."

He says to me as I move both of my hands to do what he has commanded of me.

I bring the wrist closer to my lips I force my fangs into the flesh and as I continue to feed I am so hungry.

Marrick moves closer to me he is sitting next to my head. He places his hand in my hair to comfort me.

"I am so glad that you are here with me."

I say to him as I send my thoughts to him.

"Please forgive me Renee! This is all David's doing. He tried and almost succeeded in destroying our existence he almost destroyed us. He was also trying to separate us as well."

Marrick goes on to explain to me.

"You must know that it was Luna she had found us. We would have been destroyed if she had not saved us. David had set a trap for us and we fell right into it. But we had finally destroyed his human followers and the vampires that he created. David came at us one by one picking us off as if we were but a single insect. We would have been stronger fighting him together. He left us all to parish in the sun's first light but his plan did not work because Luna was able to burry us into the ground. I cannot help but wonder as to what Maryann had done do to change her? You had told me that you could feel Luna. The night you buried her, your blood tears fell upon her face. She absorbed your blood into her and that is how you are able feel Luna. I did believe you when you had said to me that you could honestly feel her after you buried her. I could feel it from you as well. I thought it was because you were grieving for her that you desperately wanted her to be with you once again."

Marrick says to me as I continue to lie here upon the ground.

I am listening to his words but the blood from this body that he gave me to feed from tastes so sweet and delicious.

I am so weak I want and need more human blood.

I am finally starting to heal from what David had done to me last evening.

Marrick knows that I have now completely drained this body from the last ounce of blood. Marrick removes his hand from my hair and takes hold of the wrist to remove it from my face. He pushes the body away from me so that he can move himself closer as I continue to lie on the ground looking at his beautiful pale white face. Marrick slides his hand under my shoulder and he places his other hand on my arm. He helps me to sit up.

I can still feel as if David's hand is still inside of me crushing my bones. I am trying so hard not to think about it but it is very difficult because he has invaded my body once again. I do not want to be weak and venerable I need to be strong and powerful. With Marrick once again by my side I can be.

We are close enough to the pool that Marrick reaches his cupped hand into the water he moves it back to me. He begins to wash the blood from my skin. I lay myself up against his body as he cleans my face.

Marrick quickly places both of his arms around me his grip becomes tighter as I can feel the bones of my ribs starting to fuzz themselves together as I continue to heal. I quickly move my legs close to me I place both of my hands his arms squeezing him as I can feel the pain becomes stronger.

"When will it stop? It feels as if it is happening all over again."

I say to him as Marrick continues to hold me through this pain.

"Renee you must try to relax. The pain of your body healing allows you know that you still have a soul. The moment when you feel no pain will be when you have lost your soul. We must all fight to keep ourselves together as we battle to destroy David. He was a human born without one."

Marrick says to me as he continues to hold me as I try to relax my body.

As the pain starts to ease up I loosen my grip that I have on his arms. Marrick continues to keep hold of me. My eyes are filling up with blood tears and I can now feel them as they begin to stream down my pale white face.

I am able to control myself as my tears are flowing from my eyes.

"Marrick did David succeed in destroying anyone that was with you? He told us that he had destroyed everyone's including you and Damon."

I say to him as I rest my body against his.

My clothes are still soaked from being in the pool. Marrick's clothes are also wet from allowing me to rest against him as he holds me in his arms tightly against his beautiful sculptured body.

"I am sad to say that we lost Paul along with the ones that had just completed their transformation into a full vampire. We lost 4 people all together Renee."

He replies to me I can hear the concern in his voice for us all.

"Marrick I am so sorry."

"Renee there is no reason for you to apologize for something that you had nothing to do with."

He replies to me.

"Marrick since Luna was with you last evening that explains why she was not here."

"Renee you must know that we were following you David somehow figured that out."

He replies to me.

"Marrick it seems like he is always a step ahead of us. Because I have his blood within me he will always know where I am at."

I say to his as I begin to feel once again that this is my entire fault.

"No Renee you must not think or feel this way. It is not your fault for what he had done to you."

Marrick replies to me.

As I continue to rest against him I am going to change the subject.

"Do you know who closed the pool?"

"Yes Renee it was Stu. If he would have pulled you out of the water after the sun had raised your existence would have ended. He did the right thing by closing the pool to protect you from the first light."

"Marrick I am so grateful to him. I just did not know who it was. Did the back of Stu's neck completely heal from the injury that David placed upon him?"

I ask to him.

"Yes Renee Stu's neck is completely healed and so has everyone else. We were able to bring more human bodies for everyone to feed from."

He replies to me.

"Please tell me that these humans that you brought back to us are criminals."

"I can assure you that they are Renee. They were with David."

He replies to me as he continues to hold me to close to him.

"Marrick if I were to lose my soul would I be able to somehow get it back again?"

"No Renee when you lose your soul it is gone forever. I have seen vampires who had good souls like you. When something horrible happened to them they completely lost themselves in revenge. I watched as a good friend of ours let his soul slip away little by little. This was around one hundred years ago his village was destroyed along with his family. All he could think about was destroying the one who had done this. Marco could not think of anything else. He completely lost everything not only did he lose his soul Marco lost his own existence."

"Marrick was that David's doing as well?"

"No Renee it was not. There is another that is far worse than David."

Marrick explains to me.

"This depresses me even more I hope that we never cross paths with this being."

I say to him.

"How is it that you and Damon were able to keep your souls?"

"Renee we made a promise to our father to destroy David. We also wanted revenge for what he had done but it did not consume us. We were also willing to destroy ourselves after David's death."

He explains to me.

Marrick releases his grip on me as I move myself to stand up he now stands beside me.

I have a very bad feeling growing inside of me and it is once again mixed with fear as my body begins to tremble.

"Marrick I must tell you that I have an extremely bad feeling. David is close and he is making his way back here. We did what we could to make him weak last night hoping that we could destroy him.

But we were not very successful with our task. We were the ones that he severely hurt and we became very weak. We wanted him to be the one damaged so that we could kill him."

I say to him as I look up into his eyes.

I can feel that the pain within my side is now completely gone. I can feel Sarah I look toward the house and I see her standing at the sliding glass door. I also see that Damon is standing directly behind her. I close my eyes because of this sick feeling in my stomach that I have once again.

"Marrick I must tell you that David is now here! I can feel his evil. We need to end his life David has caused to much destruction!"

I say to him as I open my eyes again.

I turn my head to the left and I see David casually walking out of the woods he is making his way toward us. His body has healed itself but his clothes are covered with his dark red vampire blood.

"Marrick tell me, how was it that you and Damon were able to escape the sun? I will just have to remove your heads from your bodies this time."

David says to him as he walks closer to us.

"Your plan did not work out as you had wanted it to. You are going to be the one who is going to die not us!"

Marrick replies to him as David moves himself closer.

I stand here looking at David as he continues to make his way toward us I can see his glow it is such a very dark red that it almost looks black.

I can feel Marrick taking hold of my arm I place my other hand upon him.

I hear the sliding glass door open up and as quickly as they can all move everyone is now in the back yard.

I cannot help but feel sadness for Paul and the others that David had killed.

As quickly as David can move he is making his way very fast to the speed of light toward Richard.

What is he doing?

I cannot help but ask to myself.

As quickly as David moves past him Richard's body is falling to the ground and Lizzie is holding the head of her grandfather. There are streams of thick blood as it drains from his severed head.

Lizzie has a horrible look upon her face as she looks into Richard's gray eyes. She is in shock and covered in his blood.

Once again I remember how Keith reacted as David murdered Fred.

"Stu you must get Lizzie back into the house NOW! You must stay in the safe room inside the basement."

Sarah yells to him.

Right away Stu moves very quickly as he takes hold of Lizzie in his arms. He is forcing her back into the house. She is still holding Richard's head but this time she has a very tight grip upon it as she holds it to her body.

"David if you survive this evening I will make it my mission to hunt you down so that I can FUCKING KILL YOU!"

She yells to him as Stu holds onto her while they now stand at the sliding glass door.

"I must say that I do enjoy listing to a promise that you will not be able to keep. But I promise that I will have my way with you Lizzie and you will be begging for me to end your life. But if by some chance you survive I will make you mine for the rest of your existence I will complete your transformation."

David replies to her with a twisted smile upon his face.

David is raising both of his hands into the air as if he is catching something. He is now lowering his hands down to his chest. David is quickly moving one of his hands I am having trouble watching what he is doing but I can now see what he is holding. Lizzie threw Richards head back to David. He is holding something in his other hand that he was moving. David slightly raises his eyes and tilts his head to his left to look at Logan as we all stand here watching him. What he is doing he is moving his fingers around.

Why is it that they are not attacking him!

I ask to myself.

"Logan I have something that I would like for you to have. Call it a small memento. It is something for you to always remember Richard."

He says to her as we see him move his hand just slightly upward as he tosses something to her. David does not take his eyes off of Logan. She reacts to what he has tossed to her she moves her hand to catch it. Tears of blood are now streaming down her beautiful pale white face as she stairs into the palm of her hand.

"David, why did you end Richard's existence? Why are you doing this?"

"Logan, have you not learned by now that you are not meant to be with anyone."

He replies to her as he continues to look upon her.

My non-beating heart just dropped into my stomach.

That is such a horrible thing to say to Logan. He has to be destroyed.

I say to myself as I continue to stand here next to Marrick.

"You will not survive this evening David."

Thomas says to him with anger in his voice.

"Oh now tell me you do not like to gift that I gave to Logan? She will always be able to gaze upon his gray eyes. Look at her she is still gazing at them as she holds Richards eyes in her hand."

David replies to Thomas as he starts to walk around.

"This will be the last time that we will look upon you David."

Robert says to him.

"I must agree with you brother. I have grown very bored from your attempts of trying to destroy me."

David replies to him as he moves closer toward Robert.

The both of them are moving closer to each other. Robert has a knife it is made out of wood and he is aiming to stab it into David's chest but David dodges out of the way so quickly. Robert turns around as fast he can but as he does David is moving toward Robert with a look of shock upon his face. David turns his head just slightly so that he look at his brother and then moves his head down to look upon his own chest.

"I am very impressed with your effort my Dear brother but I must say Robert you have missed my heart."

David says to him as Robert looks to where he has stabbed David.

"Tell me David can you feel the pain that I have just inflicted upon you?"

Robert asks to him as he takes hold of the handle to force the wooden blade closer to his heart cutting David's chest open. His thick vampire blood is starting to escape from him once again. David moves his hand very quickly and places it open Robert's hand. I can see him forcing Robert to push the wooden knife further into David's own body. David is no longer allowing Robert to move the knife closer to his dead heart. David cannot feel the pain that is why he has forced Robert to push the knife straight into his own chest. He would have dropped to the ground on his knees from the pain.

"Oh Robert I do love giving pain to others and that is exactly what I am going to do to you once more but this time I will not leave you to die in an alley. I will rip you completely apart exposing your insides then I will leave you to burn in the sun."

He whispers to his brother with a smile upon his face.

I know have a horrible and scary shiver that is slowly creeping thru my body.

How could Robert have missed his heart?

I ask myself as I start to feel sick once more.

Robert quickly moves his hand away from under David's as he releases the handle of his knife leaving it in David's chest. David moves his fingers to place around the handle he is pulling the wooden knife out of his chest very slowly. After the tip is out David raises it up to his face and places the blade upon his lips. He moves his tongue out of his mouth we are all watching as he licks his own blood from the wooden knife. I cannot continue to watch so I close my eyes as I lower my head.

I find the courage to open my eyes again but as I do I see that Logan is moving very quickly toward David and Sabrina and Thomas are doing the same.

Please kill him!

I say to myself.

David is so strong and quick he moves out of their way. I do not see him where did he go?

"I suggest that you stop or she will die."

David says to them as he is now standing directly behind Sarah with one hand on her throat with his other hand he has a wooden knife holding it over her heart pushing the tip of it in her pale white skin. I can hear her flesh ripping as he continues to slowly push the knife in her chest.

"David you sick son of a bitch let her go!"

I say to him as I move away from Marrick's side.

"Now tell me my Dear Renee why should I let her go? You do realize that she is going to die."

He replies to me as he holds Sarah tightly to him.

Oh my stars what do I do!

I ask to myself.

"David, please allow me to take her place. I do not want her to die."

"Renee have you forgotten that I had said to you that I am saving you for last. I want you to watch as I kill your family. Can you feel her fear?"

He asks to me.

"I suggest that you do exactly what Renee had asked of you David, release Sarah now!"

Damon says to him as he is now standing right behind David with a knife at the side of his neck.

"Very well Damon if this is how you want to play it."

David replies to him as he very quickly pushes Sarah away from him.

David turns around so fast that he looks like a very tall pale white blur. Damon is prepared for him to move. Damon presses the sharp blade of his knife into the skin of David's neck as he moves very quickly. David is bleeding once again. Maybe we now have another chance to kill him.

David turns from Damon very quickly once more and with the wooden steak still in his hand David throws it directly at Sarah.

I must protect her!

I am moving as fast as I can toward her and I push Sarah out of the way. I see her fall to the ground as I fall with her. The wooden stake entered my body from my back.

I am in pain again but my existence has not yet ended.

Sarah moves her head to look over to me.

"Renee!"

She cries out to me as she moves herself.

"Sarah you must pull it out!"

I say to her as she moves very quickly over to me.

She takes hold of the knife and as quickly as she can Sarah pulls the knife out of my back.

I am doing everything that I can not to show weakness I do not yell out as the knife is removed from my body. I can feel it being removed from the bone of my spine.

"Renee you saved me from David. Please tell me that you are ok."

She says to me as she sits next to me on her knees with one hand on my back. Sarah is trying to apply pressure to stop the bleeding.

Sarah now has the wooden knife in her hand.

"I need to lay here for a moment."

I reply to her.

I can feel my back starting to heal as I continue to lie upon the ground on my stomach.

I can feel a strong force coming closer it is such a familiar feeling. I am moving myself to sit up Sarah is now helping me to stand up. This feeling is becoming stronger. I look to my right I focus my sight into the woods. I am now watching as Luna is moving very quickly through the trees. She is coming to help me to protect me. I can hear her growling as she is running out of the woods. I can see her dark black eyes they are no longer light blue. She is showing her teeth her

K-9 teeth are longer and I can see that the point of her fangs can rip us all apart.

As I watch Luna run as quickly as she can, that if I was a still human her appearance would seem like a long black streak cutting through the air as she moves to the speed of light.

Damon is still fighting with David as I continue to watch Luna make her way toward them. Luna runs right into Damon forcing him out of the way as she is now directly standing in front of David ready to attack him.

"Oh little black wolf are you here for your revenge?"

David asks to Luna as he begins to laugh.

Luna is in her attack position. Her feet are planted upon the ground with her nose lowered to the earth as she has her eyes fixed upon him watching his every move.

Luna now has David's full attention and Michael and Thomas take advantage of it. They are both moving very quickly toward him. But David can hear them moving and turns from Luna to fight them but before he moves Luna lunges toward David and she clamps her mouth upon his wrist pulling on him with all of her strength. Luna is trying to remove his hand from his body. David moves his leg very quickly to kick Luna. The force from his foot going into her side is so great she releases her hold on his wrist. Luna is sliding on the ground away from David as she pushes her paws into the ground to stop herself. David's blood is dripping from Luna's mouth.

I can see his wrist David is losing a lot of blood from what Luna had just done. I can see that David is finally beginning to weaken.

I am moving as fast as I can toward Luna I need to make sure that David did not hurt her more than what he has already done. As Luna is moving herself to stand up she looks over to me.

"Luna, are you ok?"

I ask to her as I fall to the ground on my knees in front of her.

As she stands looking back to me I move my hand toward her I want to touch her one more time. As my hand moves closer to her she moves away from me. I stand back up I turn to watch her. I am now looking at everyone fighting David together as I stand by myself.

I begin to walk toward them and as I am making my way over I notice that there is a wooden knife lying upon the ground. As I continue to move I bend myself down to the ground and I pick it up.

"We are going to kill you David even if you do escape again we will hunt you down."

I say as calmly as I can as I continue to move toward them.

"My Dear Renee, give it your best try."

I hear his reply to me.

As I am now closer to them as David is fighting them all. I see Marrick move very quickly behind him. Marrick moves his hand and places it upon David throat digging his nails into his skin. Marrick is now holding a knife directly over David's evil non-beating heart digging the blade into his flesh. What Marrick is doing to him is the same thing as to what David had just done to Sarah.

I am looking at all of the wounds that have been placed upon David's body. But I can see the wounds on everyone else as well. I look over to Sarah I can see that she has a slash mark in her neck and there is a rip in the skin of her arm. She is also losing a lot of blood as well.

"Luna moves herself toward me she is now walking in front of me as we are both moving toward Marrick as he is holding David very tightly to him.

"My Dear David it seems as if you will not escape from us this time."

I say to him as I cannot help but smile to him.

"Oh Renee you should know that I always have a card up my sleeve."

He replies to me.

"You have no cards left to play David your deck is no more."

"Are you sure about that my Dear."

"David that next time that you call me that, I will rip out your tongue!"

As he continues to look at me there is a smile forming on his face from ear to ear. I do not want to look at him but I must not show him how scared I am.

I must be strong!

"What is he talking about he has no one left to help him he has no one left to command."

I say to Marrick as I am now standing in front to them.

Luna is still in front of me she is not allowing me to get any closer.

"We must be prepared for anything."

I hear Marrick as he sends his thoughts back to me.

I am holding onto this wooden knife so tight that that the sharp points of my nails are going into the skin of my hand.

Luna is beginning to growl once again.

I can hear the sliding glass door open and close there is someone moving very quickly behind me but it is only one person. I know that this is not Lizzie.

"Stu how is Lizzie?"

I hear Sarah ask him as he now stands beside of me.

"She is resting."

Stu replies to her.

"How were you able to get Lizzie to rest?"

I ask Stu.

"She is very upset and it was the only thing that she is able to do right now."

He replies to me as he moves his head to look at David.

As I continue to look over to him I notice that Stu is holding weapons in both of his hands.

"David it seems that you have been over powered."

Stu says to David as he looks at him.

"Yes it does seem that way doesn't it but I can tell you that their hold on me will not last too much longer."

David replies to him.

As I still hold the knife in my hand I am trying to move forward but Luna still will not allow me to get any closer to David. I raise my right hand up that is holding the wooden knife and I gently toss it upward into the air and as I catch I am now holding the blade in the palm of my hand. As quickly as I can I move my hand just slightly above my shoulder as I am focusing my gaze upon David. I am now pushing my arm forward releasing it from my hand watching it as it moves very fast through the air flying right towards David chest.

Right away David moves his gaze upon me as he smiles. Without saying a word he begins to move. He moves his head forward and then David pushes his head back as hard as he possibly can as he hits Marrick in the face with the back of his head but Marrick does not release his grip on David. Marrick is now forcing his knife into David's chest. There is a loud thump my knife has just landed in David's chest as well right next to Marrick's knife that he just forced into David's chest.

"Why is he not dead?"

I ask as I lower my head to look at the ground in anger.

As I look back up David has somehow escaped Marrick's hold on him.

I do not understand as to what is happening.

David is once again in a battle with everyone. Once again I have no weapon except for my long sharp nails. I am moving myself toward them I am going to push my way into the fight. I want to destroy David as well.

As I move closer to them I can hear Luna growling she sounds so different since she has changed into what she is now. Her growl is deeper with such a very powerful sound.

I am now with them as I am dodging everyone's moves as they continue to fight with him. David has his back turned toward me this is my chance to kill him.

I am moving very quickly toward him I jump onto his back I warp my legs around his waist to hold onto him. I raise my hands to his neck and with my fingers slightly bend I am forcing my long sharp nails into the skin of his neck. I am going to rip his head off just as he had done to Beauty.

I am moving my fingers as fast as I can to slice his flesh with my sharp nails. I can feel his blood flowing over my fingers and down his body as I still have my legs wrapped around him.

"You are going to die tonight!"

I say to him with anger in my voice as I continue to cut his skin.

I can feel David falling to the ground he has landed on his knees but I am not going to let go. David moves his hands as quickly as he can to place them on my wrist he is trying to pull my hands away from him. I am not going to let go!

Luna is very slowly moving toward David as I am still on his back trying to remove his head. I hear a thump once again someone just shot David in the chest with an arrow.

How is it that he is not DEAD?

I say to myself.

Luna is now directly in front of David she moves very quickly. She has just clamped onto the flesh of David's stomach right under my leg. David removes his hands from my wrist and he places them upon Luna. He is picking her up as he is now throwing her across the back yard. I can feel David as he becomes weaker. Luna has bitten a piece of flesh from his body. I move my gaze to look at her just to make sure that she is ok. Luna is eating the skin that she just took from David's body.

I am still doing everything that I possibly can to slice the skin of his neck to remove his head from his body. I have half of his neck sliced open. The sight of his blood escaping from his neck is making me crave blood. I am moving my head closer to his neck and I place my mouth where I have been cutting his skin with my sharp nails. I am now feeding on David's vampire blood.

I can feel David places his hands upon each side of my head trying to get me to release my grip on him. I am not going to let him go. I still have my nails buried into his neck trying to kill him as I am also feeding on his blood. I will do everything that I can to succeed.

My hair is flowing around the front of my face.

What is happening? Am I falling backwards?

I ask myself as the back of my head hits the ground so hard I can see a red flash behind my closes eye lids.

I have such a horrible pain going through my head that I release my mouth from his neck. I am having trouble keeping my nails in David's neck.

I remove my hands from his flesh and I place them on the back of my head. I cannot tell if this is just David's blood or if it is mine as well. I am in such pain. I can feel David removing himself from me as I continue to lie upon the ground.

I move my head to the right as I open my eyes and I find myself lying next to the marble birdbath. I look at the flowers that are fully bloomed I notice that there is blood upon a rose. The blood is all over the petals dripping onto the leaves and slowly making its way down the stem. As I continue to gaze upon it I realize that the full moon is right behind it and the rose is a shape of a heart.

I must say this is something very beautiful to gaze upon. But I do know that the blood upon this rose belongs to David.

We can kill him!

I say to myself as I begin to sit up next to the roses listening to them as they fight with the monster once again.

I place my hands upon the ground and I move myself to stand up. I do not feel weak is this because I fed from David? He said that vampire blood will only sustain us. Maybe if we all feed from him, drain his body of his vampire blood we can leave him to burn in the first light as the sun rises in the sky.

I can feel blood running down the back of my neck I know that my skull has been cracked upon. As I begin to move toward them once again I notice that David has no fighting chance this time. Every one of them is taking a piece of him little by little. Marrick has just forced his hand inside of David's body he is crushing the bones of David's ribs the same way that David had crushed mine. How can you make a monster like David who has no soul and cannot feel any pain. How can he be made to suffer?

I am now making my way toward them as they are now standing around him. I stop as I am now standing in between Sabrina and Logan. As I look upon David he is on his knees once again Marrick and Damon are both holding onto him. They each have a hold of his arms forcing him upon the ground. He looks so weak. As I look upon him I can see that the damage that I had done to his neck is not healing and his blood is now slowly leaving his body from Marrick forcing his hand inside of David's side paying him back for what he had done to me.

David has his head slightly lowered to the ground but he raises his eyes to look at his brother Robert and I am thankful that he is not looking at me.

"You are all sadly mistaken if you honestly think that you can destroy me!"

David says to us with his voice calm and steady.

"Tell me my Dear David why do you believe that we cannot destroy you? You are now weak and your body is not healing."

I say to him as he now moves his eyes to me.

"Have you not realized that I always have a plan?"

He replies to me as he smiles.

"You have no one left to help you David."

"Then allow me to prove you wrong Renee."

He replies to me as Marrick and Damon still have him on his knees.

"Please KILL him now!"

Logan begs to them.

Robert and Thomas moves very quickly toward David with their weapons straight out in front of them aiming for his neck to cut his head from his body. Marrick and Damon both take a step backward as they both still hold onto David's arms moving out of their way forcing David to thrust his chest out. Robert and Thomas are both starting to raise their weapons as they prepare themselves to slice his head off from his neck.

"I COMMAND YOU NOW!"

David yells out.

David is gone.

Robert and Thomas stop as quickly as they can they are now standing directly in front of Marrick and Damon.

"Where did David go and what plan did he have for escape?"

Sabrina asks as she is now walking toward Thomas.

"Someone is missing! Stu is no longer here."

Sarah says as she is looking around for him.

"Oh my stars we need to check on Lizzie."

I say as I begin to run toward the house I can feel that Luna is following me.

As soon as I get to the sliding glass door I open it up and then Luna and I make our way down into the basement. I am moving as fast as I possibly can. I am getting closer to the room and I can see Lizzie lying upon one of the cots. I am now inside and I stop as fast as I can. I bend down to Lizzie and I can hear her heart slowly beating. I am so happy that she is still alive. Stu did not kill her.

"Marrick she is still alive."

I say to him as I send my thoughts.

"Renee we are out searching for them."

I hear his reply.

As I stand here looking at her resting upon the cot I can smell blood. I lower myself to her as I sit on the cot that she is laying on. Stu has hit her in the head to knock her out. I place my hand on her head so that I can see how badly she is hurt. The damage to the side of her head is not severe she will be ok as I continue to listen to the sound of her heart that is half dead.

I am so happy that she is safe.

I say to myself as I turn to quietly walk out of the room so that she can continue to rest.

She has been through so much this evening but we are here for her we know how she feels. David murdered her grandfather Richard. Logan must be full of anger as well from what David had done. The words he said to her makes my skin crawl.

"You are meant to be alone" are the horrible words that David spoke to Logan.

Luna is leaving my side she is moving away from my right side but she remains inside of the house as I am now walking out of the house and into the back yard. Sabrina is very upset for what has just taken place.

"How is it that we were able to be deceived? We trusted Stu he has been with us for at least a year. We should have known that Stu is with David."

Sabrina speaks out as she has such great anger in her voice.

As she stands here with her weapons in her hand Sabrina tightens her grip on them. She has a knife in one of her hands. Sabrina rises her hand up close to her ear and she moves so quickly. She releases the knife and I can hear it flying thru the air followed by a very loud thump. Sabrina's knife is inside of a tree all I can see is the handle. The knife is completely inside of it. She walks over to it she raises her hand to take hold of the handle and she pulls it out and then she walks over toward Logan.

Logan is still holding Richards gray eyes in the palm of her hands. She is still not saying a word but I can see revenge on her face as she moves her head to look at Sabrina. I do not think that I have ever seen Logan so upset since I have known her.

Luna is coming up behind me I turn myself to look at her I want a really good look at her. Luna looks so very strong and powerful that I almost feel intimidated by her. If she is able to injure David in such a powerful way than what will she do to us if she becomes angry with me or someone else? The way that she moves I can see the strength that Luna now possesses.

This is something that I should not be thinking about because I do trust her.

I say to myself.

We found Stu.

Marrick says to me as I hear his thoughts.

Not only can I feel my anger but I can also feel the strong hate and anger from Sarah and Marrick.

Luna leaves my side very quickly as I can now hear a faint cry traveling through the air. This sound has come from Stu. I remain in the back yard as everyone else begins to move very quickly to where they are at.

They do not have David because Marrick's words to me where that they found Stu. So where did David go?

As I continue to stay in the back yard I begin to walk toward the birdbath I am gazing upon the heart shaped rose that has David's blood upon it. I close my eyes but I realize that I still have his blood on my hands as well as my lips because I fed on his blood.

I am going to try to feel as to where David is I know that I can do this.

He knows as to where I am at so I must be able to do the same.

I say to myself.

With my eyes still closed I stand next rose that has David's blood upon it. I concentrate on David's blood that is on my skin. I can feel the blood as it is starting to tighten as it begins to dry. Feeling the blood on my flesh I begin to think about him. The first thought that is coming into my mind is when he succeeded in distracting me last night. When he held my wrist to his lips and kissed it. I allow this thought to remain in my mind as I now try to feel him.

"Where are you David?"

I whisper into the wind as it starts to gently blow through my hair.

I continue to concentrate as I feel his blood continue to tighten on my skin. As I begin to open my eyes I know where he is. I slowly turn to my left there is a smile that is forming on my face as I turn myself to look at David.

"I can now feel YOU."

I say to him.

"David you are now weak and broken."

"Help me to heal Renee and I will allow you to continue your existence."

"I will never help you!"

I reply to him as I continue to look at him.

I open myself to allow Marrick and Sarah to feel what I am feeling allowing them to know that David is alone with me.

"I want to kill you David I have no desire to help you and if I die in the process then so be it."

I say to him as my smile disappears from my face.

As I continue to stand here I begin to feel Luna she is coming closer and moving very quickly.

"I cannot help but say to you that I am no longer frightened by you. I am not scared of you anymore."

I say to him as I realize that what I have just said to him is true.

"You only feel this way because I am weak at this very moment."

He says to me as he moves himself closer to me.

I am going to stand my ground I am not going to back away from him.

Luna is almost here and I am going to do everything that I can so that he does not realize it. I know what it is that Luna wants to do.

David moves his arm very quickly as I can hear soft footsteps upon the ground. David has placed his hand around my throat and with his other hand he places it upon the side of my body picking me up from the ground and into the air. As he still has his grip upon me he is moving very quickly as the back of my body hits the side of the house. He now has me at his eye level looking into my eyes with my body up against the house. My feet are just dangling down I no longer have the ground under me. As I look back into David's eyes I do not see anything at all. They say that the eyes are the window's to look upon the soul. What I have been told about David is true he honestly has nothing inside of him except pure evil.

"Tell me Renee do you see your death as you look into my eyes?"

"David I see nothing at all."

I reply to him.

"Then me DEAR RENEE allow me show you."

He says to me as he moves very quickly to place his mouth upon the flesh of my neck.

I can feel the pain as he forces his fangs into my neck as he rips my skin. He is feeding on my blood. He is pressing himself against my body so that I cannot move. As he tightens his grip on my neck with his mouth I can feel my blood being forced from my body as he continues to feed from me. I cannot move.

As David still has me pinned up against the house the soft footsteps are getting closer. David removes his other hand from the side of my body and places it on the top of my head forcing my head to rest upon my own shoulder. He is digging every one of his teeth into my neck so that he is able to feed on my blood more quickly. I am becoming weak I need help.

I hear a very hard and loud thump. David removes his mouth from my neck and he allows me to completely fall to the ground but I am able to steady myself on my feet I do not fall.

"I see that Stu did not follow his instructions. He was commanded to kill you Lizzie."

He says to her as he begins to move toward her.

He is removing a knife that Lizzie used to stab David in the back of his neck.

I move myself so that I can help her but as soon as I take a step David is quickly moving away from us and he has fallen to the ground. I move my head to look my beautiful black wolf has a hold of him. Luna has him pinned to the ground. She is not allowing him to move. She is growling showing her teeth to him as she is allowing her saliva of blood to fall upon his face. David moves his head to look at her. David cannot move to free himself from her as she stands on his body. Luna has her front pawls on his shoulders and her back feet are on top of his thighs. I can see that she has her claws embedded into his pale white flesh. She is too strong and powerful for David.

Luna is once again using every ounce of strength forcing her weight upon his body.

"What are you waiting for you BITCH?"

He asks to her as Luna opens her mouth and very quickly takes hold of David's throat.

Luna moves herself from standing on top of his body she is now standing at the side of David with her mouth still clamped down on his neck. Luna is trying to remove his head.

David does not make a sound he does not yell out in pain.

I can hear his skin starting to rip apart and as Luna tightens her jaws upon his flesh while blood splatters upon the ground.

I continue to move toward Lizzie and as we now stand together we continue to watch Luna as she is now removing David's head from his body.

I can feel Marrick and Sarah as they return with the others. I look over and Sarah has her hold on Stu. I can see the look of relief upon his face. David can no longer control him.

Robert is making his way toward David's now headless body. He kneels down beside his brother and places his hand upon David's shoulder.

"I will see you in hell."

Robert says to him with his head lowered.

Robert is taking hold of his knife with both hands holding it in the air above David's body. Robert is now thrusting his knife into David's chest. He is cutting David's flesh to open him up. Robert is now placing his knife on the ground and he looks at his brother one more time. Without saying anything he places his hand inside of David's chest. Robert is removing the heart from his brother.

I cannot express how free that I now feel as I watch Robert move himself to stand next to David's body.

Michael is standing next to Robert with a long thick tree branch. Robert bends down to take hold of David's head. With Michael still holding the tree branch Robert holds David's head up under it are strings of his pale white flesh with thick streams of blood flowing from it. As quickly as Robert can move he brings the head down upon the top of the branch forcing David's head on top of it. With Michael still holding onto the branch he is now pushing it deep into the ground so that it does not fall over.

We are all looking at this branch with David's head upon it. I must say that I now feel at peace as I look upon his headless body still lying on the ground in a pool of blood. We have won we killed him and we are all free from him.

I look up into the sky and I can see a dark blue color the sun is beginning to rise.

"We must go inside we do not want our bodies to burn along with David's."

Robert says to us as we all start walking toward to house. As I place my hand next to the sliding glass door I cannot help but to look back at his head upon the tree branch. I can hear a loud screaming cry coming from so far away. I have a horrible feeling in the pit of my stomach as I move my head trying to figure out as to what direction this cry is coming from. I move my gaze to look upon David's head and I am frightened as to what I see.

David's head and body are missing.

I move very quickly inside of the house and I close the door and lock it. I am now running as quickly as I can down the steps into the basement. As I enter into the safe room I close the door.

"David is gone! I head a screaming cry and as I was trying to find out where it was coming from someone took David's head and his body."

I say to them as I turn around to look at them.

Marrick comes over to me and he places his arms around me to try and comfort me. Luna is now standing at my side.

"I had feared that this may happen. David's maker has taken him. Her existence has not yet ended."

Robert says to us.

I can feel my body starting to shut down as Marrick forces me to lie down upon one of the cots. Marrick lies right next to me holding me in his arms. Luna jumps on top of the both of us as she makes herself comfortable. I can feel that she is doing this to protect the both of us. I can feel Luna's body shutting down as well as my own and Marrick's.

"It took everything that we had to weaken him but in the end Luna was the one that was able to kill him. How will we be able to defeat his maker? By the sound of her crying scream she will be coming after us."

I say to Marrick as I send my thoughts to him.

"Renee I promise that we will do everything that we can to be ready for her."

"Marrick, do you know who she is?"

"No I do not but I do know that she is the one who destroyed Marco's family and village."

He replies to me.

"Renee I command you to rest your mind you need to completely rest your body we will need to hunt as soon as we wake this evening."

I hear his thoughts as he sends them to me.

As I can feel my mind starting to rest as Marrick has commanded of me I begin to think of the Blood Upon A Rose the beautiful heart shape flower with the full moon behind it.

We defeated David I hope that we can also defeat what is coming our way. The female that turned him into a vampire as well as the evil that he had created!

I say to myself as my mind is now completely at rest.

http://www.raybondmusic.com/

Ray Bond & The Black Diamond Band are from Lancaster, Ohio. Log on to their website to find out when their next performance will be at so that you can enjoy their fantastic country music live.